"Maybe we can   better, huh?"

Carson squeezed her hands, and Nola felt the warmth of his fingers. "I'm sorry we got off on the wrong foot. I didn't know Augustus had a daughter. Especially a—" He stopped abruptly, as though catching himself from saying something he'd regret.

"An Indian?" Nola finished for him, her chin going up.

Carson cupped her chin in one hand. "You do have a big chip on your shoulder about that, don't you?" His thumb came up to seal her lips as she opened her mouth to protest.

"No," he went on softly. "What I was going to say, was—especially as young and beautiful a daughter as you. That's what I was going to say, but I figured I might be out of line."

He ran his thumb provocatively along the line of her lips and added, his deep lazy drawl almost inaudible, "You asked for it, Nola Rose. You made me say it."

Dear Reader,

Welcome to Silhouette *Special Edition* . . . welcome to romance.

Last year I requested your opinions on the books that we publish. Thank you for the many thoughtful comments. For the next couple of months, I'd like to share quotes with you from those letters. This seems very appropriate while we are in the midst of our THAT SPECIAL WOMAN! promotion. Each one of our readers is a very *special* woman, as heroic as the heroines in our books.

This month, our THAT SPECIAL WOMAN! is Kelley McCormick, a woman who takes the trip of a lifetime and meets the man of her dreams. You'll meet Kelley and her Prince Charming in *Grand Prize Winner!* by Tracy Sinclair.

Also in store for you this month is *The Way of a Man,* the third book in Laurie Paige's WILD RIVER TRILOGY. And not to be missed are terrific books from other favorite authors—Kathleen Eagle, Pamela Toth, Victoria Pade and Judith Bowen.

I hope you enjoy this book, and all of the stories to come!

Sincerely,

Tara Gavin
Senior Editor

QUOTE OF THE MONTH:

"I enjoy characters I can relate to—female characters who are wonderful people packaged in very ordinary coverings and men who see beyond looks and who are willing to work at a relationship. I enjoy stories of couples who stick with each other and work through difficult times. Thank you, Special Edition, for the many, many hours of enjoyment."

—M. Greenleaf, Maryland

JUDITH BOWEN
HIGH COUNTRY RANCHER

Silhouette®

SPECIAL EDITION®

Published by Silhouette Books

America's Publisher of Contemporary Romance

To my mother-in-law,
Antonia Jacoba Henrika van Buiten-Dykstra,
who loves, and always has loved, romance.

With apologies to the people of Brocket, Alberta, for moving their
community a little closer to Pincher Creek in this work of fiction.
Still, the wonderful, windswept site of Nelson Small Legs Jr.'s
memorial powwow of 1980 is not a bad place to wake up in, is it?

 SILHOUETTE BOOKS

ISBN 0-373-09851-0

HIGH COUNTRY RANCHER

Copyright © 1993 by Judith Bowen

JUDITH BOWEN

met her husband when they were editing competing newspapers in British Columbia, and they were married in Gibraltar. She has enjoyed raising sheep and children in Fraser Valley, and still spins wool, knits, weaves and puts up dozens of jars of preserves and pickles every year. Her interests include reading, regional cookery, volunteer work, gardening and, of course, writing romances. *Paper Marriage* was chosen as the National Readers' Choice Traditional Romance for 1991.

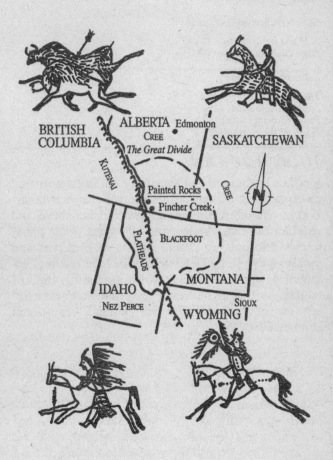

BRITISH COLUMBIA

ALBERTA

Edmonton

CREE

The Great Divide

SASKATCHEWAN

KUTENAI

CREE

Painted Rocks

Pincher Creek

FLATHEADS

BLACKFOOT

IDAHO

MONTANA

NEZ PERCE

SIOUX

WYOMING

N

All underlined places are fictitious.

Chapter One

"Whoa!"

With a sudden oath, the man on the line-back buckskin pulled up sharply, causing the mare to jump skittishly to one side. The packhorse following closely behind threw up his head to avoid bumping into her on the narrow, rocky path. Both horses, buckskin and black, tossed their heads impatiently, halters and bridles jangling.

But the man took no notice. He reached into the saddle-bag behind him and took out a pair of field glasses, making adjustments automatically as he raised them to his face.

After a moment or so he cursed again softly under his breath, and with one smooth, fluid motion, he dismounted and dropped his reins to the parched earth. He left the horses and stepped a few yards to the left of the trail, where a large boulder marked the edge of an ancient landslide. He hunkered down until he found a comfortable position, then braced himself against the rock, a tall, lean figure in jeans and a denim shirt, sleeves rolled to the elbows, a stained and faded bush Stetson on his head. Then he put the glasses to his eyes again and studied the exposed cliff ahead of him for a long time.

Damn, he'd been lucky! To just happen to ride through here exactly when he had.... He watched, not taking his eyes from the scene before him for a second. The sun sank lower, lower...until the hard edges of the Canadian Rockies splintered the light into shards of red and gold that spilled over the dull ocher of the bare hills to the east, the jagged rock formations to the north and west.

Then he saw it, what he'd been hunting for ever since he'd crossed the border a month ago. It was just the way Old Jim had described it. And that meant the telltale outcrop he was looking for wasn't far away. Victory was his, it was only a question of time.... He dragged a deep, shaky breath into his lungs, trying to control the crazy impulse that made him want to jump up and shout his victory to the sky above and the dark canyons below. His search was over...well, nearly over. He wouldn't let this one slip through his fingers.

He shifted his position and scanned the darkening valley below him. He'd need to find a good place to pitch his camp, a private place in one of these canyons. He'd need to pack in his summer's supplies, make inquiries in Pincher Creek as to who owned this land. He'd seen fences, broken wire and sagging posts but, still, that meant it was part of somebody's range.

He'd need to handle this one very, very carefully. He'd dreamed of finding this one day, just as he'd promised Old Jim he would. And it was all his. Then—what the hell? he thought—he tossed his hat high into the air. The horses threw up their heads sharply and the mare snorted.

"Ayieee-hah!"

It was an old cowboy yell, but it marked the making of a prospector's day.

"Just tell me if it's true or not, Augustus! I heard that some American prospector's been poking around the Lazy J—?"

For a moment Nola held her breath and watched the man at the kitchen table spoon the sugar into his mug of coffee, then begin to stir it thoughtfully. He stirred it considerably longer than necessary, and when he looked up, she could see a gleam she knew all too well in the faded blue eyes.

"'N what if he has?"

Nola's shoulders sagged against the door frame. Damn! Until that moment she hadn't known just how much she'd been praying what she'd heard was only gossip, just jealous talk by one of the local rock hounds who'd never been able to find anything more than bunchgrass and sagebrush and maybe the occasional dinosaur bone or two in these dusty hills. But she knew, just the way her father'd answered her, that what she'd heard wasn't only jealous talk. Carson Harlow was here in southwestern Alberta, somewhere on the back stretches of the Lazy J, and, if she read the signals right, her father was mixed up in it, too. "So it *is* true, then."

"Uh-huh." Her father took a couple of noisy drafts. He liked his coffee sweet and he liked it hot. He regarded her the whole time from under grizzled brows, his face lean and deeply carved by the sun and the wind and the thousand worries that were the lifetime legacy of a high country rancher. Prettiest country in the world, he'd always said, but pretty don't pay the light company.

"Who told you?"

"I was in Pincher Creek, Tuesday. Ran into Grizzly Sawchuck, at McLeod's?" She raised her eyebrows. Her father nodded slightly. Everyone knew the eccentric Grizzly Sawchuck. "He told me he'd seen some guy he knew named Carson Harlow up past the Wild Plum Creek last week, on your place. Some American. Said he'd run into him before, in Nevada." She paused. She could tell none of what she was saying was news to Augustus Snow. "Grizzly said Harlow was the prospector who staked the Wellsdrum strike there. Silver."

"Uh-huh."

Suddenly Augustus's silence infuriated her, and the resolve she'd nourished so carefully on the bumpy, dusty trip up to the ranch—the resolve to keep calm and reasonable with Augustus, to present her arguments coolly and firmly—all that careful determination exploded. "Damn it, Dad! You *know* about the Painted Rocks back in there somewhere. You *know* about what would happen to that country if some...some stupid mine started up—"

"Just hold your horses, young lady. What mine? What Painted Rocks?"

"You know what I'm talking about! I've heard that story since I was a kid—you've even told me—and since I've been working with the band this summer, I've heard it again, this time in Blackfoot. The Painted Rocks are back in that country somewhere, they've got to be there. And they're important, more important than any old mine could be. They've got to be located. And saved." She sensed his interest and she took a step forward. "It's history, Augustus—history! Just think. Maybe a world-class Indian historic site located right here on the Lazy J!"

"Hogwash. Bull's breath. Gopher tails. Nobody's ever seen no Painted Rocks," Augustus said flatly. "Just an old yarn somebody's great-granny told somebody else's great-granny who told a few simpleminded cousins and that was that." He got up to pour himself another cup of coffee from the chipped graniteware coffeepot on the wood stove.

"Some coffee, Nola Rose?" Out of habit, he waved the pot at Nola.

"No, thanks," she said, just as automatically. Augustus's coffee would cure snakebite. Nola bit her lip and moved closer to the kitchen table. Somehow she had to convince him.... She eased out a wooden chair and sat down gingerly, glancing discreetly at her watch. Nearly five o'clock. She'd hoped she'd be able to make Augustus see reason right away. It looked now as though it might take a while. She was hungry; she hadn't stopped for lunch in her rush to drive up to the ranch to find out if what Grizzly'd said was true. Whatever Augustus had simmering in the pot on the back of the kitchen range smelled delicious.

Nola looked around the big ranch kitchen. It looked pretty much the same as it had when she'd been a girl growing up here—worn linoleum, massive cast-iron enameled sink under the window, faded chintz curtains bellying into the room from time to time in the summer breeze, scarred oak table and chairs, big, old-fashioned wood stove that had been there since Augustus's mother's day. The only modern notes were the refrigerator and a shining white propane stove that probably hadn't been used since Martha died.

Six years. Nola passed a hand over her face in a gesture of weariness. Had it really been almost six years since she'd received that midnight phone call from Augustus telling her that Martha was dead of a heart attack at the age of sixty-eight? Nola'd been in her second year of college up in Calgary and it was the only time she'd ever heard Augustus weep. She'd wept, too, for his beloved Martha May, and the woman who'd been the only mother she had ever known. Had Augustus ever gotten over her? Nola didn't think so, and neither had she. All the more reason that it was her responsibility—duty, even—as his only living family and the person who loved him best in all the world to do what she could to protect him from the schemes of a gold digger like this American prospector. Even if the Painted Rocks turned out to be no more than an Indian fable, as most people seemed to believe. For a man of seventy-eight, nearly seventy-nine, sometimes Augustus Snow could be as innocent as one of his own newborn whiteface calves.

"Don't suppose I could tempt you to stay for supper?" Augustus was stirring at the pot on the stove. Nola felt her mouth water as the rich scent of one of his famous beef stews filled the kitchen. "I'd be awful grateful for a pan of your biscuits," he added slyly, addressing the pot in front of him. "Just for a change."

Nola smiled. Then she crept up behind him, went up on her tiptoes and gave him a big hug, resting her cheek for a moment on his worn plaid shirt. He smelled of wood smoke and horses and the peculiar tang of that revolting Copenhagen tobacco he chewed.

"Guess you could," she said, stepping back lightly and smiling as he turned around. "You've got plenty enough for two there and I can whip up some biscuits in a minute." Besides, she thought, tying on an apron from the kitchen drawer where they'd remained since Martha's day, sharing a meal with her father would give her a chance to strengthen her case. The American had to go. Her first concern, she had to admit, was to make sure the Painted Rocks site was left alone until it could be documented and preserved, but a close second was her need to protect Augustus from himself. It wouldn't be the first time her gruff but surprisingly tenderhearted father would have fallen for some pie-in-the-sky scheme...nor would it probably be the last.

It wasn't until she had her arms in a basin of flour and lard and baking powder that he mentioned there'd be a third at the table. His new partner, in fact. Carson Harlow.

"What?" she yelped, skipping back a step so that bits of biscuit dough scattered onto the floor. *Partner!* "Augustus! Why didn't you tell me you were expecting company?"

Nola pushed irritably at a damp strand of hair that had fallen out of her braid and stuck to her cheek. She felt hot, and sticky, and all of a sudden she was burning up with annoyance at the way Augustus had outfoxed her. Why was he doing this to her? Didn't he realize that she was only trying to help him, that she had his best interests at heart?

"Kinda sounded like you've made your mind up on this Harlow fella from what Grizzly told you and I thought you might reconsider once you get a chance to meet him," he drawled, giving her a conspiratorial wink that made her want to scream. "Besides, I got a sudden hankerin' for a plate of your buttermilk biscuits, sugar. Don't get near enough now that... now that Martha May's gone."

It was his mention of Martha that had the heat ebbing from her cheeks as swiftly as it had arisen. She sighed. So much for her chance to probe her father a little further on the subject this evening, maybe talk him around to seeing her point. She'd hoped to avoid the prospector altogether, if possible. Augustus was the one to deal with him.

Now he was joining them for supper. Glumly, Nola picked up a pan of biscuits and shoved them into the oven. From what Grizzly'd told her, the American was good at what he did, and there's no way he'd be up here north of the 49th parallel unless he figured he had a pretty good chance at hitting pay dirt somewhere. And if that pay dirt turned out to be up near the Wild Plum... Nola shuddered. If she couldn't convince Augustus to give up this prospecting nonsense, at least for the rest of the summer...

"That oughta be him now," Augustus said with satisfaction.

Nola could hear the distant growl of a truck's engine coming up the lane.

Her father eyed the kitchen clock. "Right on time, too."

Ignoring her floury hands, she grabbed her father by the arm as he went toward the kitchen screen door. Outside she could hear Rupert and Melba barking up a storm as a pickup drove into the yard.

"Listen, Augustus." She licked her lips in apprehension. Lord! She hadn't had a moment to patch together any kind of a plan. This was like her worst nightmare—walking into court late to make her final pitch to the jury only to discover her painstaking notes had turned to blank pieces of paper. Maybe she should take advantage of the situation and try to convince the two of them together? But she wasn't ready. And she didn't *want* to deal with the prospector. The prospector, whoever he was, needed Augustus's permission to trespass on his land. The prospector was nobody—it was Augustus she had to convince. This business was between her and her father, no one else. Why was something that should be so straightforward and simple getting so balled up?

"Don't say anything about the Painted Rocks," she whispered quickly, the words tumbling out as she cobbled together a plan in her head. "That's between you and me. I—I don't want any strangers in on it until . . . well, until I get a chance to talk things over with the elders." In a childish gesture, she crossed the fingers of one floury hand behind her back. That was an outright fabrication; the elders wouldn't expect her to consult with them, nor would any member of the tribe. "Promise?"

"Trouble with you, Nola Rose, is you worry too dang much. You gotta grab onto opportunity when it rides by." He touched the tip of her nose with one gnarled and calloused finger, as he'd done as a gesture of affection since she was a child. "You gotta take things the way they come, like I do."

She glared at him, and stood her ground.

"All right, all right," he grumbled. "I promise not to mention it if you don't. Fair enough?"

"Fair enough." She raced for the sink to wash the biscuit dough from her hands. And her hair! Nola glanced in the spotted, broken mirror that hung on the wall to one side of the sink and quickly ran damp fingers over her hair, smoothing the stray strands, black and shiny as silk, into her braid. Not that it'd matter much to some cocky, know-it-all corporate geologist. Or to some crusty old prospector who probably hadn't had a bath himself since last spring.

She turned and stretched up to reach the plates in the cupboard, hearing the rough sound of male laughter from the porch outside the kitchen door behind her. Melba was whimpering with excitement, and Nola knew she'd be jumping around the stranger's legs in bliss. Rupert, she hoped, would show a little more loyalty.

One, two, three, she counted out the dinner plates. Nola bit her lower lip and stretched even higher, trying to reach Martha's good cream and sugar set. Might as well do a decent job of laying the table.

"Need a hand?"

Nola nearly dropped the plates, whirling at the deep sound of a man's voice just behind her. He'd startled her, that's all, coming up behind her so quietly. Their eyes met, locked, and Nola's nervous laughter died in her throat. She felt her palms, damp and slippery, clutching the plates against her middle.

He was frowning, but he couldn't be half as surprised as she was. This man wasn't bewhiskered; he wasn't crusty-looking; he wasn't old. Nor did he look like what she thought your average corporate geologist-turned-prospector fronting for a big mining company might look like. He was tall and straight and shaggy blond and rugged-looking in faded jeans—very clean, she noted—and a richly beaded, fringed, buckskin jacket that she knew instantly was the genuine article. Nola focused on the jacket, unable suddenly to look up at the man any longer. He was too close. He was too...too male. Her breath felt painful in her throat, and she felt heat bloom in her cheeks again.

Where was Augustus? The moment seemed to last forever, but surely only a few seconds had passed.

"Here, let me reach that for you," the prospector said. Not waiting for her reply, he took another step toward her and easily lifted down the cream and sugar set. Nola hadn't moved, still shocked at her first reaction. Her reaction to Carson Harlow, the man. Not the prospector—the man. Nola felt the ends of the fringe on his jacket sleeve fan her cheek lightly, he was so close. The faint scent of his male body, of leather and plain soap, surrounded her and she squeezed her eyes shut for a split second, praying for her pulse to slow, for the heat to die in her cheeks. She prayed for reason, for sanity.

"Thanks," she managed to croak as he set the cream pitcher and sugar bowl on the counter. Anger brought her to her senses. She was behaving like a schoolgirl! And—the jacket. Why was this white man wearing a jacket like that? It looked like old Flathead beadwork, from the Bitterroot Mountains of southern Montana. That kind of garment was a cultural artifact, it belonged in a provincial museum, by rights, not on the back of some white man.

"Carson? I'd like you to meet my daughter, Nola Rose." Augustus came into the kitchen smiling broadly. "My pride and joy." He was plainly delighted at his role as host and...and what? Nola's eyes narrowed suspiciously. Matchmaker? Surely not, she thought, horrified. But she knew him too well to put anything past him.

Nola had to respond. She moved quickly toward the table and put the plates down. Then she wiped her palms on her apron and took a step toward the two men. She took a deep, calming breath and somehow managed a smile.

"Nola, this here's Carson Harlow, that American you was so worried about."

Nola shot a dark look at her father, and extended her hand in formal greeting. The American took it. "I wasn't worried, Augustus," she lied. "Not a bit. Welcome to Alberta, Mr. Harlow."

He nodded. "Thanks. My friends call me Carson," he said softly, that lazy American accent sliding down her spine like melting vanilla ice cream on a summer picnic.

"Carson," she repeated politely, with another smile and a nod. *Friends!* She wanted to say he was no friend of hers, never would be.

Was it her imagination, or had that dark, gray-green gaze flickered with humor at Augustus's remark, and at her quick reply? Darn Augustus, anyway! She might have known he'd try to stir things up, even if he had promised not to mention the Painted Rocks.

Augustus had called him his partner. Surely that wasn't really the case, surely he'd said it just to annoy her. But, regardless of what cockamamy plan this American had cooked up with her father, her own best plan was to win Augustus over. Never mind the prospector. After all, he needed Augustus's permission to prospect the Lazy J. She'd just have to see that he didn't get it. Partner, indeed!

With dismay, Nola realized the stranger still held her hand in his, his grip hard and firm and warm, a faint smile on his handsome face. She pulled her hand away and quickly picked up the plates, moving down the table to finish laying the places. What a tidy picture of domesticity she must present, with one of Martha's frilly aprons on, and the aroma of fresh-baking biscuits and beef stew wafting from the cook stove as she scurried about getting supper ready for the menfolk. Not exactly the picture of an up-and-coming Indian rights activist lawyer, which she was.

Nola hadn't lived at home for years, but when she was at the Lazy J she never minded fussing over Augustus. He appreciated it, it comforted him in his deep loneliness since Martha had died; she knew that, and she had nothing to prove by refusing. Still . . . what it must seem to this American. Though why it should matter if the prospector got the wrong impression, she didn't know exactly.

Surreptitiously she studied the two men as she finished setting the table and went to the refrigerator for butter and milk. The American had taken off his jacket and hung it casually on one of the pegs just inside the kitchen door where Augustus hung his work coats and his hats. Then he'd joined her father at the big aerial map pinned to one side of the kitchen and stood, rocking back on his heels, his hands jammed in his pockets as he and Augustus studied the map, side by side. The prospector was nearly a head taller than her father. At first she was troubled by something in the way he moved, almost silently, with complete confidence and control, his calm, sinuous grace unusual in such a tall, broad man. Then she saw the plain leather moccasins he wore, scuffed and well-worn, and she felt her blood rise again.

That's why he'd been able to sneak up on her the way he had. Why did he wear Indian clothing? It was as plain as the sun-bleached hair on his head, as the flashing green devil's own eyes in his handsome face, that there wasn't a drop of Indian blood in his veins. It wasn't right . . . traditional Indian clothing and artifacts belonged to native Indians, no one else. Nola knew the collections of provincial museums could come under similar charges of cultural appropriation, of grave robbery, but at the same time, public collections helped to save some of the fast-disappearing past for future generations. Then, as Indian pride grew, as it was growing today, the new generation could reclaim its past. But for a white man to own such a jacket, to adopt Indian clothing...

It was an insult to every aboriginal since Columbus who'd suffered the white man's yoke; a visual reminder of every treaty that had been ignored, every Indian child who'd grown up in wretched poverty, every proud warrior herded onto a reservation, caged like a beast in the land of his forefathers.

Strong views, yes. But she had every right to hold such strong views. She glanced at the American's back, blue chambray shirt stretched taut across broad shoulders, lean thighs strong in form-fitting denim. She tossed her own glossy black braid back over her shoulder and allowed herself a slight smile of triumph. And pride. Indian pride. Had he already guessed?

"Sit down, young fella!" Augustus waved his guest to a chair opposite the one Nola usually sat in. "Sit yourself down." He took his usual place at the head of the table, rubbing his gnarled hands together. "Fresh biscuits! Ain't that a treat? And nobody makes 'em like my Nola Rose. Sink your teeth into one of these, Carson." He offered the plate proudly to the younger man.

"Oh, Augustus," Nola began, blushing furiously. "Don't be silly. I've offered to show you how to make biscuits often enough, and it's your own fault that you're too stubborn to try." She took her seat at the table, wishing she didn't have to face the stranger throughout the meal.

"Please, go ahead," she said, gesturing politely to her father and Carson to begin. Carson was sitting quietly opposite her, those clear, gray-green eyes not missing a thing, she knew, although she didn't risk more than a quick glance to find out. "Coffee or tea with your meal?" she asked them both, addressing the salt shaker. "I'm having milk."

"Milk, please," Carson said, holding out his cup for her to fill from the milk jug. Nola held her breath, willing her hand to steady itself. She just nodded quickly at his quiet "Thank you," not trusting her voice.

This was crazy! She was acting like some backwoods ranch girl who'd never seen a good-looking man in her life. Handsome is as handsome does, everyone knew that. She was nearly twenty-six, for heaven's sake, she'd dealt with plenty of good-looking men before. In the courtroom and out of the courtroom. Better looking, some of them, by far, than this man. But none of them, she realized with growing dismay, had caused this odd feeling in her middle, this fear—or was it something else?—trickling along her veins. Nola took a deep breath and deliberately pushed the crazy thoughts out of her head.

She poured milk for her father and sat down again. The men helped themselves to the stew pot, which Nola had brought to the table, and for a few minutes there was silence as they began their meal. Nola's mind churned as she ate. Telling herself to put the man opposite out of her mind was one thing; doing it was quite another.

The stew was delicious—Augustus's beef stew always was—and she was starving. It had been a long day since she'd arisen at dawn to drive into Lethbridge to try to locate some missing Peigan band records, without success. Then she'd sat in on a two-hour meeting of the band council before joining some of the younger Peigan women and their children on a long-planned expedition to pick the wild strawberries that were ripe now and growing along the dry creek beds. They'd filled several ice-cream buckets over the course of the afternoon, then she'd driven like a madwoman up to the Lazy J to see her father.

And the day wasn't over yet.

"I didn't know you had a daughter, Augustus."

Nola looked up to see the prospector regarding her intently, a slight smile on his face that softened his tanned, rugged features and was sexy as hell. Did he have any idea what that smile might to do a woman's insides? Probably, she decided instantly.

There'd been a slight question, a hesitation, in his voice that Nola didn't miss. Nor did she miss his lazy appraisal of her own features, including a slight narrowing of his eyes as his gaze rested on the jet-black braid that hung over her left shoulder.

Augustus laughed. "There's quite a lot you don't know about me, Carson, when it comes right down to it. Yessir-ree, Nola's my only daughter. She's a big-shot lawyer these days, Indian rights and all that stuff, you know," he said proudly, winking at her. "Ain't got much time for her old dad anymore. Nope," he went on, "never had no sons. Never had time to miss 'em with Nola Rose around, my wife always said." He gazed fondly at Nola and she met his smile, feeling the love swell inside her, as always, for this ornery old rancher she called her father.

"She must take after her mama," the American said. It was a polite way of asking how a grizzled, old, sunburned, blue-eyed rancher had begotten a dusky-skinned, sloe-eyed, raven-haired daughter. And it made Nola mad.

"Could be," she answered coolly before Augustus had a chance to speak. "I never knew my mother, you see. She died on skid row in Calgary of tuberculosis before I was three years old, a pretty common story with my people, I've discovered. Augustus and Martha adopted me when I was eleven. My father was a white man, or so the social workers said. I don't know, he never stuck around long enough to get to know me. A lot of people tried their darnedest to turn me into a little white girl over the years, before I came here to live with Martha and Augustus. But it never worked." She heard Augustus's hoot of laughter somewhere in the background, but all she saw was the stranger's eyes, all she felt was the strength of his gaze holding hers, hers holding his. "I'm half Indian. My mother was a Blackfoot. From Gleichen."

As she spoke she felt her spine stiffen and her chin rise proudly. She'd never felt shame about who she was or where she'd come from. The Snows had helped her find her pride again after those long horrible years of being shifted from one foster home to another. The Snows had given her back her life, they'd taught her how to love, she'd never forget that. *Ever!*

But as she spoke, she saw the veil of some emotion she didn't understand enter Carson's eyes. Where before his gaze had been acute and clear, it now held something hidden, something he refused to share with them. His gaze held anger, too... deep, cold anger.

She regretted her outburst. Maybe she'd been too hasty, too quick to flaunt her pride. She'd never hidden her background; most people around this particular part of southwestern Alberta knew all about the feisty, wiry, little Indian girl the Snows had adopted out of the blue one day. But, still, there was a polite way to go about these things. He was a stranger, after all. More than that, he was her father's guest.

She could tell she'd offended him, although he was too polite to say anything. His silence shamed her. Suddenly all she wanted was to leave, to get back to the normalcy of her summer home with the band, to leave the hard, cold gaze of this stranger behind, this man who'd confused her with his very presence, who'd managed to fracture the serenity, the very tenor of her confidence in less than an hour, a confidence so carefully built over the years, so carefully nurtured. How had everything gone so...so terribly wrong?

Augustus broke in with a comment about the part of the country Harlow was apparently prospecting. It sounded like the Wild Plum area, she thought with a sinking feeling as she listened to them talk. Just as she'd suspected. But this was no time to say anything about the Painted Rocks site. She'd have to salvage what she could from this situation and let the matter ride until another time. Soon. She'd have to see Augustus alone. Some woman's instinct deep within told her the less she saw of Carson Harlow, the better.

Excusing herself from the table, Nola cleared the dishes away and quickly washed them in the deep, old-fashioned sink. Neither man offered to give her a hand, although Nola felt the American's gaze burning into her shoulder blades. She didn't turn around and she didn't bother to dry the dishes, just left them on the drainboard for Augustus to put away later. It was nearly seven o'clock. And she had another half-hour drive to get back to the reservation.

"Goin' so soon, Nola Rose?" Augustus said, sounding surprised as he saw her pull on her boots. "I thought you might like to stay and visit for a while. Get to know my new partner a little better. You'll be seeing quite a bit of him this summer, I expect."

"Not tonight, Augustus. It's a long drive back, and I, uh, I've got a million things to do tomorrow. Thanks for the supper. It was great—as usual."

Augustus beamed. Harlow regarded her levelly, not even a trace of a smile on his handsome features. She didn't want to see quite a bit of him over the summer; she didn't want to see him ever again.

She turned from his gaze and reached for her hat. The American's beaded buckskin jacket glowed next to her old tan Stetson. Her fingers itched to touch it, to caress the soft, Indian-tanned deerskin, to trace the ancient designs of the beadwork, to run her fingers loosely through the worn leather fringe. She clenched her fingers and resisted. "Nice to have met you, Carson," she said lightly, hoping her tone covered the lie.

"And you, Nola Rosa," he said softly, nodding. Her cheeks flamed at the sound of her name on his tongue, at the slight mispronunciation that made her name sound mysterious, exotic, the sound a man might whisper to a woman in the dark. It was the first time he had addressed her directly.

"Uh, by the way, where did you get such a beautiful jacket?" she asked suddenly, partly to cover her own confusion and partly because she just couldn't resist one final question. Her own voice sounded false and brittle to her ears. "I-it's very unusual."

He regarded her levelly for a couple of very long seconds, his eyes like ice. She felt the challenge between them, thick and raw as a physical thing.

"I got it from a dead Indian," he said.

Chapter Two

I got it from a dead Indian!

Even days later, every time she thought of the cool challenge in his eyes, the deliberate soft drawl as he threw the words at her, she felt angry all over again. He'd meant to bait her, to make her mad, she knew it in her bones. Well, he'd done that, all right. After she'd recovered from the initial shock, she'd tried to smile, as her father did, while Carson explained. But it was a pretty feeble attempt and she hated herself for even trying.

"A couple of years back I spent a season trapping with a fellow down in the south Bitterroots, an old Flathead Indian," he'd said, turning to Augustus with a smile. "I don't know why... it was a change, something to keep me busy over the winter. Then a year or two later I heard that Old Jim had died and left this jacket to me. Another prospector we both knew in Hamilton kept it for me until I happened back in that country. I've kept it with me ever since. Kind of a reminder, I guess, of those days with Old Jim...."

Nola hadn't stayed to hear the rest of the story. She'd just grabbed her hat and left, with a final wave to Augustus. Her last impression was the sight of her father, happier than she'd seen him in years, laughing with the younger man, and about to share his own tales of trapping in the Rockies, she knew. Her last glimpse of Carson Harlow's expression was equally unmistakable: he didn't look as if he liked her much at all.

The feeling was mutual, Nola thought as she viciously punched out a few digits on her telephone. She'd been trying to reach the provincial mining department all morning. Fact was, she didn't like Carson Harlow, either. Not one bit. As for the razor-sharp recognition she'd felt the instant she'd seen him, she discounted that heavily. He was attractive—he knew it, she knew it—but he wasn't the first attractive man she'd ever met. As for him, he probably didn't meet many women trudging around in the hills all summer long.

Besides, he was a white man....

The fact was, a man such as Carson Harlow scared the hell out of her. She'd seen versions of his type before, in the courtroom. Sometimes it was opposite counsel attacking her case with the instincts of a shark and the tenacity of a tiger. And arrogance. That kind of man always knew what he had and knew how to use it. Sometimes it was the man in the dock—a bank robber, a hit man, a man who'd slipped through the clutches of the law before, and would again.

Harlow was definitely on the offensive, too, with that cheap shot about his jacket. He must have realized that she might interfere in whatever game he had going with Augustus. She was glad Augustus had told him she was a lawyer. Maybe he'd think twice about trying to mess around with them both—

"Yes? Sorry, could you repeat that?" She leaned forward in her chair as she listened. She was trying to dig up as much information as she could about prospecting activity in the area. Carson Harlow *had* to represent more than he appeared to represent. She had a hunch he was just the front man for big mining interests, interests that preferred to keep their activity secret, for very good reasons. These days it was a little harder for a mining company to just come in and bulldoze over everybody else, as they'd always done. A little harder, but not much.

"I said, to be valid, a claim has to be staked by a Canadian citizen, ma'am."

"You mean, a company can't stake a claim, or...or a foreigner?" What was this? Nola tried to keep the note of excitement out of her voice.

"Nope. Companies will sometimes grubstake a prospector, but then the prospector has to stake the claim in his own name." The bureaucrat paused. "You're familiar with the term 'grubstake,' ma'am?"

She was. She knew that sometimes a company gave a prospector funds in advance to finance a field season, in exchange for first crack at whatever the prospector found. "Uh-huh. So an...an American, say, couldn't stake a claim, even if he found something worthwhile?" She wanted to be absolutely sure.

"Nope," was the flat response.

"I, uh, suppose, in that situation, there'd be nothing stopping him from getting someone else to stake for him." Nola's initial jubilation at learning that Harlow couldn't legally stake a claim in Alberta was giving way to a sort of dawning horror. "A...a Canadian."

"That sort of a situation could arise, yes, ma'am."

Nola hung up. This was worse than she'd suspected!

Carson Harlow was an American, a foreigner. He couldn't stake a claim. But surely Harlow wouldn't have overlooked that particular little item. His reputation, which was considerable and had preceded him to Canada, according to Grizzly, hadn't been earned by disregarding the laws of the land. And that brought to mind the worrisome thought that perhaps Augustus had meant exactly what he'd said when he'd referred to Carson as his partner. As a Canadian citizen, and a prospector himself years ago, Augustus knew all the ropes and would be able to stake a claim legally, if there was one to stake.

The very thought made Nola sick with anxiety for her father. All her reservations, real and imagined, about the kind of man Carson Harlow was boiled up again. He was using her father! He'd probably already finagled some kind of agreement out of Augustus, making sure of his control if a claim were staked.

Imagine! Taking advantage of a lonely old man such as her father, filling his head with crackpot ideas, crazy dreams of striking it rich. And she knew Augustus would be tempted. The Lazy J didn't make much money, never really had over the years. Talk of some big pot of gold at the end of the rainbow would have its appeal. Martha, as she well remembered, had spent half her life talking Augustus out of get-rich-quick schemes.

Nola remembered the chinchillas in the basement one fall and winter. And there was the time he'd put all his spare cash into a quarter share of an exotic breed bull that was supposed to make all the local ranchers rich. The bull, a big, white brute from Italy, had died its second winter. Poor fella, just couldn't take the cold, Augustus had said philosophically. His job driving the local school bus was the only thing he'd ever done that had actually brought extra money in, but he had given that up years ago, before Martha had died.

No, once a gambler, always a gambler, and that went for prospectors more than most, Nola knew. Even more than ranchers, who risked everything, every year, on the weather and the price of beef. It was in some men's blood, like a disease.... Her father was no exception.

Even if she'd had no interest of her own in the Painted Rocks site, she had to get involved. For her father's sake.

What kind of relationship had this stranger already established with him? Harlow looked to be about in his mid-thirties, he could be the age of the son Augustus had never had...which could be dangerous, too, to a lonely old man. Augustus had never said he'd wanted a son. Which meant, Nola suspected, that he was just too careful of her feelings to say so.

The truth was, it had warmed her heart to see her father's pleasure when she'd left him the other night, exchanging backwoods adventures with the younger man. She knew he needed the company of other men, of kindred spirits, rough, tough men in their prime, as he'd once been. Nola felt torn. Augustus was so lonely these days with only his dogs and horses and the transient, seasonal help on the ranch. Her job had taken her away from the area the past few years and she regretted that. She didn't doubt for a minute that Augustus was now reliving part of his youth through Carson Harlow. And why not, she thought with a frown, if it gave him pleasure?

She sighed. Too bad she, his own daughter, would have to put a stop to it. Still, some things were more important than the passing friendship of a stranger. Loyalty to her father was more important. Saving the Painted Rocks was more important....

Two days later, she was on her way back to the ranch. Her work investigating some of the historic documents of the Blackfoot Confederacy—the Blood, Peigan and Blackfoot tribes, Indians who'd lived generally peaceably together in history, and shared a language—for court challenges, had been delayed, leaving Nola with the chance to take a day off for the first time since she'd begun work with the Peigans two months ago. She had a one-year contract, with the possibility of extending it if all went well.

If all went well. Nola shuddered to think of what the fallout might be if some big American mining company managed to get rights to an ore body near a site held to be sacred in the long, oral tradition of the Blackfoot tribes.

And she was the daughter of the man who owned the land! What irony. Certainly the elders wouldn't blame her, but if she couldn't stop her own father from allowing a mine of some kind into the area, what chance did she have of convincing others of the importance of preserving historic Indian sites elsewhere? It was absolutely essential that she put a stop to Augustus's plans, at least until the end of the summer, until she had a chance to try to locate the Painted Rocks and perhaps have it declared a historic site by the provincial government, off-limits to any kind of development.

Nola glanced at her watch as she slowed for the turnoff to the ranch. It wasn't quite noon yet. She had decided not to call Augustus because she suspected if she did, he'd make up some excuse to avoid her. It was better this way. With luck, she'd be able to spend a few hours with him, maybe overnight, and have this whole business taken care of today.

When Nola drove into the ranch yard a few moments later, she noticed, as though seeing the place for the first time, how shabby and run-down everything had become. The buildings, the corrals—nearly everything, including the house—could use a new coat of paint. Was Augustus strapped for cash more than usual? He'd never said anything to her.

Nola frowned. She didn't see his truck parked in the shade of the big cottonwood by the house, where it usually stood. The dogs ran up to her vehicle joyously, tongues lolling, tails wagging. She got out and slammed the door, standing for a moment absorbing the faint hum and buzz of dragonflies and grasshoppers that was the sound of the remote high country in mid-summer. For a few seconds she tensed as she thought she heard the rhythmic ring of steel on steel, a muffled sound, then she shrugged. It must have been her imagination. Her father's old Chevy stood silent and dusty in the ancient doorless shed that passed for a garage at the Lazy J. Augustus never used the car, hadn't since Martha died.

Nola poked her head inside the screen door of the house. "You home, Augustus?" she called. Silence. The unlocked door wasn't unusual. No one locked their doors in the country, never had. Nola could see dishes neatly stacked on the drainboard: lunch for one. One plate, one cup, one fork and knife, a magazine opened on the kitchen table as though the solitary diner had been catching up on the feed prices in the local stock weekly, or "Who's Suing Whom" in *Western Report.*

Nola let the screen door slam shut. Maybe someone had borrowed Augustus's truck, maybe he was out in the barn or somewhere.

She walked across the yard, and around the garage toward where the big hay sheds were, and the barn. Then she stopped dead.

There was a Ford pickup parked there, beside a mower, but it wasn't Augustus's. It had Montana plates, a locked toolbox built in just behind the cab and a horse trailer, empty, hitched behind.

"Hello!" she called. Not a sound. Annoyed, Nola strode over toward the barn, toward the big door opened halfway on its overhead runner. Rupert bounded ahead of her, whining with excitement.

At first she couldn't see in the huge dark interior, then she heard the unmistakable ring of metal on metal again, off to her left, toward the rarely used smithy. It had a door that connected to the barn, one that Rupert was scratching, and a larger one to the west, that opened directly to the outside. Nola went up to the connecting door and reached out to open it. *What the—?*

The door opened before her hand closed on the latch and she nearly fell forward. Her breath caught in her throat, so painful suddenly that she could barely breathe.

"Looking for someone?"

Carson Harlow was stripped to the waist, his bare chest not ten inches in front of her nose, the dark hair on it glistening and flattened with rivulets of perspiration. She looked up. He had a red, sweat-darkened bandanna tied around his sun-bleached head, and his face gleamed dark and mysterious in the hot glow from the forge. A blacksmith's leather apron covered him loosely from mid-chest to mid-thigh. He looked wild and glorious and strong and completely, totally, uncompromisingly male.

Nola took a slight step back, dismayed to hear what she realized was a gasp, and that it had come from her own throat. She wiped suddenly damp palms against the sides of her jeans.

"Y-Yes, I'm looking for my father."

"He's gone to town."

"Oh." *Oh?* She didn't know what else to say, and realized she must look awfully foolish standing there just staring at him, which she couldn't seem to stop doing.

"He should be back soon." Carson took a step back and opened the door fully. "He's tracking down a part for the mower." She could see the other door, the one to the outside, open, and a horse tethered to a post outside. A buckskin mare was tethered just inside the shop, shifting her weight nervously from side to side. He made a weary half gesture and motioned Nola inside.

"Come in. Maybe you could give me a hand." She entered, and he shut the door behind her.

She could barely breathe at his nearness, at the potent male scent of him, at the scent of horses and smoke and leather and hot iron. It had been years since Augustus had used the smithy, although he occasionally loaned the shop to neighboring ranchers.

"Now that you're here, you might as well hold Shasta. I'm having a hell of a time getting her back feet shod. She's just a baby, she's not used to this yet."

Carson walked to the mare's head, murmuring soft, soothing sounds deep in his throat, sounds that made the skin at the back of Nola's neck prickle with tension. She took the lead he handed her. She felt like an idiot. Her heart was thumping so loudly she was sure he could hear it, but he seemed blessedly unaware. If he knew what she was thinking, what she was feeling, if he even hinted that he was, she'd ... she'd die!

"There you go, baby," he said quietly to the mare, his voice deep and low. Nola felt every vibration of his voice brush down her spine. "Hold still, now, for the pretty lady. We'll have new shoes on you in no time and you'll be back outside with Buddy." He stroked the mare's head. *Pretty lady.* Nola knew he was just talking nonsense to soothe the animal's nerves, but his description of her hit her warmly, pleasantly, somewhere in the region of her midriff, just below her heart.

He went back to the forge and picked up a glowing horseshoe out of the white-hot furnace and positioned it on the anvil with the tongs. He began to bang at the horseshoe rhythmically, shaping it, molding it so that it would fit the mare's hoof perfectly.

"How old is she?" Nola called out, hearing her own voice brittle and high. This man had unsettled her right down to the soles of her boots. He was the last person she had expected to see today, but now that she saw him, she couldn't seem to drag her eyes away from the gleam of his smoothly muscled arm as he adjusted the position of the shoe in concert with the hammer's rhythm, from the tendons sculpted in his strong neck and shoulders as he lifted the heavy smith's hammer and brought it down again and again.

"She's four years old. A range pony," he yelled back, not looking at her. "Never wore shoes before. I bought her off an outfitter near Cardston who hadn't used her much. She's a good mare, but she's still a little green. Needs handling." He looked up suddenly and grinned at her and Nola felt her heart nearly leap out of her chest. "I can soon fix that."

She had no doubt that he could.

She watched him put the last touches to the horseshoe and toss the finished shoe into the water tank to one side of the forge. At the tremendous hiss of steam, the mare jumped sideways.

"Whoa, Shasta," Nola said, running her hand down the mare's neck and feeling the fine tremors of fear flicker beneath her palm. "Settle down, sweetheart. You're going to be all right."

She loved the feel of the mare's soft hide under her hand. How she'd loved the horses when she'd been growing up out here on the Lazy J. Now, although she was good at it, she rarely had a chance to ride. First the city had claimed her, then the thousand and one details of her job. It seemed there wasn't much time anymore for just plain, simple pleasure in her life. She stole a glance at Carson. He didn't look like the kind of man who'd ever done anything that wasn't exactly what he wanted to do. He looked perfectly focused, perfectly competent, perfectly capable of finishing whatever he decided to take on. No question, a man like that would be a formidable challenge to her own plans. She shivered, feeling the same flicker of instinctive fear she knew the mare must be feeling.

She watched him move to the side of the buckskin, run his hand gently over her flank, then cautiously down her left hind leg, each action smooth and slow. His back was to Nola, broad and tanned and smoothly muscled. "Okay. Hang on to her now," he warned, glancing over his shoulder. He took a few farrier's nails from the pocket of his apron and stuck them between his teeth.

Then, with a quick movement, he picked up the mare's hoof and held it between his knees, hunching over it and supporting it firmly. The mare struggled for a couple of seconds, a quick, panicky, terrified movement that pulled at Nola's heart. Carson held tight, the cords in his neck tightening as the mare tried to jerk her foot away. Then, quivering violently, the mare stood still as Nola patted her neck and murmured softly to her.

It took less than a minute for Carson to rasp the hoof smooth, trim the frog in the center, seat the shoe properly and, with a couple of quick, sure strokes of his farrier's hammer, drive in the nails that held it securely. Nola was reminded of a childhood ditty. "For want of a nail the shoe was lost . . ." In the song, for want of that nail, a kingdom had ultimately been lost.

"There!" He straightened and turned to Nola, lifting one arm to wipe the sweat from his face. "That's a tough job finished," he said. He gave her a half smile that did strange things to her insides. "Thanks for your help." She wondered how he'd managed to shoe the mare's other feet by himself.

"Not many people shoe their own horses these days," she said, more for something to say, to fill the silence, than anything else. He made her nervous. More than nervous.

She watched him thrust his hands into the tank of water, then splash it up over his face and chest. He shook his head and the drops flew in a high glistening arc from his shaggy head.

"Maybe not," he said, straightening. He pulled the sweat-darkened bandanna from his head and wiped his wet face with it, his eyes not leaving hers. Then he added, "But I've lived long enough to know it's easier to do a job yourself than count on somebody else to do it."

He walked over to the wall, chest streaming with water, and slowly, methodically, hung the tools he'd used on the dusty hooks hammered into the wall. The apron he hung on its own peg. "My brother and I learned how to shoe a horse before we got out of school." He laughed, a rough sound with not much humor in it. "Had to, I guess."

He turned around and Nola tried hard not to suck in her breath. He looked magnificent. Utterly magnificent. She'd never seen a man look sexier or more...more absolutely at home where he was. Wherever he was...here or roaming the hills. He was a roamer, a rambler, a dreamer who searched for gold. A mountain man. Home was nowhere to him, home was everywhere.

She realized now, seeing the dark hair on his wet chest, that he wasn't a natural blond, that the sun had bleached the hair on his head to that nearly straw color on top, leaving it much darker underneath. She wondered how it would feel, would his hair be coarse and springy in her fingers, or soft and thick and warm as silk? She met his level, inquiring gaze and tried desperately to will the color from her cheeks.

She'd never met a man whose presence was so boldly, so aggressively, so potently male. She wasn't alone, couldn't be—any woman, no matter how experienced or inexperienced would feel like a schoolgirl in the presence of a man such as this. Each careful argument she'd constructed on the way to the Lazy J, each charge she'd planned to make with regard to his relationship with Augustus melted from her mind. She felt her cheeks grow hotter, her throat drier. This man was trouble . . . big trouble.

And it wasn't just because of the Painted Rocks site. Or Augustus.

Chapter Three

She had to say something... anything!

A brother... he'd said something about a brother. "Uh, where are you from, anyway? I know you're from the States, but I don't think Augustus said exactly where..." She could have kicked herself for the way she was babbling. She had to get a grip on herself. After all, she was a lawyer, she had been trained to control her emotions, to present her arguments soundly, to find a way to resolve conflict in disputes far more tangled than this one.

As Augustus had said, she'd probably be seeing more of this man this summer. And if she couldn't convince Augustus to cooperate, maybe there was a chance, slim, but still a chance, that she could convince Carson Harlow. She had to mend her fences with him, after her disastrous beginning the other night. After all, she had no real objection to Augustus's friendship with this man, it was the prospecting around the Wild Plum and the idea that he might be using Augustus for his own ends that had her upset.

"I'm from Idaho, originally." He moved to the mare's head and took the lead from Nola's suddenly nerveless hands. "The Sawtooth Valley. Ever been there?"

He looked at her, one eyebrow raised.

"No. But I've heard that it's very beautiful," Nola said. "It's near Ketchum, isn't it?"

"North of Ketchum."

He led the mare outside. Nola followed him, relieved to get outside. She took a deep breath. Out here in the sunshine Carson Harlow wasn't a giant, a primitive male god, dark and splendid in the hot glow of the forge. Her reaction to him had been a product of her overactive imagination, that's all. Out here, he was a man, just like other men.

Carson tied the mare to the rail beside the black, then put his shoulder to the door of the shop to close it securely. "There's skiing there, a lot of ranching. Yeah, you could say it's a pretty place." He shrugged. "But so are a lot of other places."

And he'd seen a lot of other places, she knew that. The itinerant life of a prospector meant chasing your hunches, following your heart.

"Why'd you leave?"

He looked directly at her, eyes suddenly interested. "Why do you ask?"

"I—I don't know." She patted the black gelding nervously on his shoulder. She really didn't know why she'd asked him, it had just come out. "Just curious, I guess."

"Look."

Carson came up to where she stood by the horse and stopped in front of her. She had to look up at him to avoid staring at his bare chest, which was right in front of her eyes. He reached for her hands and held them. Nola felt her eyes widen, not in fear, she knew. Surprise, maybe...

"There were a lot of reasons I left the Sawtooth Valley, none of them all that interesting. There was a woman involved, and some bad blood between me and my brother, and a few other things that I don't really feel like talking about."

That was fair enough. Nola felt a faint flush creep up from her throat at his words. *Mind your own business.* It couldn't be clearer.

"Now." He squeezed her hands slightly and she felt her pulse quicken. "The way I figure it is this. You and I are going to be running into each other this summer. Maybe a lot. Maybe we can try and see if we can get along a little better, huh?"

What was he saying, exactly what she'd been thinking?

"I'm sorry for what I said the other night. That stuff about getting my jacket off a dead Indian and all that."

He squeezed her hands again, and Nola felt her heart squeeze, too, as she registered the warmth of his fingers, the strength in his hands holding hers. Then he released her.

"Something you said at the time kind of bothered me and I... well, I won't go into the reasons for that, either." His eyes searched hers. "I guess I was surprised to see you there in the first place. I didn't know Augustus had a daughter. Especially a—" He stopped abruptly, as though catching himself before saying something he'd regret.

"An Indian?" she finished for him, her chin going up.

"My, my, my." He reached up and cupped her chin in one hand and smiled slightly, his eyes darkening. "You certainly have a great big chip on your shoulder about that, don't you?" His thumb came up to seal her lips as she opened her mouth to protest. Nola felt her heart race frantically, this time with fear. He was too close, his touch was too intimate.

"No," he went on softly. "What I was going to say, was—especially as young and beautiful a daughter as you turned out to be. That's what I was going to say, but I figured I might be out of line. But now I've said it."

He grinned and his eyes dropped to her mouth. He ran his thumb provocatively along the line of her lips; then added, his deep lazy drawl almost inaudible, "You asked for it, Nola Rosa. You made me say it."

For one shocking second she thought he was going to bend down and kiss her. She felt her cheeks flame with color. Then he laughed and released her chin. "And, just think—a beautiful daughter who's a rip-roarin', crime-stompin', big city lawyer to boot. Augustus sure is one lucky dad."

She stared at him, desperately wishing she hadn't thought what she'd just thought, or heard what she'd just heard. She wished he hadn't touched her at all, never mind in a way that had made her quiver inside. What an...an annoying man! What an annoying *white* man, she reminded herself.

He shrugged, then turned and walked toward the ranch house. Nola hesitated, then followed a few steps behind him, pretending she didn't see the shifting muscles of his bare tanned back, the easy lithe grace of his body as he moved, long legs in faded denim, moccasins on his feet...and seeing nothing else. Her heart was pounding like a hammer mill. She felt as if she were going crazy.

"Would it have made any difference if I was...if I was old and ugly?" she shouted when he was about twenty feet from her. *And married,* she barely stopped herself from adding. Lord! she thought wildly, how had she managed to get herself into a slanging match with this man? She hadn't planned anything like this at all—

He stopped and turned around, a devilish grin transforming his handsome features. Not that handsome, she told herself firmly. He needed a shave.

"Any difference?"

And his gaze dropped slowly, deliberately, to look her over from the top of her head to the toes of her dusty boots. Nola held herself stiffly, not allowing her gaze to waver, not allowing herself to flinch even the tiniest bit under that slow, appreciative, insolent inspection.

"You bet it would. All the difference in the world," he finished softly, then turned and resumed his leisurely pace toward the ranch house.

A blind, hot fury swept through her. She felt like taking off one of her boots and throwing it at him. Darn Augustus, anyway, when was he coming back? Why did she have the rotten luck to keep running into Carson Harlow every time she came to the Lazy J? Why didn't he just . . . just go back into the hills and poke at rocks or whatever it was prospectors did? Why was he always hanging around here?

Nola pretended she'd suddenly forgotten something in her car and stalked off toward it, waiting there five minutes before following him into the house. When she finally went in, she could hear the shower upstairs running and all her anger returned as the image flashed into her mind of him standing there, buck naked, the water washing down his powerful shoulders, over his back, spraying his lean, flat, tightly muscled belly—She shut her eyes tightly, held her hands over her ears and let out a tiny scream, knowing no one but the dogs could hear her. What was it about this man that was making her crazy?

Ten minutes later, still fuming, but telling herself it was in her best interests—everyone's best interests—to get her emotions under control, Nola sat at the kitchen table flipping rapidly through a magazine. Every page looked exactly like the one before. She heard a door slam upstairs and looked up to see Carson come down the stairs, two at a time. He'd shaved, too, and with his hair slicked back and wet, and with a clean shirt on, he looked almost civilized.

Almost . . . the shirt wasn't buttoned. Nola resolutely kept her eyes from it.

He stood there for a full minute, which seemed an eternity to her, balancing lightly on the balls of his feet. His gaze held hers, head high. She met his eyes square on across the expanse of the kitchen, across the scrubbed wooden table where they'd shared their first meal. Then, with just a shadow of a grin and a quick "See you later," he was gone.

It was a little anticlimactic. Nola sat at the table a moment longer, examining her feelings, wondering why disappointment outweighed relief. Then curiosity overcame her resolve and she ran to the window to watch him leave.

He was loading the mare into the horse trailer. Nola watched as he eased her in slowly, talking to her the whole time. The black gelding, obviously used to the procedure, entered readily. Nola was pleased to see that he loaded his horses back to front. It was much safer for the animals in case of a sudden stop. She didn't know why it mattered to her, but she knew it did. It showed consideration for his animals, concern. She liked that. And despised herself for even caring.

She watched the plume of dust rise behind the departing truck and trailer, then listened to the gathering silence as the sound of the truck's engine faded in the distance. She felt a strange sense of let-down. She had to admit, whatever else this man did to her, he certainly got her blood moving. It reminded her of the adrenaline rush of a good court fight, the thrill of knowing you'd blocked the opposition with an airtight argument of your own, the cat-and-cream satisfaction of watching the Crown's counsel blunder on, knowing you had him dead as soon as it was your turn to address the jury. Few experiences in life equaled the excitement of that kind of moment. Nola had a good notion that a knock-down, drag-out tangle with this man might just measure up to it. But she wasn't sure that she wanted to find out for sure.

By the time Augustus arrived, an hour and a half later, Nola had had a chance to reason out her position again and muster her forces. She greeted her father with a hug and a smile as he stomped up the veranda steps.

"Thought that might be your car," he said, giving her a suspicious glance, but returning her hug warmly. She knew he knew darn well it was her car. "Carson still here?"

"He left a while ago," Nola said lightly. She hoped it sounded as though she wasn't much interested in Carson Harlow's whereabouts. Which, of course, she wasn't. She took her father's hat and twirled it in her right hand. "Sit down, Dad. I'll bring you out some lemonade I just made. It's such a hot day, maybe we can sit here in the shade for a while. Have you had lunch?"

The dishes in the sink, she'd surmised, had been Carson's. She pretended not to see her father's mounting suspicion. She knew he didn't trust her one bit when she called him "Dad." It had just slipped out. Ever since she was a child she'd called him "Dad" when she especially wanted to soften him up for something. A new doll, a trip to the cattle auction with him, permission to camp out by herself under the stars.

"Some lemonade might be nice," he allowed, and sank into one of the white-painted Adirondack chairs on the veranda with a muffled grunt. Nola knew her father's rheumatism bothered him more each year. Those long years in the saddle, in all kinds of weather, had their toll eventually. High country ranching was not an easy life.

"Here you go!" She put down a tray with tall glasses of lemonade decorated with sprigs of fresh mint from the overgrown garden out back, and tinkling with ice. On a plate was a ham and cheese sandwich she'd quickly slapped together.

"Humph." Her father gave her a wary look and reached for the sandwich. "Thanks."

Nola pulled one of the other chairs a little closer to his and sat down. She reached for a glass, then held it up and smiled brightly at him. "Cheers."

"Cheers." He held up his own glass and winked. A sly grin creased his weathered face. "So, Nola Rose. What's on your mind?"

"Oh...nothing." She took a long swallow of the icy cold drink and put her feet up on the peeled lodgepole pine timber that formed the edge of the balustrade. From between the toes of her stockinged feet she examined the familiar view of the Rockies rising hard and bright behind the ranch, snowcapped and eternal. It was the prettiest picture in the whole world, a view that money couldn't buy.

The headwaters of the Wild Plum Creek were up there somewhere. The Painted Rocks were up there. She frowned and took another swallow. Then she rattled the ice in her glass, swirling it around and around. "Well, actually, Augustus, I've been thinking quite a lot about this business of your friend prospecting around here—"

"My friend?" He shot her a mildly amused look. "You mean, Carson?"

"Well, yeah—"

"He ain't just my friend, sugar. He's a hell of a wonderful guy and a damn fine prospector from what I've heard. I got a lot of respect for him. Why, Grizzly was telling me a while back that—"

"Dad!"

"This guy knows what he's doing, Nola." *That* she didn't doubt. Not for a second. "He's not just any old rock hound, I can tell you that. And I've got to admit I'm tickled pink the way he tracked me down like he did, asked my permission to prospect the Lazy J, like a real gentleman, and offered me a pretty little deal if he hit pay dirt. Not a lot of prospectors woulda done that, Nola. Lots of 'em woulda snuck around here like a bunch of weasels, hoping I wouldn't catch 'em at what they were up to—''

"Dad!"

"Huh?" He finally looked at her. His eyes were shining. Nola groaned inwardly. No doubt about it, Augustus had it bad, he had it real bad.

She chose her words carefully. "Look, Augustus. What if this guy isn't what he seems to be? Have you thought of that? You know how secretive the mining business can be. You know how one company hates to let another company know what it's up to. What if this American is just a front man for some big mining company?"

"Carson? Hell, no—"

"Dad, we don't even know what he's looking for! Do you want to see some . . . some big strip mine for coal up here, maybe—big machines and crushers and rail spurs going in there where you like to go fishing?"

"He ain't looking for coal, Nola. That's the beauty of it. He's looking for something else—"

"What?"

"He won't tell me, exactly. But it ain't coal—"

"Well, there you go. Why won't he tell you? Because he doesn't want you to know, that's why!" she said triumphantly. "He's keeping secrets from you, too, Augustus. If he won't tell you what he's up to, what makes you think the rest of what he's telling you is the truth?"

"I just got a feeling, that's all," Augustus said stubbornly. "A man lives long as I have, he gets to know when he can trust his gut. And, by God, I believe Carson Harlow's a man you can trust."

Funny, deep down she'd had the same feeling. She'd felt scared in the smithy, scared and yet . . . safe. She knew how that mare must have felt, quivering with fear, yet allowing the man to shoe her. Despite her own awareness of danger, deep personal danger, Nola had instinctively trusted him. She couldn't help herself. She'd felt his warmth and his strength and his affection for the mare, and had known in some deep, fundamental way that she could depend on him, too, the way a woman dreams sometimes of depending on a man. She knew exactly what Augustus meant. Carson Harlow was a man who made you feel safe. And at the same time she knew he was trouble, with a capital *T.* Big trouble. She needed to think about this, sort it all through...later, when she had more time.

"Okay, okay. Well, let's just figure for a minute that Carson's who he says he is, he's not working for any mining company—and I don't for a minute think that's not the case, you understand?" She shot her father a warning glance. After all, the best con men had that talent, too—charisma, charm, the trick of making their victims feel safe. "But let's just say he is working on his own. Did you know he couldn't stake a claim because he's an American citizen?"

"Yep," her father said with satisfaction. "And we've got that all figured out."

"You have?" Nola knew what was coming, but she quickly crossed her fingers in the hope that she was wrong.

"Yep. Carson finds what he's looking for, I go in and stake the claim. We got an understanding. I told you, we're partners on this."

An understanding. Nola closed her eyes and uncrossed her fingers. Lordy, Lordy. Carson Harlow had the man totally blindsided.

"You got something written down?" She gripped her glass tightly, and took a deep, calming breath. How could a man of seventy-eight be so...so *stupid* sometimes?

"Aw, Nola, sugar. 'Course not." He shot her a wounded look. "This is what comes of all your fancy education. All this distrust of your fellow man. It ain't wholesome. Now what counts here is, K. Carson Harlow's a man of his word and so is Augustus M. Snow. That pretty well says it all, as far as I'm concerned. We don't need nothing written down. His word's plenty good enough for me." He shook his head as he looked at her with pity—as though she hadn't seen a thousand and one vicious ramifications fought out in a court of law over agreements just like the one he supposedly had with this prospector.

She sighed. "Another glass of lemonade, Dad?"

"It's pretty good stuff," he said as he handed her his glass. She went into the cool, dim quiet of the house, mind working furiously. There had to be a way to get through to him—there just had to be! When she came back, Augustus greeted her with a big grin.

"I'm awful glad you're startin' to show some sign of sense over this prospecting business, Nola. I always told you, you can't tell how far a frog will jump just by looking at him. You got to give this guy a chance, sugar. I was getting a little worried after that set-to you had with Carson the other day—"

"That's just it, Augustus. I'm not." She leaned back and took up her cold glass. She studied the scene before her with narrowed eyes, and absently rubbed at the condensation on her glass with her thumb. She didn't want to hear any more about how wonderful K. Carson Harlow was....

"Not what?"

"Not showing any sense, as you put it. The fact is, Augustus, I'm the only one who *is* showing any sense about this man." She sat up straight in her chair and put her glass down again. She held out her hand and counted her points off on her fingers. "Listen, here. A stranger shows up one day and says he might have found something valuable on your ranch—gold, coal, uranium, God knows what. Does he tell you what he's looking for? No! Does he give you any references, any past partners you can check out? No! Does he offer you a written agreement so, just in case he does find something out there, you don't get burned? No! Whose word have you got on this guy? Grizzly Sawchuck's, for Pete's sake. Grizzly!" She let her shriek of disbelief speak for her opinion—and most of southwestern Alberta's opinion—of Grizzly Sawchuck.

"'Trust me.' That's all Carson Harlow says—" She thought, guiltily, that she'd felt she could trust him, too. But she had the sense to know better, not to let her heart rule her head. And she had the benefit of considerable courtroom experience and an education that told her that there were reasons for binding agreements, duly witnessed. Darn good reasons. Especially for someone as vulnerable to a certain kind of appeal as her father.

"That ain't true. Carson's never asked me to trust him. I just do. Look here, sweetheart. Just think..." Augustus was leaning toward her, his gnarled hand on the arm of her chair. "If this here prospect pans out and, don't say I told you, but I figure it's got to—Carson's got some kind of inside edge, a map or something, he won't tell me exactly—" He lowered his voice in confidence, and Nola shot him a look of pure alarm. "We're gonna be rich. Rich! You and me!"

He slapped his knee and laughed. "Just think! All these years of scratchin' on the Lazy J, and sitting out there behind us the whole time, up in a bunch of scrub pasture and dry gulches that was only fit for losing good beefsteak in—land that gave nothing but damn-it-all trouble and aggravation—all these years there's been something sitting back there just awaitin' for a smart young fella like Carson Harlow to come along. You'll see, sugar. You just gotta give him a chance."

He paused, apparently contemplating the splendid vision of what lay ahead for them both. "Yessirree. I shoulda found something like it myself back when I was a young fella prospecting, but I never did. Woulda made Martha May's life quite a bit easier, too—''

Her father's voice broke off and Nola quickly looked at him to see him blinking hard, his eyes shiny. So this was what it was all about.... Heart full, she reached over and took her father's calloused, veiny hand in hers. Deep down, she'd known that this was what was behind her father's determination all along. He was living his dreams through Carson Harlow.

"Oh, Dad." Her voice broke. "I—I know you'd have liked to make things easier for Ma, but . . . but that's all behind you now. And you know Ma didn't care." She patted his hand, hating herself for upsetting him, and hating herself for letting her carefully thought-out argument go so badly astray. "You know Ma was happy here. She loved you, she loved the Lazy J just the way it was."

"And you. She loved you, too, sugar."

"Yes. I know. She loved me, too." She felt her eyes fill with tears and she laughed, shakily. "And I loved her, Augustus. I always will. She's the only real mother I ever had. But that's all behind us now. Behind us both. You know I don't care about money or anything like that. You and Ma helped me get through college and . . . and now I've got my career ahead of me. I'm good at it. I love what I do, Augustus! I'm happy. I—I don't want anything more from you. You know that."

It was hard to say exactly right. Money! She didn't give a fig for money. Besides, she made a decent living. What Augustus and Martha Snow had given her had a value far beyond mere dollars. They'd given her back her pride; they'd given her their love; they'd taught her how to love again. All the riches buried in the mountains behind them couldn't have given her that.

He squeezed her hand and gave her a crooked smile. "Still, a man likes to do the best he can for his family, Nola

Rose. Give 'em everything they deserve. I'd like to have done more for you both, you and Martha May.''

"I know, Augustus. I know." She sat quietly with him for a few more minutes. They both looked out toward the mountains and the lengthening shadows of the afternoon.

"Staying the night, Nola? I always keep your room ready for you." Augustus cleared his throat and reached for his glass. His voice was gruff.

"I know you do." She considered a moment. Why not? It would be good to spend the night at the Lazy J again. She might even get out on one of the horses after supper for a ride with her father. They used to do that a lot, just the two of them, while Martha read or did her needlework in the last of the long summer daylight. "I think I will, if you're sure it won't be any trouble. They're not expecting me back at the band site tonight."

"You could call." He paused. "You like your work with them?" Augustus's gruff inquiry gave her the opening she needed.

She told him about some of the projects she was working on, projects to do with land claims, irrigation and water disputes with white neighbors, and long-overdue wrongs that needed to be righted in court some day, if the tribes of the Blackfoot Confederacy decided to press their case. Her job, and the job of one of the band members, Ben Walking-Bow, was to accumulate and coordinate information regarding such possible cases, and make recommendations to the various band councils as to the chances of success if the matters were pursued. Then, if her contract were renewed next spring, she might actually pursue the matters in court herself, as legal counsel for one of the tribes.

After supper—Nola cooked, to her father's delight as he said a man could get awful tired of beef stew—Nola brought up the subject of the Painted Rocks again. She brought it up more to clear her own conscience. After her

earlier session with Augustus, she didn't think he was going to change his mind about Carson Harlow. He'd made
his position plain. He certainly wasn't going to run the
American off the place.

And she was right. Augustus said, first of all, he didn't
believe the Painted Rocks existed; second, that there was no
way he was going to call off Harlow over the notion that
they just *might* exist; and third, he hoped she'd have a lot
better argument than she had before she bothered to bring
the subject up again. The picture Nola painted of the disastrous consequences of a working mine going in next to
a historical site of such importance as the Blackfoot rock
paintings, he pooh-poohed completely.

"Hell, Nola. Everybody knows only one prospect in a
thousand amounts to rock worth mining. Ask me again
once we know if Harlow's made a strike."

The only concession she got out of him was his reluctant
agreement that he wouldn't interfere if she wanted to con-
tinue to investigate the American's background, within
reason. Nola still wasn't convinced Carson Harlow wasn't
a front man for a mining company. If she uncovered real
evidence that he was, she knew Augustus would cave in.
He'd be hurt, terribly hurt that Harlow had misrepre-
sented himself, and she was sorry for that. But he'd get over
it. And the Painted Rocks would be safe.

The next day she drove back to the reservation with a
lighter heart than she'd had since she'd heard about Carson being sighted prospecting on the Wild Plum. Why she
felt the way she did, she didn't know. It wasn't that she'd
had any success at convincing her father. She hadn't. But
she had slept well in her narrow bed under the eaves at the
Lazy J. She'd awoken at first light to a morning hush
pierced only with the shrill calls of magpies and larks and
the other early risers, and had lain there for a while, smiling.

She loved the life she led now, the excitement, the thrill of pursuit, the joy of victory at a case won, the secret tears at a case lost... but sleeping at her father's house had reminded her of how happy she'd been as a child, too, growing up wild on the Lazy J. She'd been fed, she'd been clothed, she'd been loved. They'd left everything else up to her. It was worth spending the occasional night here with Augustus, just to remember. It had been a perfect childhood, exactly the kind she'd want for a child of her own one day.

A child of her own one day. An Indian child... with an Indian father. It was her deepest, most secret, most precious wish. A wish she had held carefully, closely, for many years, in her heart. A child who'd grow up safe and secure in the knowledge that he, or she, belonged wholly and completely to one of the great Blackfoot tribes, hunters of the buffalo, warriors of the Plains. And her own shameful secret, the white blood of the father who'd abandoned her, would one day be forgotten.

One day.

Chapter Four

A father for her child.

Unbidden, the cool green eyes of Carson Harlow, the shadow of his slow smile, slipped into her mind, blurring the road in front of her as she began the last descent toward Pincher Creek. Determinedly she pushed back the image.

The statement of pride she'd blurted out to Carson at her father's table that night hadn't been the whole truth. She'd paid a price for the fierce pride she'd regained as an adult, a pride that was no more than a mask for the pain and fear she'd suffered as a child, moved constantly from one foster home to another, alternately welcomed for the government check she brought with her and reviled for the Indian blood that flowed in her veins. It had been a living hell for a child, any child, and especially the sensitive child that she had been. When the Snows adopted her it had been a miracle from a heaven she didn't believe in anymore. They'd loved her, truly loved her, and for the first time in her short life, she'd learned it was possible to give love back.

Then, when she was thirteen or fourteen, a visitor passing through had shown her an *i-nis'-kim*, a tiny piece of stone shaped like a buffalo, had told her it had come from an old Indian and that it contained powerful magic . . . and the desire to find out who she really was had been born in her heart. That desire had consumed her life.

She'd gone to law school and had specialized in aboriginal legal issues. She'd learned the nearly forgotten Blackfoot language, an accomplishment that had opened many doors for her with tribal elders, some of whom suspected the motives of this half-white crusader, the abilities of this very young woman. Then she'd added a final goal to her dream of regaining her birthright one day: she intended to marry an Indian from one of the Blackfoot tribes and wholly rejoin her mother's people.

It was a dream she'd barely articulated to herself, so dangerous did it seem to tamper with matters of the heart. But this was much more than a matter of the heart. This was a plan, a good one. And plans had always worked for Nola Snow. She knew what she wanted: a kind man who would be loyal and true to her and who would be a good father to their children one day. She already had a potential candidate or two in mind.

A kind man. She thought of the man she'd met three days before, the man she couldn't seem to push completely out of her mind ever since she'd met him. Carson Harlow. He'd been polite enough, but did that make him a kind man? There was something raw in him, something primitive and wild that scared her half to death. She supposed, really, that it was because of what he represented: a considerable obstacle to her own plans to secure a historic designation for the Painted Rocks site. And he looked as though he could be stubborn, mighty stubborn.

She bit her lip and applied the brake as she rounded a long gravel curve in the road. Well, he'd discover she could be pretty stubborn, too. She frowned, suddenly annoyed with herself. Why was she even thinking of him in this context? It was only her own stupid physical reaction to the man that told her she was attracted to him. And why not? He was a very attractive man. But definitely not marriage material. Not for her. Not for any sensible woman. He was a drifter, a loner, a dreamer, a man with a shady past, by the sounds of it. And he was a white man. She intended to marry an Indian. That's all there was to it.

Most women, she knew, looked for love when they thought of finding a man and settling down. Not Nola Snow. But then she'd learned the hard way. Sometimes you got lucky, as she had with the Snows adopting her all those years ago. But most of the time, she'd found, love wasn't something you could count on.

One day at a time. That's the way you achieved your goals in life. One day at a time.

She wrenched her mind to the task ahead of her. This morning would be busy, going over the notes of the researcher in Lethbridge. It looked as though they might be onto something with the old timber lease rights, something good. She felt excitement bubble inside her. The fight for justice, for truth—that's what this was all about.

The researcher, Marie Crowfoot, was waiting for her, and Nola spent the rest of the morning single-mindedly going over the documents Marie had collected. Then they had a quick lunch in the tiny kitchen behind the office and settled down for another stretch. By three o'clock, Nola's head was spinning and she was happy to finally get up from her chair when Marie told her that Ben Walking-Bow had just returned from Pincher Creek, and that he'd been to the bakery.

"Mmm," she said, stretching and bending to work out the kinks in her spine. "I think I'll go back and see if Ben remembered the custard doughnuts."

Ben Walking-Bow. He was a kind man, and an Indian, one of the young, college-educated Peigans, only a couple of years older than herself. The kind of man who was on her vague mental list of what she'd want in a man when she finally decided to settle down. She thought Ben liked her, too. So far, they'd only worked together. Nothing even remotely resembling a "date" had occurred, but Nola wondered if it was just because they were both too busy. Once this business with Augustus was out of the way, maybe that would change.

Ben *had* remembered. She'd just selected a pastry, the biggest one in the box, and was laughing with him over something he'd read in the Pincher Creek *Echo* that morning, when Marie came into the kitchen.

"Nola," she said, brown eyes twinkling and a wide grin on her round face. "There's a guy here to see you. Better come."

"Me?" Nola mumbled, surprised, her mouth full of custard and delicious, fresh, springy, sugary doughnut. She wasn't expecting anyone.

"Yeah. A real hunk, too." Marie giggled. "And he looks like he's in an awful hurry to see you."

Hunk?

With sinking heart, Nola hurried to the office, swallowing quickly and wiping the sugar crystals from her chin with the back of her hand. She could hear Ben following behind her.

Carson! What was he doing here?

A man in a hurry, all right. He was striding back and forth in the small office and when he heard her, he whirled, eyes glittering, green and hard as jade. She saw his gaze shift once, over her shoulder to take in Ben, saw a muscle tighten in his jaw. His face was impassive, carved in stone, but his eyes burned into hers.

"Carson—"

"I want to see you, Nola." His voice was hard and low, and Nola could feel the raw anger beneath it. His look was unmistakable. "Alone."

She looked around helplessly. What was going on? There wasn't much room in the band office. "Maybe we could—"

"Outside."

"Hey, you know this guy, Nola?"

She turned and smiled at Ben, grateful for his concern, but before she could say anything, Carson broke in.

"She knows me."

"It's okay, Ben," she said, laying her hand lightly on her colleague's arm. "Really." She felt a rush of warmth toward Ben, and cold fury that Carson had answered for her the way he had.

"Okay," she said lightly, hoping her tone covered the turbulence she felt. She turned to Carson again. "Let's go outside."

He held the door for her. She walked out, of her own free will, it seemed, but she was no freer than if he'd grabbed her up in his arms and marched out the door with her. She was seething. Just what did he think he was doing, ordering her around like he was?

"Get in." He held open the passenger door of his truck. It was parked just outside, in a yellow No Parking zone. Figured, she thought sourly. Rules were for other men.

For a second or two she hesitated. Then, intrigued, she decided to go along with him. What was this all about, anyway?

She climbed in, aware of Carson watching every movement that she made. Oops! Drat the pastry. Accidentally dripping some of the custard on the dash as she got in, she quickly wiped it up with her finger and licked it before he could comment. Not that the cab was a model of tidiness. It was dusty, and there were tools and ropes and chisels and various chunks of rock on the floor of the passenger side.

Carson got in the driver's seat, slammed the door, and started the engine. Suddenly he seemed very large and very imposing, and very close beside her. Suddenly she wasn't sure this was such a good idea.

"Hey! Just a minute," she said, reaching out to touch his arm before he shifted into gear. It was an automatic gesture. "Where are we going? What's this all about?" He looked at her hand touching his arm lightly and she instantly removed it. He met her gaze square on, a muscle in his jaw tightening as he put the truck into gear.

"I thought we'd come to an understanding yersterday, you and me." He gave her a hard, sideways look. "Seems I was wrong. So we're going someplace where we won't be disturbed, so we can clear up the, uh, *misunderstanding* that we seem to have. For once and for all."

Misunderstanding?

He raised one eyebrow sardonically. "I talked to Augustus this morning and I figure you've got a little explaining to do."

Nola grabbed for the dash as he let out the clutch and stepped on the gas, hard. Then she sat in silence as he gunned the engine and steered the truck recklessly off the gravel road a hundred yards from the band office, across a shallow ditch and up the other side to the top of a low, windswept ridge that bordered the settlement. She could just imagine what Augustus had told him.

Despite the turmoil in her mind, one part of her noticed that he drove the way he seemed to do everything—with his own unsettling blend of grace and forcefulness. He wrestled the pickup over the bumps and hummocks of the ridge for another hundred yards, then abruptly slammed on the brakes and switched off the ignition.

All she heard was silence...too much silence. Nola took another bite of the rapidly collapsing pastry. Carson watched her, and Nola felt her stomach clench with nerves.

"So?" she mumbled through the mouthful, raising her shoulders in a brief gesture of invitation. Somehow she didn't think that this was a time when the best defense was a good offense. She frowned. So why didn't he just say what he had to say? She had to get back to work.

Cautiously, Nola risked a glance behind her, relieved to see that the band office was in full sight. Not that she was worried, not really. He hadn't exactly kidnapped her. Still, if she had to, she could get out of the truck right now and walk back, her dignity intact. She decided to play it straight. "So you talked to Augustus. What's on your mind?"

"On my mind!" Carson exploded, and turned away from her, his large hands gripping the steering wheel tightly. She could see an old scar running down the side of his left thumb, jagged and pale. Then he sighed, a deep sigh of exasperation mixed with frustration. "Look, you really want to know what's on my mind?" he repeated softly, ominously.

He turned to her again, just as she nervously opened her mouth to take another bite. His intense gaze on her mouth, on the half-eaten pastry, sent the heat flooding into her veins. Changing her mind, she raised the doughnut slightly, nervously, in his direction. "Want some?"

His eyes darkened and something very hot and very male rushed between them until she felt unable to move, unable to swallow, unable to do anything. The moment hung trembling between them, forever it seemed, then the muscle tightened again in his jaw, once, twice, and he turned his face away abruptly, to stare grimly over the windswept barren hills. "No."

He didn't say another word nor did he look at her again until she'd taken the last bite and wiped her sticky fingers on her jeans. Nola raised one arm to scrub at her mouth with her sleeve. Childish, maybe, but she wasn't going to face him with confectioners' sugar all over her face.

When she dared to look at him, he was watching her, a queer expression shading his eyes, twisting his mouth. She had the feeling that either he'd successfully hidden something from her again, something vital, as he'd done that evening at her father's house, or that he was actually going to level with her. Give her the straight goods. Nola didn't know which she preferred.

"You want to know what's on my mind?" he said again, softly.

"Yes." A woman would, she thought, being dragged away from her place of employment by a large crazy prospector, a virtual stranger— "hunk," Marie had called him, but Nola had an idea she was easily impressed—who was about to bamboozle her aged father and maybe ruin her entire future career as an advocate for her people by accidentally triggering a minor gold rush or something similar in those hills back there.

"You're on my mind," he went on, still softly. *"You."*

Nola tried to hide a tiny gasp as she registered his answer. *Her?* What could he possibly mean?

"You've been on my mind ever since the moment I met you with your sweet little apron on and your light-as-a-feather buttermilk biscuits in the oven at your daddy's house. The last thing I ever expected to see on the Lazy J was a woman like you. Maybe you've heard it said that the way to a man's heart is through his stomach. Well, don't believe everything you hear," he continued over her gasp of astonishment. "Mind you—" she thought she saw a flash of humor in those gray-green eyes "—those were damn fine biscuits. Good cooking never hurts. Maybe you already know that. But I figure it's about time somebody set you straight on a few other points—"

"What!" Nola didn't think she could sit there a moment longer and listen to this . . . this—

"I'm not finished. Here's another one you might want to remember. Just because you dream something up in Technicolor in that pretty little head of yours doesn't mean it's true. You might be a hell-for-leather, hotshot lady lawyer on your own turf—and I've got nothing against that. I admire you for what you do, if you want to know the truth. And if I was in the market, you might be the kind of lady a man on the wrong side of the law would lay awake at night dreaming about. But I'm not. At least, not at the present."

He paused and studied her. Again, Nola glimpsed that flash of private amusement. It made her blood boil. "I guess what I'm saying, sweetheart, is that what you happen to do for a living might impress the average guy all to hell, but it doesn't mean a damn thing to me. None at all. So get off my case."

Nola couldn't believe what she was hearing! She wanted to cover her ears. She wanted to scream. She wanted to smack him right across that handsome face, right across that sexy, arrogant mouth. She wanted to jump out of the pickup and walk back to the band office, head high. To hell with him! *Dignity!* She knew she'd be lucky if she made it all the way back without breaking into either tears or a dead run.

"Ever since I met you, you've been on my mind." His voice was low and urgent. "Day and night."

Nola's shocked gaze swung to meld with his. She felt her heart thudding, echoing in her own ears. There was heat in his gaze, there was anger, there was frustration and distaste, there was something that stopped her from reaching for the door handle and simply walking away.

"One of the disadvantages of prospecting—some might call it an advantage—is that a man in my line of work doesn't meet many women. Not unless he's looking for one. And right now I'm not looking for one. But I haven't been able to get you out of my mind since the night I met you, and I have to say I don't like it one damn bit." His gaze searched hers and suddenly his eyes weren't cold, they were hot. Dark and hot and full of promise. "I don't want to be thinking about you, about..."

He paused and Nola felt his gaze drift slowly over her face, her shoulders, her hands gripped tightly in her lap—so tightly the knuckles showed white. "Don't say anything," she whispered desperately.

But he ignored her. He raised his head a little and looked down at her, his eyes hooded. "I've been thinking about what you'd look like with your hair flying free, what you'd look like with a smile on your face."

He paused again, and when he went on, his voice was hard. "I don't want to waste my time thinking about you, Nola Rosa. I just want to do my job, do what I'm good at, and I want to get out of here. Head back to Montana. Just as soon as I can.

"So, do me a favor. Stay out of my life. I thought we'd settled that yesterday. You don't like me—that's plain to see—and I...I don't want to see any more of you than I have to, considering."

What did *that* mean, considering?

"What's between me and your daddy is just that, between me and him. It's none of your damn business. Do I make myself clear?"

He didn't give Nola enough time to either nod or object.

"So don't go bothering Augustus behind my back with questions he doesn't know the answers to," he went on with a pained expression. "Don't bother making phone calls checking up on me. Don't bother prying into where I come from, or where I'm going. What I'd like you to do, lady lawyer, is just butt out. From now on, as far as your daddy's business with me goes, I expect you to keep your nose out of it—"

"*This is outrageous!*" She couldn't contain herself one second longer. "Absolutely outrageous! Me keep out of *your* life—who just burst into my office and marched me out of there like some child who'd misbehaved? What do you mean, keep my nose out of it? Who the hell are you, anyway, Carson Harlow? What makes you think that what happens to my father is none of my concern? Who's going to look out for him if it isn't me? It isn't going to be the likes of you!"

She'd leaned forward on the bench seat as she spoke, trembling with fury, until she was just inches from his face. She saw his nostrils flare slightly as he looked down at her, as he fought to control his anger. She didn't care, she didn't give a damn what he thought—

"Just what kind of man are you, anyway, Carson Harlow? What kind of man takes advantage of an old, lonely man like Augustus?" she finished on a low note, her voice quavering with emotion.

"What kind of man am I?" He grabbed her shoulders and held them in his powerful grasp. "You tell me. What kind of man do you think I am?"

She heard the raw edge of pain, pain and fury, in his question.

Nola's breath stuck in her throat. Her chest was heaving, she could feel strands of hair stuck to her face in the heat. And more, much more than anything, she felt the iron strength of his hands gripping her upper arms, the heat of his body flowing into her through the fibers of her shirt, connecting her to him. She held his gaze as steadily as she could, knowing instinctively that not flinching was part of winning.

Then, horrified, she felt the full rich strength of the intimacy between them, the heat of his breath on her face as he waited for her answer, and she knew, deep, deep in her woman's soul, that she wanted him to hold her closer. She wanted him to kiss her. She'd never, ever, wanted a man to kiss her, to hold her, the way she wanted this man to. All she had to do was lean forward slightly, just another inch or two....

She dropped her gaze, terrified that he'd seen what he mustn't see—what had to be written there in her eyes, naked, a message any man could read. Giving in, being the first to look away was better than the risk of letting him glimpse her sudden need for him, her shame, the deep, unexpected longing she had to be held by this man, to be kissed, to be soothed, caressed. As soon as she looked away, he released her.

She rubbed her arms automatically, holding herself tightly. She took a deep breath. Something inside her had snapped, some tightly twisted lie she'd told herself forever, it seemed, until she believed it to be true. And she hadn't known, until this moment, that the lie even existed. "I—I don't know what kind of man you are," she said finally, her voice very small.

Carson sat back and took a ragged breath, the ragged sound telling her that what had just happened had shaken him, too, although perhaps for different reasons. He ran his fingers wearily through his thick sun-bleached hair and for a very long moment he didn't say anything. Then, staring out the dusty windshield ahead of him, he said flatly, "I'll tell you what kind of man I am.

"I'm a man who likes his own company, who prefers to walk among strangers. I don't have too many enemies, but neither do I have many friends. I've hurt women in my life, and women have hurt me. I don't value much that other men value. Loyalty matters—'' he looked at her swiftly, then away again ''—and courage. And standing on my own. Loyalty matters because it gives the other virtues perspective. I'm not a real terrific guy. I've lied, and I've cheated, and I've broken the law. But I've never cheated my friends, or my family. . . or my women.

''I like horses and I like dogs.'' He gave her a crooked smile and she felt her heart falter. ''And I like kids. I like spring better than fall. Once in a while I get damn lonely. That's about it.''

He shrugged and smiled again at her, wryly, and this time she smiled back. It was a faint smile, but she couldn't help herself. Something in her wanted to connect with this man, no matter what or who he was. Something in her, something true and deep and generous, wanted to offer this stranger at least the possibility of friendship, of simple hospitality, a white flag for the few short weeks their lives would cross.

''I—I have to ask you some questions. You know that.''

''Yes.'' He turned to her, one arm against the steering wheel, one stretched along the back of the seat. Nola sat a little straighter, mostly to establish the distance between them even though only inches separated his hand from her shoulder, from her disheveled braid.

''Does this mean you're going to let Augustus be?'' he added.

''About you?'' she asked cautiously. She kept her fingers crossed. That meant she wasn't promising to lay off Augustus about the Painted Rocks.

He nodded.

''I promise.''

''Okay. Shoot.'' He smiled again and the sunshine seemed to brighten the already bright blue summer sky.

''First of all, are you a professional geologist?''

"No."

"Are you working for a mining company?"

"No."

"Are you working with or for anyone but yourself?"

"No."

"Are you looking for gold?"

He laughed. "Sure I am. Every prospector looks for gold, he can't help himself. But, no, I'm not actively searching for gold. That's not why I'm up here."

"Are you going to tell me what you're looking for?"

"No."

"Are you about to stake any claims?"

"I can't tell you that."

"Won't, you mean."

"Yeah," he admitted, with a flash of devilment. "Won't."

"Are you going to hurt my father?"

"Not if I can help it."

"Are you telling me the truth?"

"Yes."

"Would you tell me if you weren't?" she ventured.

"Yes." He grinned.

"Good," she said. She met his eyes steadily for a long moment, a moment in which it was painful to breathe. It was as Augustus had said, and as she had felt from the moment she'd met him—he looked like a man who could be trusted. *Dear Creator Sun and Mother Earth,* she sent up a quick Blackfoot prayer, *let what my heart tells me be true.*

She looked back over her shoulder and shifted uncomfortably on the vinyl seat. "Now, maybe you could drive me back to the band office. Ben brought me some stuff from town I've got to deal with and I've got a couple of other things I need to wrap up today."

"Just like that?" He grinned, that sexy grin that she almost dreaded to see for the wallop it delivered to her midriff every time she saw it. He turned the key in the truck's ignition. "No more nosy questions?"

"I'll let you know when I have more questions."

"That's better," he said enigmatically, and let out the clutch.

Yes, much better, she thought with a sigh of relief. The sooner she was back on a businesslike footing with him, the better. The sheer awful intensity of what she'd felt back there had scared the hell out of her. He'd said he didn't want to waste time thinking about her. It hurt, but at least he was honest. Well, she didn't want to waste any more time thinking about him, either. But was that the truth? It had to be—a man like Carson Harlow did not figure even remotely in the careful, attainable goals she'd set for herself. And, she hated to admit it, thinking about him day and night was exactly what she'd been doing, too.

"Ben that fellow behind you when you came out of the back room?"

"Yes, Ben Walking-Bow. And it was the *kitchen* we were in." Back room made it sound so . . . so furtive . . . like bedroom.

"Whatever."

Nola glanced at Carson with irritation.

His voice was bland as he applied the brake at the band office. "Friend or lover?"

"Friend," she snapped. *Lover?* Why had she even answered such a nosy personal question as that? As if it was any of Carson Harlow's business—

"See you around, Nola Rosa." He gave her another of his sexy grins and a wink as she clambered out the passenger door herself. He kept his foot on the clutch, his hand on the gearshift, ready to go. No gentlemanly running around to open the door for a lady, she noticed.

"Sure." She slammed the door shut and he winked again and gunned the engine. She expected him to leave in a spray of dust and gravel. As though he'd known her thoughts exactly, he gently released the clutch and drove away slowly, picking up speed when he was fifty feet away.

"And my name's not Nola Rosa, either!" she yelled, hands on hips, at the distant plume of dust he'd left behind. That felt good. She'd wanted to say that for a long time. He couldn't possibly have heard her, yet, in the distance, she heard the answering blast of his horn as his truck rattled over the cattle guard down by the gate.

And when she pushed open the screen door to the band office, she was smiling.

Chapter Five

Ah, Nola...sweet Alberta rose. With thorns that stuck out a mile. He'd never met a woman like her.

Carson slouched against the door and rubbed his jaw back and forth thoughtfully, guiding the truck expertly over the rough road with his right hand. Lord! For a moment there he'd thought he wouldn't be able to stop himself from pulling her into his arms and kissing that sweet, soft mouth until she shut up and quit arguing with him and recognized something between them that they both knew but wouldn't name. Good thing he hadn't, he thought with a slight smile, he needed a shave.

On the other hand...

His eyes narrowed slightly against the glare of the western sun, he'd have staked a winter's wages that the same impulse had crossed her mind. And that thought made him shift in his seat, sit a little straighter, aware of the effects of a plain old male surge of interest at the prospect of having a woman such as that in his arms, eager, willing....

Nope. Carson shook his head, as though to clear it. That was the last thing he needed, a summertime romp with the daughter of his Canadian partner. Things were ticklish enough as they stood, what with her putting her oar in about him with Augustus. Last thing he needed were accusations and recriminations flying around that he'd seduced the old man's daughter.

Part of the problem, he knew, was the fact that he hadn't had a relationship, not a real relationship, since Becky'd left him. That was nearly four years ago, when he'd gone back to prospecting. It had been a big mistake, leaving the Sawtooth Valley with Becky for the bright lights of Portland. He may not have been cut out for ranching, at least not working partners with his brother, Boone, but he wasn't a city man, either. Becky'd soon discovered that, and found someone else who suited her better. How could he blame her? How could he hold her back from her dreams? She'd spent her entire life trying to shake the Sawtooth Valley dust from her heels. He hadn't married Becky, but he'd come close. Looking back now, all he really regretted was that she hadn't been honest with him right from the start. Maybe that's why he'd been so hard on Nola just now—he couldn't abide the thought of another woman in his life with a hidden agenda.

There'd been a few women in the years since Becky, not many. A couple of widows that he remembered with particular pleasure, and that divorcée who ran the gift shop in Missoula. And there'd been a few ranch women along the way, women who'd been bored and willing.

But there'd been no rancher's daughters. And that's the way he intended to keep things.

Still, Carson shrugged his broad shoulders irritably as he made the turn onto the paved highway that led to Pincher

Creek, what he'd told her was true—prospecting was a lonely life, damn lonely. And sometimes he wished it didn't have to be that way.

He'd known a few prospectors who'd married, but unless they'd married the kind of women who were content to tag along with their men every summer, living out of packsacks and wearing out boot leather, it didn't always work out. Most women resented the long prospecting season with their men out in the hills. Most women—and children, when it came down to it—liked to see their men at home once in a while. He knew exactly how that felt.

Franklin Harlow, his own father, had been little more than a mysterious stranger to him and his brothers and sister growing up on the Double H. He wasn't a prospector, he wasn't a rancher, he hadn't been much of a provider of any kind. And it had killed their mother; their beautiful eastern-bred mama had died of a broken heart not long after Jesse, the youngest was born. Their grandmother, Mattie, had raised them then, and Boone had shouldered the responsibilities of a man before he turned fifteen.

Was he going to turn out like his father? Carson hated the thought of it, hated what it had done to his mother, what it had done to his whole family. Mattie always said he took after their mama, but that was just in looks. His father'd been a dreamer, a cowboy artist, happier sketching and roaming the hills and making up crazy poetry than he'd been taking on his responsibilities as a man. Was he doomed to follow in his daddy's footsteps, the only difference being that instead of a paintbrush, he carried a hammer and pick?

It was ironic, really, when you thought about it, Carson thought, pulling up at the light in the town of Pincher Creek. He rubbed his jaw again absently. Now that Boone was married, and Lucie'd found out how valuable all those dusty old paintings were up in the attic, the old man was finally pulling his share, all these years after he'd been dead and buried. Carson had sold a couple of paintings, part of his legacy; so had Jesse and Boone. Maybe Jane had, too, he didn't know. The proceeds had staked this season up here in Alberta, searching for the elusive outcropping Old Jim had sworn was here. The rest he'd left up in the attic at the Double H back in Idaho, his insurance for the rainy day when he'd need his father's help again. If that day ever came.

Carson pulled up in front of the Alberta Hotel. He noted the barber pole and made a quick mental calculation. A shave? Or, later, after he checked out the lowlife in the tavern? He was trying to round up a haying crew for Augustus. The thought of a cold beer on a hot July day was awful hard to resist. He made up his mind and headed for the entrance to the hotel bar that read Gentlemen. The other entrance had an ancient neon sign that read, quaintly, Ladies And Escorts. Inside, he knew, was just one big barroom.

Canada! He shook his head. No Wild West about it. This was the land of law and order, and they all seemed to be darn proud of it. Colored money and prickly women and nothing ever open on a Sunday. But the Rocky Mountain draft was good, and the women...well, he hadn't made his mind up on that one yet.

The first person he saw when his eyes had adjusted to the barroom dimness was Grizzly Sawchuck. He hadn't exactly been looking forward to running into Grizzly. After his run-in with Nola, the last thing he felt like was being drawn into the elaborate conversational two-step necessary to keep another prospector from sniffing out your intentions.

"Say, Harlow, you old son of a gun," Grizzly yelled. "C'mon over here and let me buy you a coupla cold ones."

"What happened, old man? You finally hit pay dirt?" Carson grinned and tossed his hat down on the table. That was another of these crazy Alberta drinking rules—you weren't supposed to drink liquor with your hat on. Nor could you drink liquor standing up. He slouched down in the chair Grizzly had hooked from the next table with his left foot. The small round table between them was covered with beer-dampened terry cloth, empty glasses and cigarette butts overflowing from flimsy foil ashtrays.

"Hell, no," Grizzly cackled, and winked at the other two men at the table. "The way I figure it, I expect you to be buyin' beer next time you come to town. I'm just hedgin' my bets! Maybe you're lookin' for a partner, eh? Meet Slim, here, and Mort Slade."

Carson nodded briefly at the others, both of whom were grinning broadly at Grizzly's reply. Then he glanced around the room, about a third full of men who didn't have anything better to do on a hot afternoon than knock back beer and work on their shuffleboard game. He watched idly as Grizzly held up four fingers to the barmaid. Nor was he surprised when she slapped down eight glasses of draft. He'd been in Alberta long enough to find out that when you ordered a glass of draft, you got two. Old Alberta tradition.

"I'll let you know when I'm looking for a partner," Carson said, drawing a glass toward him. "Might be a long wait, so I wouldn't turn down any offers, if I were you."

"What about Augustus Snow?" the little prospector asked slyly, his eyes gleaming between bushy gray eyebrows and a straggly beard. "I hear you're spendin' a fair bit of time up at the Lazy J these days. 'Course—" voice lowered, he elbowed the fellow next to him "—could be that daughter of his, eh, Mort?"

"Could be," the other man said, winking back at Grizzly. Carson had the sudden urge to haul Mort Slade—whoever the hell he was—to his feet and punch his lights out.

"Right pretty little thing she turned out to be," Grizzly went on. "Yessirree. I knowed her since she was a just a itty-bitty slip of rawhide. Rough? Why, she took more handlin' than half a dozen boys woulda done."

Carson said nothing, hoping the conversation would turn in another direction. He found himself listening to every word that was said about Nola, wanting to know more about her, but at the same time, astonished at the raw fury he'd felt a split second ago. Nola Rose Snow didn't need defending. It struck him that she was one woman who could hold her own in just about any situation life tossed her way. She sure hadn't backed down from him. None of which had stopped that wild, protective surge from flooding through his veins when he'd seen that cowboy wink.

"Yep, we went to high school together," the cowboy went on, apparently unaware of just how close he'd come to serious physical injury. "She was some wildcat, I can tell ya." He shook his head. "Nobody told Nola Snow what to do—*nobody*."

Carson felt a slight tinge of relief.

"I hear she's working for the band for the summer," the other cowboy said. Had Grizzly called him Slim?

"Yeah. Don't have nothing to do with no white guys anymore, I hear," said Mort. "Not that I'd ask her out, no way." He laughed. "Too much to handle, I figure."

White guys? Carson frowned. What were they talking about? He wasn't planning to ask.

"Say, you boys know anybody'd be interested in a week's work haying?" He looked from one to the other. "I'm rounding up a crew for Augustus."

"Why, sure," Slim said. "I could use some work myself now that they finished with the irrigating up on the Bar S. I'll be there."

Mort said to count him in, and he pointed out a couple of other men in the bar who might be interested. Carson had hoped Mort Slade would be otherwise gainfully employed. So he'd gone to school with Nola? So had half the valley, most likely. Besides, what did it matter to him?

"Thanks." Carson drained his glass and stood, reaching for his hat. "I'll tell Augustus to look for you Monday morning early."

"Say, you ain't goin' already?" Grizzly protested.

"Yeah. I'm heading out, old man." Carson settled his hat back on his head. If Grizzly'd planned on fishing for information, he hadn't received much for the price of his beer. Carson suddenly grinned at the old prospector and tossed a couple of bills on the table. "Drink up, boys. The next one's on me."

What she'd do, Nola decided, was offer a few days' work to some of the Indian boys who were hanging around the band site these days with too much time on their hands. Nola often had taken a week's holiday in the summer to help Augustus hay and, even though she couldn't spare a week now, a few days might be all that was necessary—especially if she took a crew up with her.

When she'd called Augustus to see when she ought to come up, he'd hedged a little before finally saying that he planned to start bright and early Monday morning. The fact that he seemed to be hedging didn't surprise her—she knew he still wasn't comfortable because he'd disappointed her over this business with Carson Harlow and the Painted Rocks. He hated arguments, and he'd know she hadn't given up yet. He ought to know—if she'd been a quitter she'd probably be slinging hash at some roadside diner. Setting personal goals and laying out a rational, practical plan to achieve them wasn't easy. Getting what you wanted out of life never was.

Nola shifted gears and glanced sideways at Ben Walking-Bow, his long length folded into the bucket seat beside her. It was a tight squeeze in her little hatchback, the rear luggage compartment overflowing with bedrolls and duffel bags, the two boys in the back seat. Ben had joined her and the two teenagers, Jimmy Weaselfoot and Nelson White Calf, teasing Nola that she'd most likely need some help with them. They both knew she didn't need his help, but Nola was glad of his company. After the encounters she'd had with that...that American lately, she appreciated Ben's quiet humor, his thoughtfulness, his occasional comments on the country they were driving through.

That American. She hoped she'd seen the last of him for a while. She probably had—now that she'd promised not to try to pry information about him from Augustus anymore, he'd probably disappeared back into the hills where he belonged. Chasing whatever kind of dreams men like that had. She frowned and bit her lower lip.

Not her kind of dreams. Funny, in many ways she detested Carson Harlow and what he represented, yet he fascinated her. It scared her. The man beside her, a man she'd been thinking of more and more these days as someone she'd like to get to know better, as very much the kind of Indian man she'd eventually like to settle down with, didn't have that kind of effect on her at all. She liked Ben a lot, she respected him, was comfortable with him. In many ways Ben, with his tawny skin, his straight Indian nose, high cheekbones, and his tall, athletic build, was everything a woman like her, a half-Indian woman, could want. But he didn't make her heart sing. Nola shivered inside her skin.

Carson Harlow did.

When they pulled into the yard at the ranch, Nola was surprised to see several unfamiliar pickups parked by the barn. It wasn't eight o'clock yet. Who could be visiting Augustus this early?

"Toss your gear into the bunkhouse," Nola called to the two teenagers as she got out of her car. "Do you mind bunking in there with them, Ben?'' she added, turning to her colleague, eyebrows raised in apology. ''It's probably pretty dusty.'' She wasn't sure if she should offer him accommodations in the house or not. When it came right down to it, she decided, that was up to Augustus.

Ben grinned, and shouldered his duffel bag.

''Hey, don't worry about it, Nola. Beats sleeping on the ground and it's more fun for the boys than heading back to the reservation each night. Don't worry about us, we'll manage.'' He winked and turned, following the teenagers toward the long frame building that had served as the bunkhouse for dozens of haying and branding crews over the years.

For a few seconds she watched him go, studying her own reaction carefully, waiting for even the tiniest thrill of extra interest in the sight of his tall, lean figure striding away from her. This man, an Indian, wore boots, she observed idly; the other man had worn moccasins.

Nola waited . . . then nearly pinched herself in frustration. *Nothing!* She felt not the slightest tinge of excitement, of plain old hormonal interest, of the kind of increased awareness that a woman sometimes felt for a man. A man she could get interested in.

Damn! Damn, damn and double damn. Brow furrowed, Nola turned toward the ranch house.

''Augustus!'' she yelled as she pushed open the screen door. ''Where are you?''

''You don't have to yell. I ain't deaf, least not yet,'' came the querulous reply from a corner of the kitchen.

Nola whirled, then stared at her father in disbelief. ''What the heck are you doing? You're not even dressed yet—''

''I *am* dressed. I just got my slippers on—''

''Here I've come all the way up this morning early to give you a hand with the hay. I've brought a crew up with me and—''

What if...? Suddenly appalled, she rushed over to her father, where he sat in the kitchen rocker, a worn quilted rug across his knees, a cup of coffee at his elbow. "Oh, Dad...y—you're not sick, are you?" She wanted to smooth down his flyaway white hair that stood around his shiny round forehead like a halo. She swallowed hard. He was close to eighty...she kept forgetting.

"Hell, no," he said, giving her a quick glance before taking a long sip of his coffee. Then he continued, "I ain't sick, I'm just...just taking it easy. Can't a man have a second cup of coffee in the morning without having to explain himself?"

Nola's eyes narrowed. There was something wrong here, something about the way he'd looked at her—

"Not when he's expecting a crew to arrive anytime to help him get his hay off, he can't. Now, come on—" She took the rug off his knees and carried over his workboots from the rubber mat just inside the kitchen door. "You don't have to help us— I'll drive the tractor. But I think you ought to come out and say hello to the boys and Ben—"

"Nola?" It was Jimmy Weaselfoot at the screen door. "Where should we put our stuff? There's a bunch of other guys' bedrolls in there and me 'n Nelson don't know which bunks to take."

"Other guys?" Nola swung on her heel to stare at her father. Augustus was noisily finishing the coffee in his mug. "What other guys?"

"Other guys?" Augustus looked uneasily from her to Jimmy then back again. "Well, you don't figure I was counting on you to get my hay in, do you? I hired a couple of other hands, that's all."

"Many hands make light work," Nola said flatly, eyeing him with suspicion. It had been Martha's favorite expression.

"Uh, you could say that...yes." Augustus hauled himself to his feet with a grunt. "Just throw your stuff anywhere, son," he said to Jimmy, before bending down to fasten his boots. "We'll sort it out later."

Well, Nola thought reluctantly, her father was right—the more men they had to bring in the hay off the fields and stow it in the hay sheds, the sooner they'd be finished. It didn't look as if there was any chance of rain, not a cloud in the bright blue July sky, but you could never tell when a summer storm might blow up in this country. The sooner the hay was in, the better. Nola wasn't sure, though, that she was up to handling a haying crew, if that's what Augustus had assumed. Ben and the two boys were one thing—

She heard the rough growl of a pickup's engine as it rumbled into the yard and stopped just outside the house. She heard a door slam, then heavy steps on the porch. The door opened, and she took a quick breath.

"What are—what are *you* doing here?" She'd blurted it out before she could catch herself. The last person she'd expected to see today was Carson Harlow.

"Same thing you are, I understand," he drawled, brilliant green eyes raking her from head to foot and back again. "Haying."

He was wearing jeans and boots, not moccasins, and a clean red-and-blue checked shirt with the sleeves rolled back to the elbows. He looked even handsomer than she'd remembered, if that were possible. With a haircut, he'd look almost... almost civilized.

"The boys are started on the north field, Augustus," he said, ignoring her. "Picked up your mail on my way back." He took a step toward the kitchen table and tossed down a handful of flyers and envelopes.

"So *you're* part of the crew my father's hired."

"You could say that." The two men exchanged glances, and Nola felt like stamping her foot at the quick gleam of humor she saw Carson try to hide. She was right—her father *had* known about this, had probably known about it when she'd phoned last Thursday. So why had he let her come up this morning with the crew she'd hired, and embarrass herself? Right, she thought. Many hands make light work— Any other motive she shuddered to consider. Augustus couldn't have wanted to throw her and Carson together... could he? He had to know how she felt about the American.

"Matter of fact," the American was saying, "I rounded up this crew for your father down at the hotel last week. I'm not working for your daddy, I'm just doing this as a favor to him."

"Favor?" She felt bewildered by the sudden speed of events. That reminded her, she'd been going to ask her father about Ben.

"I brought Ben Walking-Bow along with me, Dad. Remember me telling you about him?" She noted with satisfaction the brief tightening of Carson's jaw as Augustus nodded. "I thought I'd... I'd invite him to stay in the house. Especially," she added hastily, "since it sounds like the bunkhouse is full."

"Plenty of room in the bunkhouse," Carson said. He shrugged. "But he's welcome to take the sofa in the living room if he wants."

"But... but what about the spare bedroom?" she asked Augustus, angry that Carson had had the gall to answer for her father.

"Oh, Carson's bunking in there," her father answered with a grin. "I insisted he stay here in the house with me. Keep an old man company, you might say. And it's only right, him being my partner and all."

Chapter Six

Nola whirled, furious. Carson's eyes were dancing.

"Oh," she said stiffly. "I see."

"Do you?" he asked. Her father had limped over to the sink to rinse his mug and set it on the drainboard. She didn't think he'd heard.

"Yes," she said in a low, strained voice that she barely trusted. She kept her chin high. "I think I do." By the time she'd reached the kitchen door, ramrod straight and excruciatingly aware of Carson's interested gaze on her back—and backside, she thought angrily, knowing him!—she'd regained control of her voice.

"Uh, well, what do you think, Augustus?" she asked her father lightly. "Shall I just round up Ben and the boys and take them back to the reserve? Sounds like you've already got a crew and I'm sure the boys won't mind. Ben and I've got plenty to do—"

"Heck, no!" Her father grabbed his hat off the rack by the door. "We need every able-bodied man we can get. Carson, you fill her in on what you got planned for the next coupla days and I'll go and see what those young fellas are up to." With a loud slam of the spring-loaded screen door, Augustus was gone. The kitchen clock ticked loudly in the background, too loudly.

"So," she said, turning slowly, her hands braced in her hip pockets in a show of nonchalance she didn't feel. "What are your plans exactly? Sounds like you're in charge," she couldn't help adding acidly.

"You've got that right," he answered, shoving his own hands into the back pockets of his jeans. The action, seemingly casual as her own, was full of challenge. Of male aggression. Nola stopped herself—just—from taking a step backward.

"Augustus put you in charge of the crew?" It hurt, it really hurt—but she'd be damned if she'd let this man see it—that her father, her own father, would place his trust so easily in a stranger. It wasn't that she wanted to be in charge of a haying crew, not in a million years, but at the same time she resented the fact that her father had handed over his authority to Carson Harlow so readily.

"I'm in charge of the haying," he said flatly, and she noted that his deliberate choice of words defined an even broader responsibility. "Matter of fact, it was my suggestion that Augustus take it easy this morning. A man his age has got a right to relax, let someone younger take over once in a while—"

"Meaning you, I suppose."

He narrowed his gaze as he looked down at her. "Yeah, me, for one. And the rest of the crew." His eyes never left hers. "And you."

They were squaring off like a couple of bantam roosters each defending his own piece of the barnyard. The sudden image made Nola want to smile, and he must have seen it in her eyes because his faced suddenly softened. He held out his hand.

"I wouldn't be here if I hadn't promised your father I'd take care of the haying for him. No other reason. Okay?"

"I guess I can live with that." She took his outstretched hand as briefly as she could, even the second or two of contact enough to make her palm burn. Startled, she glanced up to see a shuttered look drop over his eyes as their eyes met.

She turned to leave.

"Nola?"

"Yes?" She looked back. What she saw on his face was an odd look, a tired look, a look almost of pain.

"Don't fight me on this."

"Fight you?"

"Yeah. Let's just pretend for a couple of days that we can handle whatever this is between us like a couple of adults—"

"What do you mean 'between us'?" She could have bitten her tongue. Instead she laughed shakily. "I don't know what you're talking about—there's nothing between us."

"Oh, yes, there is, Nola Rosa," he said softly. "You know it as well as I do, and I'm just hoping I won't have to spell it out to you before I head back to Montana."

He paused, and Nola couldn't have spoken or turned to meet his eyes if her life had depended on it.

"Let's just let it lie," he went on softly, his voice coming from behind her. "It'll be a whole lot easier on us, and on Augustus, since we're guests under his roof."

"I don't have to tell you that this is my home, too," Nola said hotly, turning. "I grew up here. And I guess I should know enough not to upset my own father—"

"Hey..." he interrupted. "Don't get your shirt in a knot. Of course, I know this is your home, too, and of course you know what's best for your father. I never meant for a moment that you didn't."

"Then why'd you mention it?"

He sighed. "I just wanted to remind you that it was in everyone's best interests to keep the next couple of days as uncomplicated as possible. Let's just remember that we're both up here to give Augustus a hand with haying. That's all."

He was right. There was no point in them scrapping every time they spoke to each other.

"Okay," she said grudgingly. But she was relieved, too. This...this testiness, this prickliness she felt whenever he was around wasn't normal for her, either. She didn't like it. "Sorry I snapped at you like I did," she said, glancing up at him.

"Apology accepted." He grinned suddenly. "Hey...I'd sure hate to have to face you in court, lady," he drawled, a teasing note in his voice. His smile was of admiration, and respect, and Nola felt herself smile back.

"Then just make sure you stay out of trouble," she said lightly, and pushed open the door. She heard it slam behind her, but not before she caught Carson's soft reply.

"That's going to be tough where you're concerned."

She'd pretend she hadn't heard that.

Late July and August was the hottest time in the high country, and haying had to be the hottest job in the ranching business. Nola was glad to spot Carson's pickup at the entrance to the north field just after twelve o'clock, and watch him carry several boxes over to a shady spot under the cottonwoods that lined the access road.

She saw the rest of the crew pile out of the back of the truck—Augustus and Nelson, who'd stayed behind to overhaul a second ancient tractor Carson wanted to use, and Ben and Mort Slade. Nola had been pleased to see

Mort, whom she hadn't seen since high school, when Carson had brought her out to the field that morning, but Carson had tersely ordered Mort back to the ranch to help Ben stack bales in the hay barn. She hadn't had a chance to talk with him at all since then. Nor had she seen Ben all morning. Maybe they could have lunch together....

"Looks like chow time!" she called to the men over the whine and grind of the tractor's engine. Nola had driven the old Massey-Ferguson all morning. Jimmy and a husky cowboy named—what else?—Slim had spelled each other stacking bales, and one of Augustus's neighbors, Billy O'Dale, and Tom Spanner, a silent, tobacco-chewing hand from south of Pincher Creek, had walked behind, heaving the eighty to one hundred pound bales up to the man on the wagon. It was hot, sweaty, thirst-making work.

The men gave a ragged cheer and hoisted themselves one by one onto the half-loaded wagon. Nola slowly turned the tractor and then picked up speed, bumping and jostling over the uneven ground toward the entrance to the field.

"What's for lunch?" Nola jumped down from the tractor and intercepted Carson as he pulled another box from the back of the pickup. "Can I help with anything?"

Her question brought a brief piercing look from under the wide brim of his hat. Nola hadn't spoken to him since their hot exchange that morning. She'd had the morning to think about that and had decided to show him that she, at least, was willing to put their differences behind her...for now.

"Sandwiches, doughnuts...you could bring over that jug if you want. It's got the lemonade in it." His voice was completely noncommittal, as though he, too, had resolved to ignore her presence on the haying crew.

Had he made all these sandwiches? Nola looked in the box. Ham, tuna salad, roast beef... He must have talents that included more than a nose for gold. Or whatever it was he was looking for in the hills back there.

The Painted Rocks. Nola got a sinking feeling in her stomach just thinking about it. She still had her biggest challenge ahead—somehow convincing Augustus to put a stop to the prospecting and protect the sacred Indian site. If she couldn't, how might her failure affect her career, her credibility with the Blackfoot Confederacy? It certainly wouldn't do her any good.

The sandwiches, Nola was relieved to discover on closer inspection, clearly had been made by one of the delis in town. Carson Harlow, superhero, wasn't someone she wanted to meet. Although he seemed pretty good at whatever he turned his hand to…whether it was shoeing a horse or flipping pancakes or overseeing a haying operation. For a man who said he was no rancher, he definitely seemed to know what he was doing—

"Hey, Nola!" Jimmy waved to her, a sandwich in each hand. "Come over and sit with us."

"Sure," she called back. "Just give me a chance to find some ice." Nelson and Ben were with him under one of the big cottonwoods, both with loaded plates.

"There's ice in the cooler," Carson said.

"Thanks." Nola poured herself some lemonade carefully. "Mmm. Looks good. I'm starving!"

His quick perusal of her jeans-clad figure, her old T-shirt, grimy with dust and sweat, made her cheeks burn. But he said nothing. Lord, it was hot! Why hadn't she thought to put on her shorts this morning? She walked toward the clump of trees where the others were sitting.

"Here, sit down." Ben patted the grass beside him and Nola sank down with a sigh.

"Wow! I think I'm out of shape," she said, smiling at each of the others in turn. "Or else I'm getting too old for all this hard work."

"Yeah, right," laughed Nelson, his brown eyes twinkling as he bit into his sandwich. "What are you, Nola, twenty?"

"Nelson! I'll have you know I'm twenty-six next birthday," Nola said with mock indignation. "Have a little respect for your elders."

"Old enough to know better," Mort said with a sly wink. He was sitting to Nola's left, leaning back against the trunk of the cottonwood.

Nola waved her sandwich at him. "Yeah, sure. I should be old enough to know better than to come up here every summer and give Augustus a hand with the hay! But I can't say I ever get any smarter—"

Ben said something, and Nola laughed, nearly choking on her sandwich. As she coughed and Ben thumped her on the back, she happened to glance up and saw Carson frowning. As she looked again, in dismay, her coughing fit subsiding, he slowly turned his back on the group under the tree.

Turned his back on her. Deliberately. She knew it, as absolutely certain as if he'd slapped her.

Bully for him! She sat a little straighter and took a deep draft of her lemonade. Who did he think he was, anyway, sitting in judgment on her? She wiped her upper lip with the back of her hand. A little teasing, a little fun with the guys—where was the harm in it?

She watched him sideways, from under the brim of her cap, unable to stop herself, as he picked up a couple of sandwiches and a mug of coffee and headed for a spot on the other side of the hay wagon, a good fifty feet from their group. Augustus limped along beside him, gesticulating and talking the whole way. Carson nodded solemnly from time to time, bending his head to the older man, as though he were completely absorbed in what Augustus said. Yet Nola knew, knew in her bones, that he was as aware of her, sitting where she was under the tree with the rest of the crew, as she was aware of him, of every tiny gesture, every expression.

He sat down under another tree with Augustus. Just from the position she was in, she could still see him clearly, if she turned her head to look. She felt on display, on stage, as though everything she did would be scrutinized. Instead of making her feel vaguely uncomfortable, as that sort of thing usually did, she suddenly felt elated, excited. . . .

She suddenly felt like flirting.

That shocked Nola. One of the principles of her life, one of the reasons she believed she'd always found it difficult to form long-lasting relationships with men—not only because she'd been so busy with part-time work and her law studies that she hadn't had time for them—was that she refused to play the game that many women played. She'd always wanted a level playing field, and knowing that it wasn't level, even in her profession, didn't stop her from pretending that it was, and trying harder. She'd never compromised that belief. She'd never deliberately flirted with men. She had a low opinion of women who did.

But now . . . now she found herself flirting. She laughed loudly at something Mort said that wasn't all that funny. She punched Ben playfully on the shoulder when he teased her about something they were both working on at the office. She ribbed Nelson about his latest girlfriend—

Then, when she gave the other group a quick glance to gauge Carson's reaction, some she-devil in her heart making her do it, she was shocked to see that Carson had moved, had sat down so that all she saw was his back. He'd noticed, all right, and once again he'd deliberately turned his back to her.

Then Nola felt such a rush of shame that she had to suddenly excuse herself under the pretense of getting more lemonade, curtly refusing Mort's quick offer to get it for her. She needed to walk, stretch her legs, regain the equanimity she'd spent all morning building. She was horrified at herself, as much because it was so contrary to her usual behavior as because she'd seen the light of surprise in Ben's eyes, and the interested gleam in Mort Slade's. Lord! She covered her hot cheeks with her palms.

She'd hoped, deep down, that Ben might become interested in her, as a woman not a lawyer, but she certainly hadn't ever intended to flirt with him to try to make it happen.

The rest of the day Nola managed to avoid Carson, and by evening she'd managed to convince herself that it had all been a figment of her imagination, that she'd imagined everything.

But her dreams—which, of course, were only her imagination—that night in her narrow bed under the eaves, were no less real. Mercifully, by morning they'd vanished.

The next day dawned bright and blue, and too early, Nola thought, groaning as she threw back the covers in response to the thump on her bedroom door and Carson's shout. "Breakfast in ten minutes. Come and get it."

Breakfast in ten minutes, Nola thought grumpily. Easy for him to say. She'd never met a man with more capacity for work and less need for sleep. She'd tossed and turned last night, until she'd finally heard him come in after midnight. What had he been doing until then? She'd never know unless she asked, and there was no way she was asking.

Nola sorted through the clothes she'd overturned from her suitcase onto her unmade bed and found a clean pair of cotton socks. Shorts, a loose, cotton, long-sleeve shirt to keep off the sun, her Toronto Blue Jays baseball cap to shade her eyes....

"Okay, okay," she muttered to herself. She could hear the outdoor whistle blast that Augustus had long ago rigged up from an old Mack truck horn as a signal to call crews to breakfast, to give the wake-up calls in the days when the bunkhouse was full of itinerant laborers, to raise a general alarm in case of emergency, and so on.

The kitchen was a hive of activity. Men stood leaning against the wall, men sat at the wooden table, some with plates of sausages, bacon and pancakes, some with just a mug of coffee in their hands. Augustus was manning the electric frying pan full of bacon, Carson was flipping pancakes expertly at the grill as though he juggled a busy short-order kitchen every day of his life.

"Find yourself some syrup, boys," he called to Nelson and Jimmy who had just come in and were still looking sleepy. The hands of the clock above their heads showed just after six o'clock. "Might be some in the pantry." She didn't think he'd seen her.

"Morning, Nola," he said evenly, with a quick glance over his shoulder. So he *had* noticed her.

"Good morning, Carson." Might as well maintain the careful neutrality of the previous day. Something in her woman's soul felt unaccountably disappointed by the oh-so-careful balance of the truce between them, sensible and necessary though she knew it was.

She threw her arms around her father. "Morning, Augustus." She stole a curl of bacon. "Mmm. That tastes good."

"Grab a plate, sugar," Augustus said, giving her a big grin and a wink. "This is an awful hungry crew and you'd better get some grub while you can. Coffeepot's full—"

"You make it?"

"No, Carson did."

Nola nodded and reached for an empty mug. That meant the coffee might be drinkable.

Augustus continued, "Carson's plannin' on clearing out the back field today, although I told him he's crazy. We've never cleared out that field in one day before. Two's the best we've done, and that was when I had old Pound-maker and his boys helping me that year—"

"'Course that was probably because you always got after your crews for working too hard," Nola said slyly, giving her father's arm a quick squeeze after he piled her plate high with bacon.

"I did not!" Augustus sounded indignant, but Nola could see Carson grinning to himself at the stove.

"Come on, Dad," she teased. Pancakes were next. She went toward Carson. "How many times have I heard you say, 'Slow down, boys, slow down. You're going to wear yourselves out. Don't forget tomorrow's another day'?"

Carson laughed out loud.

It was the first time she'd heard him laugh, really laugh, and it did crazy things to her middle. She felt warm all of a sudden, and full of wide-awake energy, and seized by an almost overpowering desire to laugh herself. Her eyes met his for one long second, then another. She felt an almost physical jolt at the warmth, at the friendliness in the gray-green depths. How had she ever thought Carson Harlow's eyes cold, as cold as the man?

"One?" He held up a steaming pancake on the spatula.

"Two, please," she said. He smiled, and as she turned away, she smiled, too. It was as though they'd shared something back there at the stove, something personal and intimate that included, yet at the same time excluded, Augustus. Nola had the impression that this American, this stranger, knew her father almost as well as she did herself. It was impossible, yet it felt like the truth.

Carson was helping in the field today, since Augustus and Nelson had managed to get the old John Deere overhauled and running. That meant two wagons would be hauling hay to the sheds, which meant they might just finish that field in one day as Carson had planned. But it also meant each team was a little shorthanded.

Augustus drove the John Deere, and Nola was on the Massey-Ferguson again. The two teenage boys and Ben were on Augustus's crew, with Carson. Mort Slade had volunteered to work on her crew, with Slim and Billy and Tom Spanner. Carson had given Mort a black look when he'd spoken up, but had said nothing. That had surprised Nola a little, considering how anxious he'd seemed the day before to keep Mort and Ben back at the Lazy J. Of course, today they were needed in the field. And maybe she'd just been imagining things yesterday....

But no, she hadn't imagined his reaction when she'd shared lunch under the cottonwoods with Ben and Mort. Nor had she imagined her own response to his apparent indifference, a reaction that even now made her cheeks burn.

Today seemed even hotter, if that was possible, than yesterday. Most of the men kept their shirts on, wisely, Nola knew. Carson wasn't one of them.

She caught herself again and again as her eyes were drawn to the far side of the field where Augustus's team was working, watching Carson as he bent to grab a bale by its baling twine, then heave it up and onto the wagon, his bare, hard-muscled torso gleaming with sweat, even from this distance. Then he'd walk another twenty feet, bend down to hoist another bale, wearing nothing but jeans, boots and worn rawhide gloves.... Nola felt like a complete idiot at how her attention wandered from her job of keeping the Massey-Ferguson on a relatively straight course. You'd think she'd never seen a man with his shirt off before.

Besides, he was asking for trouble. She'd seen what a day's worth of heaving bales of stiff, scratchy hay and harsh plastic baling twine could do to a man's bare skin. Still, the hot July sun made taking off as many clothes as possible tempting. She was glad she'd worn shorts, wished now she'd put on a short-sleeve T-shirt this morning—hang the risk of sunburn.

They were working in a field that Nola couldn't remember haying in before. Maybe Augustus hadn't used this field for hay when she was a girl. But she did remember that behind the west fence, just below the slight knoll of what they'd always called Krueger's Rock in the middle distance, was a wallow with a creek through it. A cold, clear creek that had its headwaters either in the not-too-distant Rockies or in some hidden up-country spring. It was less than half a mile from the ranch house and she'd often played there as a girl, making mud pies and wading in the cool water, sometimes with a friend, sometimes with just her dogs for company.

Right now the thought of an icy cold drink of pure mountain water was too great to resist.

"Time out, guys!" She jumped off the tractor. They could take a ten-minute break. Augustus's tractor had taken a full load to the ranch nearly half an hour ago and they weren't back yet. The wagon she was hauling was almost loaded. It was three o'clock, coffee time, and Carson hadn't shown up yet with the big jugs of coffee and lemonade he usually brought to the field about now.

"Where to?" Mort asked, taking off his hat and wiping his brow on the sleeve of his shirt.

"There's a creek just down there. I'm going down for a drink of water. Anybody want to come with me?"

"Nah." Mort felt in his shirt pocket for his cigarette package. Tom Spanner was already chewing his everpresent tobacco gloomily on the edge of the hay wagon, occasionally spitting tobacco juice between the toes of his boots. Billy looked as if he was asleep, stretched out in the shade, hands behind his head, hat tipped down over his eyes. "Carson'll be along any minute with the coffeepot. I can wait."

"Okay. I'll be right back," Nola said, slipping between the strands of barbed wire that separated the hay field from the scrubby bush that led down to the creek below.

Once in the cool of the trees, Nola felt a thrill of excitement. She hadn't been here for years, not since she was twelve or thirteen at least. Augustus and Martha had adopted her just a few summers before that, and it had been when she was about thirteen that some long-forgotten ranch visitor had shown her the *i-nis'-kim*. That tiny weathered piece of rock shaped like a buffalo—a potent symbol of Blackfoot history and tradition—had changed her life, even if she hadn't realized it at the time. Many times she'd come down to this creek, oddly unnamed as far as she could remember, to think about the *i-nis'-kim,* to think about her life and what the future might hold for her, a scrawny half-wild Indian brat who dared to hope. Now, she thought idly, the future was here, the future was now....

She pushed her way through the willows and stepped over windfalls, holding up her arms to protect her eyes from soft green branches that slapped at her face, unmindful of wild rose thorns that scratched her bare legs.

She smelled the creek before she saw it, cool and dank and dim beneath the overhanging diamond willows. It was exactly the same as she'd remembered, muddy banks torn up by cattle hooves, gravelly islands in the middle of the shallow stream, the ancient welcome sound of tumbling, running, life-giving water.

Nola laughed out loud to herself and waded in, canvas shoes and all. It was sheer heaven! She bent down to cup her hands together to bring the sparkling water to her mouth and drank again and again, finally ending by splashing her face all over, gasping at the contrast of the icy water on her overheated face.

She heard heavy footsteps behind her and the sound of small branches breaking. "Come on in, fellas, the water's fine!" she called over her shoulder. The crew must have changed their minds about joining her. And why not? This was the best idea anyone had had all day—

She heard the sound of more footsteps and a heavier, more solid sound of something crashing through the bush just to her left. That was strange, the tractor was over there, behind her—

My God! Nola felt all her stomach muscles clench in horror. Not thirty feet away from her, on the other side of the creek, was the biggest, wildest-looking range bull she'd ever seen, some kind of Hereford-Brahman cross. As she watched, paralyzed with fright, he lowered his massive head and idly hooked a dead branch on the path with a wicked-looking horn. The branch, a good three feet long, flew threw the air as though it hadn't weighed an ounce.

Nola tried to swallow. Couldn't. Then, horror-struck she watched as another bull emerged on her side of the creek, about thirty feet to the other side of her. He bellowed as he emerged, and the first bull answered by shaking his massive head from side to side, huge shoulder muscles rippling like iron cables under the blood-red coat.

She was between them; what could she do? Nola thought of yelling for help, but knew it was hopeless. They'd never hear her back at the tractor. And besides, her throat felt paralyzed.

Maybe if she edged casually upstream—or downstream. There was a bull in front of her and behind. Which way? Nola closed her eyes for a split second and heard her blood pounding through her head so loudly she couldn't even think anymore. Then she opened her eyes. Was that a dog she'd heard? And the sound of something else crashing through the bush? Another bull? Dear God, was she going to die here, in the middle of the creek—

"Ayieee-hah!" Nola heard a bloodcurdling yell behind her and the bull she faced threw up his head and snorted. Then there was a blur of snarling grayish-brown fur hurtling through the creek and an explosion of barking as it hit the bank on the other side.

Rupert! Nola felt her knees weaken. Thank God—

"Get the hell out of there!"

Carson!

"Run, damn you. Get out of there and run as fast as you can—"

Nola turned. Carson was yelling and waving his hat, challenging the bull on her side of the creek. Then she heard a loud crash behind her and heard snorts of rage mixed with wild barking. Rupert was putting the run to that bull, at least.

"Run!"

Nola's feet felt like lead. Desperately she tried to run, but her legs didn't want to work. She made four or five strides through the water, then fell, sobbing.

"Get up!"

"I—I can't—" She staggered to her feet, then fell again.

"Yes, you can, damn it!" Carson roared. "Now—*run!"*

With another bellow—she wasn't sure if it was him or the bull—he charged the bull, waving his hat in one hand, a large broken branch in the other. He was shirtless, and she could see a red gash along one bare shoulder that dripped blood. Images tumbled through her mind like colored glass from a broken kaleidoscope and yet somewhere, somehow, she found the strength to get to her feet.

She clambered up the muddy bank, her clothes streaming with water, her hair hanging heavy and wet down her back. Then she ran.

She ran until she couldn't run any more, on an angle away from the creek, climbing, climbing, always away from the creek. She ran until she fell again. Then she got up, brushing the sharp, dry pine needles from her palms, and looked behind her. Each breath she dragged into her tortured lungs felt like a knife piercing her side. She could see nothing but the twisting movement of leaves in the soft summer breeze. Rupert's crazed barking sounded very faint and far away. And Carson . . . whatever had happened to Carson?

She couldn't run any more. She couldn't possibly run any more. She dragged herself to the smooth, cool, white trunk of a big poplar tree and collapsed against it, her breath shuddering, her whole body beginning to tremble violently. She ought to make her way back to the tractor. . . . She ought to get help for Carson. . . . What if the bull had charged him, trampled him . . . ?

"No . . ." she wailed. She couldn't bear it. Tears ran down her cheeks. "No." The anguished sound cracked the silent summer air.

She heard something crashing through the bush. Toward her. Dear God, she prayed, let that be Carson. Not another bull—

Chapter Seven

"Of all the stupid, idiotic—" Carson growled, his voice murderous with rage. His chest was heaving, his breath as labored as hers. "Of all the damn-fool *female* things to do...."

He grabbed her by the shoulders, hard, and shook her. He was hurting her, but she didn't care... it meant she was alive. And he was alive—living, breathing, gloriously alive. The bull hadn't hooked him, hadn't ripped open that magnificent golden body with one of those evil-looking horns, hadn't trampled him viciously into the mud—

"What the hell were you trying to prove?" Through the blur of her tears she saw the smear of crimson on his left shoulder where the blood still oozed, and other bloody scratches on his chest where branches must have caught him as he ran through the bushes after her. Or as he ran down to the creek. If he hadn't come when he had ...

"Nothing. I— I was just thirsty." Her voice was hoarse and shaky and barely audible to her own ears. Her eyes filled with tears. "I wanted some water."

She looked up, blinking to clear her vision. He looked angry, angrier than she'd ever seen a man look. And she saw more than anger in his eyes, she saw fear, cold, gut-wrenching fear.

He shook her again, his hands biting into her upper arms. "Are you all right, Nola? Are you hurt?" He held her slightly away from him, then, and his eyes quickly raked her over from her head to her shoulders, and lower. She saw his eyes narrow as they took in her shirt, torn, wet and plastered to her body, the streaks of mud on her legs, the pine needles stuck to her everywhere.

"I— I'm all right. I think." She bit her lip to hold back a fresh flood of tears. She leaned her head weakly against the trunk of the poplar and looked up at him. "I— I'm sorry, Carson." Her voice broke. "I—"

She never finished. With a growl, he tightened his grip on her shoulders and pulled her closer, his hands sliding down her arms roughly. His mouth was only inches from hers, his breath fierce and hot in her face.

"Damn you, Nola Snow. I ought to...to—" He never finished, either. The next instant he pushed his body against hers, pressed her flat against the tree and spread his arms to trap her helplessly between his body and the tree trunk. Then he bent his head and covered her mouth with his.

She gasped. He immediately took advantage of her shocked indrawn breath to deepen the kiss. His mouth was hard against hers, hard and hot and unyielding, his lips and tongue demanding that she respond. She tried to turn her head away, but the curve of the poplar's trunk prevented her, its bark cool and smooth and solid against her cheek.

Nola made a weak, strangled sound that she didn't recognize as coming from her own throat. Her head was spinning, her knees sagged weakly, her hands, which she'd raised in frantic sudden need to push him away slid treacherously around his back instead. She felt the whip-cord strength of his muscles shifting smoothly under her palms, the hot dampness of his sweat-slicked bare skin.

Then, God help her, she was kissing him back.

She met each sweet, sinuous movement of his tongue, tentatively at first, then with increasing ardor as the warmth at her center deepened to heat, then to fire. She felt her heart pound fiercely, answering the rhythm of his, felt her tortured breath meld with his, the taste and feel of their mouths together, joined, and smelled the adrenaline-fueled scent of his body—acrid male sweat, the earth scent of the mud that caked them both, and his blood, fresh and sweet.

No! Somehow she gathered the strength she needed to push him away, to twist her face away from his punishing mouth—for that's what this was, wasn't it? Punishment for what she'd put them both through—

"W-what do you think you're doing?" she gasped, managing to wrench her mouth from under his and pushing him as hard as she could. Her efforts made no difference to the rock-hard muscles of his chest, to the bands of steel that were his arms, keeping her trapped tight against the tree.

"*I'm* doing?" he asked softly. His eyes, which had been green lightning before, were pools of emerald stillness now, lying deep in forest shadows, shot with sunshine and gold. He was still breathing hard, as was she. The anger was still there, just beneath the surface, but so was something else . . . something unnameable.

By way of answer to her question—and his—he bent his head again and this time, discovered almost no resistance as he sought and found her mouth. He raised one hand to cup her jaw lightly, warmly, to hold her still. Nola stretched her arms to pull him closer, closer, to bury her fingers in that silky thick hair she'd so longed to touch, to feel every inch of her body pressed against his, closely, intimately. She felt her throat suffuse with blood until she thought she'd choke, and a sudden fire swept through her veins. She wanted him, she wanted this man, this white man, in a way that she'd never wanted any man before.

Just when she felt she'd faint with the giddiness, with the crazy exhilaration that swept through her blood, just when she felt that she'd do anything for him, promise him anything, follow him anywhere...he wrenched his mouth from hers and pulled back abruptly.

Shocked, bewildered, feeling his rejection like an icy blast from those stone-cold eyes, she leaned back against the poplar, grateful for its support. She shivered despite the warmth of the summer breeze, suddenly cold in her wet clothes.

"What am *I* doing, Nola Rosa?" he repeated softly, taking a step back so that he no longer touched her at all. "You might ask yourself the same question."

Then he turned and strode back toward the trees. Rupert whined, looking from her to the prospector, then back again. Nola couldn't take her eyes off Carson's back. He was leaving her here. Alone. With God only knows how many more bulls... Then, just as he reached the forest edge, he turned, gesturing to his left.

"Head up this way. The fence is about thirty yards on. Wait there. I'll get the truck and pick you up and take you back to the ranch." Then he plunged into the trees and disappeared. With a final worried whine and a guilty look at her, Rupert bounded through the woods after him.

Even the dog had abandoned her. Nola slumped forward, sliding to her knees in the deep moss at the base of the tree. She covered her eyes and hot tears streamed from under her tightly closed fingers. How stupid could she be! She ought to feel grateful to Carson for saving her life and yet she didn't . . . she hated him! What right did he have to do what he'd done—to attack her that way? To kiss her that way?

And her . . . what about her? He was right . . . maybe she should ask herself a few hard questions. Nola's face flamed with anger again and she got to her feet, wiping her eyes with the backs of her hands. How could she have kissed him back? How could she have wrapped her arms around him, almost begging him to go on kissing her, to go on holding her? *A white man.*

She looked around wildly. She had to get out of here. Fear sent her hurrying through the woods the last thirty or so yards to the barbed-wire fence, peeking over her shoulder every couple of steps to make sure there was nothing behind her.

Lord, what a scare! She eased her scratched and bruised body through the strands of barbed wire, back into the hot sunshine of the hay field, relieved to see that her absence had not caused any apparent disturbance to the haying crew. She felt an odd sense of déjà vu. It was almost as though the entire past twenty minutes had been part of some wild dream she'd had, a forest dream that had never really happened. But one glance at her muddy, scraped shins and torn shirt told her it had not been a dream. More of a nightmare . . .

She could see the Massey-Ferguson down at the other end of the field, the crew gathered around, holding mugs. Carson had obviously brought the coffee and pastries and lemonade when he'd returned to the field, before he'd come after her, and the men were still enjoying their break. She saw Augustus's tractor turn in from the lane in the distance, on its way back from the ranch with an empty wagon, and at the same time, saw Carson's red pickup, parked a dozen or so yards from the Massey-Ferguson, begin to move toward her. Thank goodness, she wouldn't have to do any explaining to her father, not until she'd showered and changed and stuck a few bandages on her scratches. Time enough then to tell him what had happened. Besides, she didn't know yet what tack Carson was going to take.

"Get in." He pushed open the passenger door from the inside, and she climbed in gingerly and slammed the door behind her. Their close call hadn't improved his manners any, she thought, grimly hanging on to the door post as Carson navigated the pickup over the hummocks and ruts of the hay field.

She stole a glance at him. He'd put a shirt on, loosely buttoned, and she could see a deep scratch she hadn't noticed before, clotted now, just above his collar. He looked as grim as she felt. She looked away. Fact was, she was grateful for his silence. Fact was, there was nothing she wanted to say to him, either.

Back at the ranch house, Nola scrubbed her body under the shower until she hurt. She shampooed three times and swore at the pain that brought tears to her eyes as she tugged free pine needles and twigs that had twined themselves in her long, dark hair. She toweled dry and stood naked in front of the old-fashioned porcelain sink, balancing first on one foot then the other as she applied iodine to the worst of the scratches on her legs. Then she pulled on clean jeans and a long-sleeve shirt and gathered up her filthy clothes from where she'd flung them in the corner. The shorts she put in the wicker laundry hamper, the torn shirt she hesitated over when she saw the rusty smear on one shoulder that was Carson's blood, and her hands trembled. He'd marked her with his blood when he'd kissed her. *Forever,* something inside her whispered. *Forever.*

Nola shuddered and dropped the shirt into the bathroom trash basket.

She went downstairs and filled the kettle with water for tea, her hands still shaking slightly. Face it, she told herself, no matter what else he'd done, no matter what kind of a man he was, he'd saved her life.

She whirled as she heard the squeaky protest of the kitchen screen door's unoiled hinges, then a slam.

"Augustus got a first-aid kit around here?" Carson squinted slightly in the relative dimness of the kitchen after the brilliant sunshine outside. He'd showered in the bunkhouse and was wearing clean jeans, and not much else. He was carrying a shirt that he tossed onto the kitchen table. As he threw it down she could see the wound on his shoulder still oozing blood.

"Sit down," she ordered, pulling out one of the wooden chairs. She pushed her hair behind her ears. She'd forgotten to pack a blow-dryer and it was still wet, hanging in ropes over her shoulders. "I'll get the first-aid kit. That, uh, that one on your shoulder looks like it could use a stitch." She stopped, uncertain, looking up at him.

He flexed his shoulders irritably and frowned. "It's not that bad. I just need a bandage or something to keep from getting my shirt messed up—"

"Yeah, yeah—mere flesh wound, right?" She smiled and although he didn't smile back, she thought she could see that deep gleam of humor she'd seen before in the back of his eyes. It was humor that, like so many things about this man, it seemed, he didn't share with anyone.

"You could say that." He sat down heavily on the chair and leaned forward, his elbows on the table, his head turned away from her. She got out the medicine kit and spread the contents on the table.

"This might sting a little," she said, poised with the iodine wand over one of the minor scratches on his back. He didn't say anything, and she touched the wand to the cut. He winced, but still didn't say anything.

Emboldened, she painted several more of the scratches on his back and arm with the red disinfectant, trying hard to concentrate on the job at hand, trying hard not to notice the way he tensed every time she touched him, trying hard not to notice the clean male scent of his skin mixed with the scent of plain soap, trying not to notice the way his damp hair curled darkly at the back of his neck.

"Damn!" he exploded as she painted the iodine over a nasty scrape on his upper arm. She smiled, and he swore again, a little more imaginatively.

"Okay...hold still," she said, finally getting to the more serious gash on his shoulder. She eyed it critically. "It looks fairly clean—"

"I swabbed it out pretty good in the shower," he said tersely. He looked over his shoulder at her, his eyes angry. "Can't you hurry up and tape it up or something?"

"I'd better disinfect it first," she said, and reached for a bottle of Dettol. "Now, hold still." She braced her hip against his shoulder, to steady herself and him as she carefully poured the amber liquid over his wound, catching the excess with a cloth. He cursed savagely and she nearly jumped backward, stopping herself just before she spilled the rest of the bottle.

"Don't move. I'll have a bandage on it in a jiffy," she said from between clenched teeth. She knew it must sting like hell, but at the same time she felt a weak hysteria rising in her middle. She wanted to laugh. This man cursing the relatively minor sting of the disinfectant was the same man who'd challenged a half-wild range bull less than an hour before.

"What's so damn funny?" he growled.

"N-nothing," she said, pulling a square of gauze from its sterile paper wrapper. Gently she laid it over his wound. "Here...hold this while I get some adhesive tape."

He said nothing, just reached up his right hand and held the gauze steady while she cut off a piece of tape. When she bent over him to apply the sticky tape, she was careful not to touch him more than was absolutely necessary. Even touching him as she had, to steady his shoulder against her hip, had been too vivid a reminder of before, of back in the forest, of the warmth, the strength, the wonderfully solid feel of his body against hers....

"I suppose you like getting that... that iodine stuff on you," he said, glaring at her as she put the last strip of adhesive tape on the bandage.

"'Course not," she said lightly, stepping back to admire her handiwork. "It hurts."

He stood, then leaned over to grab his shirt off the table. "Thanks for fixing me up, Nola." He smiled, a shade sheepishly, she thought. "I appreciate it."

She smiled back. "It's just that... well, I thought it *was* kind of funny considering you didn't seem to think anything of charging that wild bull back there—"

"I didn't charge any wild bull."

"You sure did," she said, looking up at him in surprise. His eyes were carefully hooded again as he shrugged on the pale blue cotton shirt. "At least, it sure looked that way to me."

"Just trying to scare him off, that's all. I just yelled a little. Rupert did most of the work." He shrugged again and slowly began to button his shirt.

Nola couldn't believe what she was hearing, that he wasn't taking any of the credit for heading off those bulls, for... for rescuing her... that none of it mattered.

She turned. "I— I've made some tea," she said, moving toward the counter. "You're welcome to have some if you'd like." She detested the faint quaver she heard in her voice. She heard him come up behind her as she lifted the quilted cozy off the teapot.

"Hey—" he said softly. She felt his light touch on her back, felt him take a lock of her hair into his hand.

She kept her head turned away, bending to pour the tea carefully into two mugs, her hair falling in dark damp wings on both sides of her face. Then she took a deep breath and turned slightly to meet his gaze. His eyes had an odd look in them, a look she'd seen before, but still didn't understand. He held a lock of her hair in his hand.

"Hold still," he said, and worked carefully, eyes down, at teasing free a long pine twig that she'd missed.

She watched, fascinated. His hands, so large and work-scarred and strong. Hands she'd seen so recently wrestling huge bales of hay, brandishing a broken branch as he charged a bull—for he *had* charged the bull, she'd seen him with her own eyes— Hands that had held her roughly in his arms, close to him, as though nothing could ever make him let her go. Hands that were now infinitely patient, infinitely gentle as he untangled the piece of debris. She held her breath.

"There," he said, dropping the lock of her hair and holding out the dry, bent pine twig for her to see.

She took it from him. "Thanks," she said, her voice barely audible. Something had come up in her throat suddenly and stopped her voice. "A-and thanks for saving my life, Carson."

"I didn't save your life!" His voice was harsh.

"You didn't? Just how was I supposed to get out of there?" She swung her hair back off her face with one hand. "What would have happened if you hadn't shown up when you did? There were two bulls, remember, one on each side and—"

"Maybe they were just thirsty," he said softly, echoing her reply to him when he'd asked her what she was doing there in the first place.

"Just thirsty!" She stared at him.

"Hell, they were just a couple of old bulls, Nola," he said, running his hand through his damp hair in a gesture of exasperation. "Look. You grew up on a ranch. Surely you've been around the odd bull or two before."

Odd bull? "Those bulls were monstrous! I— I've never seen bulls like that before," she protested. It was true, they looked as if they belonged to one of those exotic breeds pictured in the *Western Stockman*.

"Okay, okay," he said, holding up his hands and turning to leave. But when he'd taken a step or two, he turned back to her. "I didn't save your life. Got that? You don't owe me a damn thing, least of all some feeling of gratitude because you think I did. I don't want it, not from you, not from anybody."

He studied her for a moment, his face grim. A muscle moved slightly in his jaw. "I know what I'm talking about, Nola. You wouldn't want to owe anybody that kind of debt, especially not me—"

"Why not?" She was outraged. Why wouldn't he accept her thanks, accept it graciously, let her put it behind her? Behind them both?

"Because I'm not a particularly honorable man," he said, his voice dangerously low.

"Is that why you grabbed me the way you did back there?" she asked fiercely. She hadn't intended to remind him—or herself—about what had happened in the forest, and she remembered with shame that it had been more—a lot more—than him grabbing her. "Is that why you...you practically attacked me?"

"Maybe." His eyes were dark and hooded and she couldn't read the expression in them at all. "Maybe I wanted you to hate me, Nola Rosa. It's better to hate a man like me than to get the idea that you owe me something you can never repay. Believe me, there's nothing worse than feeling that you owe your life to someone else."

And without another word he stalked out. A few seconds later she heard the door of his truck slam shut and the roar of the engine as he started it. Then he backed the truck and turned it with a squeal of brakes, slipped the clutch and thundered out of the ranch yard in a cloud of summer dust.

It was just as well that she wasn't going back to the hay field with him, Nola thought. She had a lot to think through.

Okay. She could handle his hostility just now. Obviously she'd pushed some kind of Carson Harlow button, something major, something to do with honor and responsibility and maybe even loyalty, the virtue, he'd told her, he valued above all. Okay. She didn't know anything about that; she didn't *want* to know anything about that.

Nola pulled some vegetables out of the refrigerator and went to the sink to wash them. She'd make a salad for the crew's dinner. Last night Carson had cooked thick Lazy J steaks on the outdoor grill and they'd all sat on picnic benches under the trees in the yard. He hadn't asked her to help—nor had she, beyond bringing out plates and cutlery. Since he hadn't presumed that as the only female in the crew, she'd naturally do the cooking...she'd lend a hand now and get the evening meal started. Besides, she couldn't go back to the hay field until the next wagon came in.

She tested her reactions carefully, underlining the thought in her mind: she didn't want to know more about what made the American tick, did she? Wrong, Nola. Dead wrong. There was a lot she wanted to know. But she wasn't having any luck at finding out so far. Nor was he telling. Asking Augustus was hopeless, plus she'd already promised Carson she wouldn't badger her father any more.

And she still hadn't got any further on the Painted Rocks business. The most pressing and important matter of all. She'd got nowhere.

She quartered and cored the cabbage she held and began to chop it savagely on the scarred, old maple cutting board. Damn! How could she solve that problem? Ben had said his grandmother had told him stories about the Painted Rocks, so it couldn't be all that long ago that some of the tribe had actually seen them. Surely someone in the band could help her out on this. Surely someone remembered something that would pin down the location. If only she could find it . . . that would prove to Augustus that the Painted Rocks really existed and then maybe he'd change his mind about Carson prospecting back there.

Still . . . She bit her lip in consternation. There wasn't much time. If Carson and Augustus started staking claims back in there, it'd be no time at all before other prospectors started swarming over the hills like locusts, staking other claims that might, just might turn out to be worth something. Prospectors were gamblers and eternal optimists. If only she knew what he was looking for. . . .

But he was as closemouthed about that as he was about everything. It surprised her, really, that he had been so straightforward back at the band site when he'd told her what kind of man he was—if that had been the truth as he swore it was. She'd believed him then, she believed him now. The day he'd told her he'd hurt women and women had hurt him. . . . Was that what was behind all this enigma and mystery? A woman?

The thought of Carson Harlow with another woman, those strong, gentle hands on another woman's body, caressing, stroking, giving pleasure . . . made something inside her twist with sudden pain.

Nola tipped the chopped cabbage into a big bowl and frowned. She had to forget thoughts such as those, images such as those . . . *blot them out*. Carson Harlow was not for her. No white man was for her. Nothing could change that. Besides, it was laughable, really. Carson Harlow was for no one—man or woman—but himself. That much was abundantly clear.

Still, there had to be some way to get through to him. Maybe she'd have to put into motion her last strategy, the one she hadn't thought about much, the one plan she'd hoped to avoid. Maybe she'd have to tell him about the Painted Rocks, pray that she could convince him of their importance, hope that he'd agree to hold off on his prospecting. . . .

But that was ridiculous! He'd told her point-blank that he wanted to accomplish what he'd set out to do in Alberta, whatever that was, and head back to Montana as soon as he could. This haying work for Augustus must be holding him up, she mused. But there'd be no way he'd put his entire prospecting season on hold. Not for her, not for anyone.

And now... after what had happened today, how could she ask a favor of him? She owed him, despite what he said, not the other way around. Nola shivered, even though she wasn't a bit cold in the sunny ranch kitchen. She wiped the counter and put the salad away in the fridge, then reached back impatiently to pull her hair into a ponytail at her nape. It was finally dry. In the back of her mind, she saw Carson's hands again, gently working free the tiny twig... smoothing her hair roughly with his fingers.

Blot it out, she'd told herself. *Blot it out.* But would she ever manage to do that? Could she? Could any woman?

"Say, Carson," Augustus said as he plunked down a couple of jars of pickles in front of Nola. "I been meanin' to ask you something..."

The men and Nola were sitting around the two picnic tables under the trees again, with plates of steak and coleslaw and beans and biscuits in front of them. Nola had given in to a woman's impulse and made a couple of pans of buttermilk biscuits that afternoon. *Not,* she told herself firmly, because Carson Harlow had complimented her on them.

"What's that?"

She heard Carson's honey-soft Idaho drawl from the table behind her and paid careful attention to her own plate. Jimmy sat to her right and Ben was across the table from her, next to Augustus.

"When did you say McCormack was coming back for them rodeo bulls? I gotta admit it makes me kind of nervous keeping rodeo stock in that back field."

The rest of Augustus's words faded into a loud buzz inside her head. She turned, stiff as a statue. Her stunned gaze met Carson's, a blaze of warning green between the shoulders of the two men who sat behind her, their backs to her, across the table from Carson. He looked up at Augustus.

"Next Friday, he figured," Carson replied in that same lazy, unhurried voice. "Saturday, at the latest."

About as lazy and as harmless as a rattlesnake stretched out on a rock in the noonday sun. He looked up and gave her another piercing glance, then casually turned his attention back to his plate. He didn't want her to say anything about what had happened that afternoon, that was clear enough.

Her heart began to pound as though she were back at Krueger's Rock right now, paralyzed with fear in the middle of that icy creek. She swallowed, her throat suddenly dry, and it wasn't from the biscuits.

Rodeo bulls?

What in God's name were *rodeo* bulls doing in Augustus Snow's back field?

Chapter Eight

Nola glanced at her watch. It was nearly ten o'clock, and she hadn't seen Carson since supper. He'd disappeared as soon as the meal was over, as soon as Nelson had grabbed her arm and said he'd help her with the dishes.

It had taken the two of them—three, with Jimmy's sporadic help—more than an hour. Nelson wasn't the fastest dish washer, handling each thick, hotel-quality ironstone plate as though it were the finest Limoges. Nola remembered the heavy, blue-rimmed plates well; she didn't think more than half a dozen had ever been broken since she'd come to live on the Lazy J.

Where had Carson gone? Nola tossed her apron on the hook by the sink and carried the damp tea towels out to hang on the clothesline. The sun was setting huge and bright and swollen just behind the highest peaks to the west, the long summer daylight nearly gone. In mid-summer at this latitude, daylight lasted nearly eighteen hours. Of course, in the dead of winter, it was just the opposite.

Nola shivered. Maybe he'd gone to the machine shed. Nola could see a light from behind the big doors. Augustus had said one of the hay wagons needed some work on a front axle. Maybe Carson was helping out. She could see lights in the bunkhouse windows, too, now that the daylight was fading. Maybe he was in there, playing poker with the men, a thick black cigar clamped between strong white teeth, green gambler's eyes narrowed to shut out the smoke. She could see him laugh uproariously, see him throw money down onto the table, see him slap one card, then another, onto the filthy wooden table in front of him, a grease-spotted queen of hearts covered by a soiled and torn king....

Nola shuddered and wrapped her arms around herself. She was cold; or was it that a ghost had walked across her grave? Ghost or goose? She never could remember. She smiled and shook her head at her fancy. Carson didn't even smoke!

He wasn't in the machine shed and he wasn't in the bunkhouse. On impulse, Nola walked toward the corral at the back of the house. Buddy and Shasta, Carson's two horses were pastured there and she could see them both grazing quietly in the distance, silhouetted against the setting sun.

She saw Carson standing near the ramshackle stock shelter that bordered the pasture, and approached quietly, breathing deeply to still her nerves. For starters, he had to accept her thanks for what he'd done that day, especially now that she knew the bulls in that field were rodeo stock, bred and selected for unpredictability and ill temper. The least she owed him was her thanks.

And the Painted Rocks. She'd made up her mind to tell him about the Painted Rocks—it was the only option she had left—and pray he'd agree to hold off on staking any claims on the Wild Plum until... Well, she didn't know until what, but something had to happen, something had to turn up to help her solve this problem before the site was lost or irrevocably damaged. Before it was too late. But first...

She walked up quietly behind him. First, she had to thank him properly.

He was leaning against the high rail fence, hatless, hunched forward, his face turned toward the last rays of the dying sun. The sun had finally slipped behind the mountains, and dusk had fallen swiftly, so swiftly that he was already just a black shadow against the fence in the time it took her to walk the thirty yards toward him. She felt shy suddenly, loathe to disturb him. He looked so... so complete and solitary standing there by himself, so private. So alone.

Nola felt her heart tremble in her breast. But it was too late to go back. Besides, she'd made up her mind.

"Carson?" Her voice was soft, timid. She cleared her throat loudly.

He turned to look at her, saying nothing, not shifting his stance in the slightest. Yet she felt an increased tension in the outline of his body, a renewed stiffness in the line of his arms braced against the top rail.

"I'd like to talk to you if...if you don't mind?" She felt uncharacteristically off balance, unsure of herself.

"Shoot."

"It's about this afternoon," she got out in a rush. He made an impatient gesture with his hand, without taking his arm from the rail, a gesture that she ignored. "Did you know about—?"

"I knew those were rodeo bulls," he interrupted brusquely. "I knew they could be dangerous, yes. I knew you probably didn't know that—"

"Of course, I didn't! Nobody tells me anything around here anymore—"

"It was my responsibility—I should have mentioned it to you, to the rest of the crew." He was silent for a moment, then he slammed his palm against the rail in a sudden explosive movement that made her jump. *"Hell!"* He turned to her. "I just can't *believe* that you'd go down there on your own like that, not when you knew it was three o'clock and I'd be bringing back drinks for the crew any minute. You must have known that—"

"I was thirsty—I told you that. And why should I have to wait for you? To ask your permission?" She was angry, hands on her hips in a classic stance. "And what do you mean 'on my own'? Why wouldn't I go down there on my own, Carson Harlow? Maybe you've forgotten that I used to live here—"

"I haven't forgotten," he growled, turning back to the fence, his face turned resolutely away from her. "How could I forget with you reminding me every step I take—?"

"I used to play down at that creek when I was a little girl— I've been there a million times! How the heck was I supposed to know Augustus would have a bunch of rodeo bulls down there? It isn't as though it's even proper pasture, it's just scrub, it's—"

"Because *I* should have told you, damn it."

Nola felt the tension in his voice, the tightly controlled anger, the raw pain beneath it all, and her own temper died as quickly as it had flared. She took a step forward, automatically reaching out to touch his arm, to tell him it didn't matter, that all that mattered was that they both were safe...but just before she touched him she pulled her hand back as though she'd been burned. *What was she thinking...?*

She said nothing. She took a deep, calming breath and deliberately unclenched her hands. She waited. Carson stared grimly out into the field, toward his horses, toward the black and jagged Rockies to the west, the Rockies that hid his future . . . and hers.

"Well," she said finally, desperate to regain some sort of normalcy. Was nothing normal? Was nothing ordinary with this man? "Well, I *am* grateful, although it must not seem like it." She laughed shakily. "Anyway, you seemed to know what you were doing—"

"I've been around bulls before," he said bluntly, still not looking at her.

"*Rodeo* bulls?" Surely not!

"Rodeo bulls."

"Oh." What could she say? Her stomach clenched to think that maybe he'd . . . maybe he'd— "A-at rodeos?" Her voice squeaked on the rising intonation.

He turned his head toward her. Could he see her, as she saw him, just a dim moon-shot outline?

"At rodeos."

"You didn't ride bulls!" She was horrified.

"Yeah, I did." His voice was slow and soft in the darkness, as though he were remembering, and liked the memory. "It was a long time ago and I wasn't all that good at it. Back when I was young and crazy and thought I'd live forever. Bull riders believe they'll live forever, you know, or they wouldn't ride bulls—"

She felt more than saw him turn his head toward her, felt him smile at her. She was suddenly grateful for the darkness.

"I— I knew they had to have *something* seriously wrong with them." Bull riding, everybody knew, was the craziest, most dangerous event in a rodeo. And rodeo was a sport packed with dangerous events.

"It gets in your blood, Nola," he continued quietly. "It's like a disease. There's no cure. Each bull is the ultimate challenge, and when that bull's behind you, whether you've ridden him or not, the next one's waiting for you. It can be tough to give it up—''

"Thank goodness you did!"

"I got tired of breaking ribs. And maybe you could say I finally figured it was time I grew up." He paused. "Have you ever felt like that, Nola?" he added softly. "Have you ever had something like that get in your blood, until it was all you thought about, all you dreamed about?" Why did she think it wasn't bull riding he was talking about at all?

"Not really," she answered. Was that the truth? She looked down, stubbed the toe of one sneaker against the hard dry ground. "I've always been a pretty rational person, I guess. Ask Augustus. I look over my options and I decide and make plans and then ... then I go for it—''

"Makes you a good law lady, I guess ..." he said. But he'd hesitated, and Nola could tell he'd left something unsaid.

"I hope it does," she answered simply.

"Funny," he said, still so softly she had to strain to hear his deep voice in the darkness. "That isn't what I thought you'd say."

She felt oddly disappointed. What answer had he expected her to give? She'd never ask, and somehow she knew he wouldn't tell her unless she did ask.

This wasn't getting her anywhere. Her head was beginning to spin. She took a deep breath. "Look, Carson. Now that I know just what was involved this afternoon, with the rodeo bulls and all, I want to thank you properly—*really* thank you."

He swore and swung to face her. "I didn't save your life, damn it! I told you this afternoon the last thing I wanted was for you to feel you owed me something. It was my fault, don't you understand me? If I'd told you those bulls were in there, like I should have, you wouldn't have gone in there. Right? Do you expect me to take credit for something that shouldn't have happened, that was my fault in the first place?''

"Well, it happened the way it happened, didn't it?" she said stubbornly. "And if you don't let me thank you...I don't know what else I can do..." Her voice trailed off and she felt the tears very near again, just as she had that afternoon. "I'd do anything to repay you, if I could—anything!" She bit her lip. *Anything*? "I know just saying thank you isn't very much, but—"

He took a step toward her as she spoke. He didn't touch her, but she felt his presence as closely, as tautly, as though he held her in his arms. She felt her pulse quicken, her breath catch. His mood had changed, she could feel it.

"You want me to admit I saved your life," he said flatly.

"Yes. If you hadn't been there—"

He made an impatient gesture with one hand. "Okay. Have it your way." He paused, then went on softly, "You could repay me, Nola. You could walk away from me right now, free and clear."

"I—I could?" She swallowed, afraid suddenly.

"If I told you that you had it in your power to give me what I wanted more than anything in the world right now, that you could repay what you consider to be your debt to me completely, that it would cost you nothing...would you do it?"

"Y-yes," she whispered.

What could he be talking about? She wished she could see his face. She wished she could see what was in his eyes, what was behind his eyes.

"Will you do it?" His voice was stronger, deeper.

What had he said, *that it would cost her nothing?* She believed him. "Yes," she answered. "I'll do it."

He straightened, and again she felt the tension in his body, in the line of his shoulders against the dark sky, in the deep breath he took. Again she was glad of the darkness that hid him from her.

"What?" She was truly bewildered.

"Kiss me again."

His voice sounded hard and distant. *Kiss him!* Nola felt her heart shrink inside her like a frightened bird. *No!* How could she kiss him after what had happened this afternoon? How could he say that a kiss would repay what she owed him—her life? He must be teasing her, he must not be serious—

He looked serious. He looked very serious. The moon came out from behind a cloud just then and she saw his face, hard-etched in silver and shadow. She couldn't see his eyes, saw only that he was standing straight and rigid before her . . . waiting for her answer.

"That's all?" It was her own voice she heard, thin and shocked.

"That's all."

She took a step closer to him. Maybe it would be a good thing to kiss him. Maybe she'd find that kissing him was really no different than kissing any other man, that what she'd felt this afternoon had been caused by the state of her nerves, the residue of her fear of the bulls, the rush of adrenaline from the long run up the hill. Maybe a cold, businesslike kiss like he'd proposed would free her from at least her own imagination.

"A kiss doesn't have to mean anything—"

He laughed, a short, hard laugh. "Of course not. I told you it wouldn't cost you anything."

"All right." *Still my trembling heart, Mother Earth.* She came closer, bewildered that he seemed so cold and distant. He wasn't even going to meet her halfway.

"Oh!" She stumbled against something in the darkness and lost her balance for a second or two. She automatically reached out to steady herself and put one hand on his chest. He made no move to help her. She felt the deep thudding of his heart under her palm, beneath the warm fabric of his shirt, and it gave her courage . . . and a kind of daring.

She leaned forward until her cheek was nearly touching him and put her other hand on his chest, softly, tentatively. Had she imagined it, or had he tensed as she'd leaned toward him? Stood even straighter? He certainly wasn't giving her any help, the muscles of his chest hard as stone beneath her palms, the beating of his heart the only sign that he wasn't a statue but a warm, living, breathing man.

Where did the rhythm of his heart leave off and hers begin? She lifted her face, went up on tiptoe. He must bend toward her if he meant for her to kiss him, but he didn't move beyond a quick intake of breath as she leaned against him fully and raised one hand to reach toward his face in the darkness.

"Come closer." Was that her own voice, whisper-thin? The moon had gone behind a cloud again, and she was glad. She touched his face, felt it lightly as a blind woman might remember another's features, and slid her hand gently to the side of his head, curving her fingers in his thick hair, feeling it cool under her fingertips.

Obliging, he bent his head slightly and, on highest tiptoe, straining to reach him, she touched her lips to his . . . finally. His lips were cool and dry. He hadn't moved a muscle, and that gave her courage, too .

She moved closer, pulled him down toward her, harder, until she could finally slip one hand behind his head, to hold him to her. Then she moved her lips slightly on his, felt a tremor run through his body . . . and still he didn't respond.

Any fear she might have had of him, any thought of the terror of that afternoon, or of the shock as he'd pushed her against the tree trunk and thrown himself against her and assaulted her—for she still believed that that is what he'd done in the guise of a kiss—vanished in the sudden, unstoppable, atavistic challenge of making him respond.

Nola had never experienced a situation such as this between a man and a woman—never—and it excited her beyond all belief. To make him kiss her, as he'd made her kiss him this afternoon . . . to reveal to him the strength of her ancient woman's power. Could it be done?

She relaxed her mouth ever so slightly against his and again felt a powerful tremor run through his tightly held body, so hard, so powerful against her. She slid her hands to his shoulders and felt his muscles tense under her touch, turn to iron. Her ancient woman's power . . . She was suddenly intoxicated with it, with its thousand mysterious possibilities, and she rocked her body, in the tiniest motion, against his.

With a fierce growl, he put his hands on her waist as though to push her away, then suddenly slid them around her and hauled her into his arms. She felt the sudden iron strength of his arms around her, warm, strong, and it felt right, so right, to be in his arms, held this way against him, to feel his heart pounding against hers. It felt so right to have him pull her closer, tighter, more intimately, than any man had ever held her before. He groaned, a savage primitive sound that sent her blood soaring, and opened his mouth under hers and she felt the heat, the sweetness, that she'd tasted once before, and she was lost, utterly lost to the fire that swept between them. He was kissing her. She was kissing him back, insistently, recklessly, gasping for breath, her heart hammering in her temple and in every pulse point of her body. She could feel her breasts pushed so hard against his chest they hurt, and she didn't care.

"Oh, Nola Rosa," he gasped, burying his face in her neck, his voice muffled by her hair, loose and wild. He must have loosened it as he'd kissed her. "Sweet woman. God knows how you do what you do to me...."

Nola closed her eyes, feeling the tumult of her blood, the ache of her breath as she filled her lungs with cool night air, the pleasure at the sound of her name said incorrectly in exactly that tortured way... pleasure followed by the high, sharp edge of something else. Grief, she knew. Tears yet to come.

This wasn't right... this wasn't what she'd wanted to happen. *Wasn't it?* a tiny voice inside her asked. This wasn't the cold, impersonal kiss he'd demanded to claim her debt. This was... this was craziness!

But she couldn't have pulled herself away from him for anything; her legs wouldn't have borne her. He was still saying something, his words tangled in her hair.

"Oh, God, Nola... I didn't want it to be this way," she heard him mutter hoarsely. "Not after this afternoon, not after today. I wanted to find out that I was wrong about you. I thought—"

He raised his head abruptly and stared down into her eyes. She could see his, pools of darkness in the moonlight, could see the glitter in their black depths.

She thought he'd kiss her again; she turned her face up to his, expecting it....

"Nola!" She heard Augustus's faint, querulous cry in the background, by the house. "Nola, where the heck'd you get to?"

Carson released her instantly, so quickly that she almost fell backward. He was no more than a black shadow again, a black shadow that stood tall and hard and unforgiving in the darkness.

"I'd... I'd better..." She took a step backward, away from him.

He said nothing.

She turned and ran.

Trouble was, this wasn't something she could run away from. Over and over, as she tossed and turned on her lumpy mattress, finally punching her pillow in silent fury as sleep evaded her, the thought nagged at her. She hadn't done what she'd planned to do. She had to talk to him about the Painted Rocks.

She couldn't duck her responsibility. No matter what had happened last night in the shadow of the stock shelter—and her skin burned with embarrassment and disgust with herself at the memory—she owed it to the Blackfoot Confederacy, she owed it to herself, to the Indian blood that ran in her veins, to do everything in her power to protect the sacred rock painting site. And the claims Augustus had hinted this American prospector was about to stake were the single biggest obstacle to achieving that goal.

She had to swallow her pride. She had to marshal her best arguments, coolly, carefully, and convince the American to hold off. She had to do it despite every woman's instinct that warned her to run, run, run, as fast and as far as the winter wind to escape him, that this American, this white man, endangered far more than her dearest dream of saving the Painted Rocks for future generations.

It seemed forever that she waited, every nerve screaming, for him to return, to hear his heavy tread on the old wooden floorboards outside her door. She waited, feeling somehow that knowing he had come back to the house, knowing that he slept, too, finally, alone in his bed in the room across the hall, would ease the confusion in her mind. She waited and waited and heard nothing. Finally, tear-stained and exhausted beyond endurance with the events of the day, she slept.

Chapter Nine

Carson swore softly under his breath, then louder and at length when he'd raised the field glasses attached to a thong on his belt. He studied the tiny figure in the distance. A mirage? No... a horse and rider were silhouetted clear and sharp against the distant ridge of rolling hills that ran right up into the box canyon to the south. The tiny black figure on horseback had to be a good mile off, maybe more.

What the hell was *she* doing out here?

He felt his jaw tighten at the same time as the skin at the back of his shoulders tensed, and he felt a knot rise in his belly that was a feeling so rare these days that he barely knew what it was. But he knew, all right, he'd felt it many times before: it was fear. Plain, simple fear. This woman had him running for his life.

Why couldn't it be another prospector scouting him out? Another prospector wouldn't have been so foolish as to ride along the skyline that way, but another prospector he could have handled—would have enjoyed handling. A nest of mating scorpions he would have enjoyed handling, just for the change.

But not Nola Snow. Nola Snow was trouble.

Carson took a deep breath and let his field glasses fall back onto his hip. He turned to the horse beside him and unbuckled the straps that held the packsaddle in place. Grimacing, he lifted it off, muscles straining, and set it down heavily in the long grass. He had camping gear and enough supplies to last him a week. Just then, the horse swished his tail smartly and caught him across the face.

He swore and jumped back a step, his hand to his cheek. "Stand still, you ugly, fly-blown, son of a no-good cayuse," he muttered, rummaging in the pack for the leather hobbles that would allow the horse to graze without straying. "I ought to sell you for dog food, you know that? Worse—cat food. You're way overdue, Buddy, I'm warning you—"

The black gelding swung his big, rawboned Roman-nosed head around to gaze with mild interest at the man behind him. It was just love talk. A little cursing and muttering was the worst he had ever had from the man. He flicked his tail again.

Carson knew it wasn't Buddy that had made him mad, it was that... *that woman.* What in God's name was she doing up here? He was tempted to pull out his battery-operated mobile phone from wherever he'd stashed it in the pack and call down to the Lazy J and find out just what was up. He was tempted, but he wouldn't do it.

No way. Whatever Nola Snow was up to was her business, not his. This was her daddy's property, she was free to travel where she wanted. Whatever Augustus Snow was up to was his business, not Carson's. He didn't want to know what was going on down at the Lazy J. He'd helped Augustus with the haying, as he'd promised, and that was that. The fact was, he'd already wasted too much time on that particular outfit and a week or two lost over the course of a field season could mean success or failure in this business. He couldn't prospect in the snow.

Winter! Hell, he planned to be out of here by Labor Day. Head back to Montana, look up a couple of women he knew—maybe—find himself a place to hole up for the winter, perhaps even have a look around a few of those sweet green valleys he and Old Jim had found back in the Bitterroots, maybe even find a place he might be able to call home one day. If he ever took the notion to settle down in one place.

He wasn't planning to go back to Idaho, not after what he'd been through with Boone. They were brothers, but they were cut from different cloth. Brothers such as that were better off keeping out of each other's way. Respect, yes. Consideration, yes. Maybe even affection, the deepest ties of the blood. But they couldn't spend their days working together. The world Boone had chosen, a world of duty and responsibility and the joys and sorrows of raising a family, wasn't his world. It wasn't Carson Harlow's world at all. Besides, he liked Montana. Liked the open spaces, liked the way they left a man alone.

He frowned. Funny, he'd never thought Boone would just up and get married like that. Settle down all of a sudden. Kind of shook him, when it came right down to it. He'd always kidded his brother that he wasn't the marrying kind. Boone was one man who didn't need a woman to settle him down: he'd been settled down since the day he was born. And then little Lucie had walked into his stubborn brother's life one day and turned it upside down. Or so Boone had told him, proud as hell.

Carson supposed it could happen to a man like that...some men. He thought of his sister-in-law—he'd made it back to the valley for his niece's christening—saw the love again in those big, blue eyes as she'd looked at his brother, saw the love as she gazed at the child in her arms, a child created from that deep and abiding love...the kind of love that lasted forever.

Yeah, he had to say, yeah, maybe Boone was lucky. Carson was surprised to find just how much he meant it. A few years ago he would have scoffed, but now...well, by the way a lot of men measured success, his brother was a lucky man.

Now, take his life. He liked it all right, always had, but he'd meant it when he'd told Nola that it could get damn lonely sometimes. He seemed to feel it more and more as the years went by. Did he want to end up like some of the backwoods loners he met up with from time to time, lonely, suspicious men who drank too much and hated strangers? In his heart, he knew he didn't.

Carson pulled out the lunch he'd made himself early this morning before he'd loaded up the horses and left his main camp to explore one of the neighboring canyons. Two sandwiches, an apple...what he wouldn't give for a cup of coffee. Regretfully, he eyed the handful of sticks he'd thrown down earlier with the idea of lighting a fire and brewing up a pot of campfire coffee.

He wasn't going to risk that now. He didn't want Nola tracking him down by the plume of smoke his fire made. Would she even have the sense to do that? He doubted it. Half Indian or not—and she was too proud of that particular fact by far—he didn't think she had the first idea of what it took to survive the way her ancestors had survived. For starters, no Indian he'd ever known would have ridden along an exposed ridge that way, for anyone to see. Too easy to be taken by surprise.

Taken by surprise? He had to smile. Who'd be laying in wait for her? After all, this wasn't a TV Western. And the fact was, she'd picked a good place to ride if she was trying to see as much country as she could...if she were looking for someone. Someone who wanted to be found, that is.

Him?

He flung himself down under a tree and finished the last of his sandwich, staring up at the clear sky, a solid bowl of blue above him. It was hot, too hot to ride for a couple of hours, and he'd planned to have lunch, think a little, maybe take a nap—he was still tired from missing a night's sleep the night before last, the night he'd left the Lazy J—then push on in the late afternoon, when the sun was lower.

Why would she be looking for him? Carson frowned, pushed his hat down low over his forehead, and shifted his body irritably from side to side, trying to get comfortable. The ground was hard under him, despite the cushioning of the long grass, but at least he'd found some shade in this little coulee. And the horses had a chance to graze.

Women.

His mind turned to that divorcée that ran the gift shop in Missoula he'd met last year. Sandra. Maybe he'd look her up when he got back...china-blue eyes, short blond curls, an innocent look that had meant nothing, absolutely nothing, when they'd finally tumbled into her king-size bed. He smiled to himself, waiting to feel the familiar surge of male pride and fond remembrance at the pleasure he'd found in her arms, satisfaction given, satisfaction received. She'd had beautiful breasts, he recalled, full and smooth, and skin like fresh cream....

And the memory didn't do a damn thing for him anymore. Not a damn thing. Carson viciously smacked the palm of his right hand against the crown of his hat to seat it more tightly against his face, to blot out the light. He crossed his arms on his chest and shut his eyes firmly and deliberately. He had stuff to think about, stuff to plan...serious stuff.

But all that filled his mind was a waterfall of black hair, shining and smooth as silk in his hands, spilling wild and free from that godawful braid she favored, and tawny Indian eyes flashing with fire and passion. Passion for justice not served. Anger at the injustice of a white man's world that had served her people so badly... anger at him, for being part of it.

That's why he'd kissed her, wasn't it? To prove to her that she didn't know herself half as well as she thought she did? Trouble is, that little experiment had shown him something he hadn't figured on finding out: neither did he.

Two hours later, Carson rounded up the horses. Buddy was easy to catch; the old reprobate came whenever Carson held out his hand. Probably thought he had oats, Carson smiled. Worked every time.

The mare was a different story. He had to approach her quietly, he had to talk softly to her the whole time, gentle her with his voice, lull her suspicions, or at the last frustrating moment she'd leap away from him and stagger off awkwardly, her front legs shackled. It irritated him when she did that, that she still didn't trust him. Then he'd sigh. What did he expect? She was young, she was green. She had the makings of a good pony but she had a lot to learn. Nobody'd ridden her before this summer. Trust was something he had to teach her, slowly, patiently.

Today she came quietly. "That's it, sweetheart," he said, pleased that maybe he was finally making some progress, knowing the sound of his voice kept her calm. He threw on the saddle blanket, an old Navaho blanket that was his good luck charm, his talisman. Then he put on the saddle and tightened the cinch. For once she didn't hump her back, didn't fight it. "Good girl!" he said, and stroked her neck affectionately. "You're finding out it doesn't hurt to take a chance, does it, baby? You're growing up."

He led Buddy over to where he'd thrown down the packsaddle. He stopped, looked up at the sky. It was nearly five o'clock. How far would he get today? And what was he planning to do, sneak off and leave her here? Damn that law lady, anyway!

He tied Buddy to a cottonwood sapling and mounted the buckskin. The mare threw her head up, pricked her ears, danced sideways on stiffened legs, pulled at the bit. He kept her head high and wheeled her toward the far ridge, feeling a suppressed need for violent physical activity.

"Okay, sweetheart, let's see what you can do," he muttered, his jaw tight with the sudden decision he'd made, the decision he'd *had* to make. The mare leapt forward, trembling, eager to run for once without the packhorse behind to slow her down.

Carson knew exactly how that felt. With a wild yell of encouragement, he gave the mare her head.

Nola had almost resigned herself to spending a night out under the stars... almost.

She cursed herself for her stupidity in not bringing any emergency supplies, a bedroll, extra food... anything! It wasn't like her. She'd always thought a situation through clearly and carefully and took the kind of precautions that ensured she didn't get surprises. It would have been easy enough to strap a sleeping bag behind her saddle—just in case. Some extra food. A flashlight. A book of matches.

But she hadn't. Which just went to show you, she thought with irritation and a rising sense of unease now that the sun was going down and the shadows were suddenly looming ominously all around her, how that...that darned *American* prospector had disrupted her perfectly happy existence.

Oh, she knew she'd be all right. She'd find a dry spot under some trees, cover herself with Ted's saddle blanket.

Somehow she'd get through the night, even if she probably wouldn't get a wink of sleep, and tomorrow she'd make her way back to the ranch. She just hoped Augustus wouldn't worry too much. Ted was limping badly, and if the gelding's leg wasn't better in the morning she might have to walk most of the way back.

Not even any matches! And she was hungry. The lunch she packed had been eaten six hours ago and she desperately wished she still had the half of that soggy tuna sandwich she'd tossed to a curious magpie. She looked around. She'd eaten roasted wild onions once with Ben's grandmother. They'd been surprisingly tasty, and maybe a person could eat them raw—if a person knew where to look. She eyed the long grass, the cottonwood leaves twirling in the light breeze. Were they edible? She wasn't that hungry yet. An Indian, a real Indian, wouldn't go hungry in a situation such as this. Don't be dumb, Nola, she told herself wryly, a real Indian probably would have had the brains to bring along a few cans of beans.

She should have listened to Augustus. He'd said she was crazy to take off after Carson. And maybe she was...

Yesterday morning she'd come downstairs early, hoping to catch Carson before the rest of the men came in for breakfast. She wanted to speak to him privately about the Painted Rocks. She didn't want even Augustus to know.

But when she got downstairs she'd found Carson's note on the table, informing her father that he'd gone back to his camp and that he was sorry for the sudden departure but he knew the crew would have no problems getting the rest of the hay in that day. That was it. Not a mention of why he'd left—although she blushed to think that maybe she could think of a reason or two—not a mention of when he'd be back. If he came back at all.

Nola started breakfast and by the time Augustus came down, her mind was made up. She was going after Carson.

She was going to find him and tell him about the Painted Rocks, and do her best to convince him to hold off on his claims. She didn't have a whole lot of confidence about her chances for success. In fact she didn't think there was one chance in ten that he could be convinced, but she knew she couldn't face Ben or the elders if she didn't try. Nor could she live with herself.

She had stayed to help with the hay, and set off early this morning. Augustus had tried to call Carson on his mobile phone, with no success. The two men had a prearranged system of times during the week to contact each other in an emergency. Dawn on the morning Nola left wasn't one of them. Probably had the dang thing turned off, Augustus had muttered. Probably didn't want nobody bothering him, he'd said with a dark accusatory look at Nola. She'd ignored him.

And look where it had gotten her.

A vague idea of finding him somewhere on the Wild Plum Creek range was just not enough, she'd realized once she'd left the ranch behind. There was a lot of country out here, big and rough and wild, and finding Carson Harlow was going to be like finding a needle in a haystack. Still, she had to make the effort.

If she didn't succeed...well, she'd make her way back to the Lazy J and try to think of something else to stop him from staking his claims. What she wasn't going to do was give up.

Nola felt fear flicker across her heart as Ted raised his head suddenly and pricked his ears. She wasn't usually a nervous person, but since the episode with those bulls... And there were cougars up in these hills. Maybe even a few bears.

Ted tossed his head up and down and snorted, and then trumpeted a joyous welcome. He limped a few steps in the direction he'd been watching so intently. Her heart slowed.

He must hear another horse, she thought . . . and a horse probably meant a rider. She scrambled to her feet, brushing the sand from her knees and backside. A rider would mean help. . . .

Oh, thank goodness!

But her joy at hearing the rapid sound of trotting hooves approaching and the jangle of saddle and bridle turned to utter astonishment when she saw Carson ride into the clearing on Shasta, ducking his head to avoid a low-hanging branch.

And then astonishment turned to joy once again. She'd found him—well, maybe not found him. He'd found her. But it amounted to the same thing, didn't it? He didn't look all that happy to have found her, though. Of course, he couldn't have known what kind of a fix she'd managed to get herself into—

"Carson!"

"What are you doing here?" Arms crossed, he leaned on the horn of his saddle and stared down at her, frowning. Some greeting. Wasn't he even going to get off his horse?

Nervously, Nola patted Shasta's velvety nose, unable to answer. The mare flung her head up and blew heavily. She'd been running; Nola could see that her tawny flank was dark with sweat.

"Well?" He straightened suddenly and dismounted in one smooth, fluid motion.

"I was looking for you," she answered simply. The last thing she wanted to do was to annoy him further by evading his question. She needed his help. Desperately.

"Me?" He frowned and loosened the mare's cinch a few inches, not looking at Nola.

"I had a few things I wanted to talk over with you."

"You did?"

This time he did look at her, and Nola's heart sank to see the hard look on his face. Was this the man she'd kissed?

Who'd kissed her until her knees had melted? Who'd held her in his arms as though he'd never let her go?

This definitely was not the best time to tell him about the Painted Rocks. "Uh, I—"

"Never mind," he interrupted with an impatient gesture of one hand. "Whatever it is, it can wait."

He looked around at the little clearing, at the saddle lying under a tree that she'd planned to use for her pillow, at the bay gelding she'd ridden who was nuzzling his mare's neck in the friendliest horsey way. She saw his eyes narrow as Ted lurched when he took a step forward. "What seems to be the situation, Nola? Were you planning to camp here?"

"Not really. I hadn't planned to, anyway. Ted—my horse—is limping pretty badly, so I figured I'd better stay the night here and walk him back to the ranch tomorrow," she said quickly. He must think she was incredibly incompetent—

"What's the matter with him?"

Carson walked over to the bay and ran his hand down the gelding's left foreleg. She felt a quick twinge of such instant heartfelt relief that she wanted to hug him. Of course, he would know what to do with Ted! She saw the touch of an expert in the way he ran his hand down the gelding's foreleg, feeling carefully, gently, for any sign of what might be wrong with the horse.

"I'm not sure. He started to limp about two miles back, but I couldn't see what was wrong with him," she said, kneeling down beside where Carson had squatted by the horse's leg. Ted moved sideways a little and she heard Carson calm him in his deep, quiet voice. The horse stood still. That voice had magic in it....

"Looks to me like he's got a little swelling here by the fetlock," he said, frowning. "Maybe bruised it."

Nola couldn't see any swelling.

"Did he hit his leg on something? A rock? Did you go through any creek beds where he might have banged into something?"

"I don't think so. We did cross the Wild Plum farther down, but I don't—"

She bit her lip as Carson lifted the horse's hoof and used a stick to dislodge the sand and debris packed into the semicircle of the hoof. He reached into his shirt pocket, pulled out a pocketknife and skillfully flicked it open with one hand, then probed carefully around the horse's frog. Holding her breath, Nola peered over his shoulder, fascinated with what he was doing, but all too aware at the same time of just how close she was to him, how she could breathe in the faint male scent that was his alone, mixed with sweat and horses and pungent foliage crushed underfoot....

"Hold him," Carson muttered, not looking at her. "I think I've found the problem."

Nola scrambled up to hold Ted's halter. Oh, thank goodness, Carson knew what he was doing. Thank goodness someone did. But it was still too late to head back to the ranch. She'd have to spend the night out here.

Ted flung up his head suddenly and snorted and tried to pull his foot away from Carson. But the man held it firmly and a few seconds later, Nola heard his grunt of satisfaction.

He stood. "Here." She saw a small triangular stone on the palm of his hand. "This was wedged up in his hoof. Hasn't cut him, that I can see," he continued, with a glance at the horse, "but it'll be tender for a while."

He tossed the stone away and turned to her, folding his knife and putting it back into his shirt pocket. "You won't be going anywhere tonight."

"I— I kind of knew that," she said. At least Ted was going to be all right. She'd been so worried that he'd maybe done some serious damage the way she'd ridden him today in her burning need to track down Carson Harlow.

Now, here he was...

"I'm prepared to stay the night."

"I can see that." His raised eyebrow said it all as he looked around her campsite.

She felt herself flush and saw that he'd noted it, too. Which made her redden even more.

"You'd better come back with me," he said brusquely, not looking at her. He walked over to pick up her saddle and blanket.

She grabbed Ted's bridle. "Where are you staying?" she asked nervously, following him back to the gelding. She could hardly argue. She might not want to spend a night out here with him, exactly, but neither did she want to spend it out here by herself.

"About two miles from here." He gave her a hard look as he threw the saddle on Ted's back. "We'll have to take it slow, but we should make it back before dark."

Take it slow. It was the longest two miles of Nola's life. When she'd gone to scramble up on Ted, Carson had stopped her with an outstretched hand as he wheeled in an effort to control the nervous mare.

"You can't ride Ted, not with him limping like that. You'll have to double up with me. Here—" He shook his left foot free of the stirrup and held out his hand. Nola took it, her heart in her mouth. She managed to get the toe of her boot into the stirrup iron, just, then he leaned down and put his arm around her waist to hoist her up. Nola clung to his neck and felt his arm tighten as he started to lift her up behind him.

The mare snorted and pulled wildly at the bit, rolling her eyes, and lunging sideways. Nola jumped clear and Carson swore savagely as he reined the mare in. His jaw was grim as he looked down at Nola.

"She's green and she's pretty spooked. She's never ridden double before. I think you'd better ride in front. It'd be safer."

Nola knew what he was getting at. Riding behind the saddle, holding on with just her arms around him and nowhere to put her feet meant the mare's center of balance would be pushed back. Since she was such an inexperienced mount, Carson obviously didn't want to risk Nola sliding off if the mare reared or acted up on the trail. Especially with another horse, Ted, following closely behind.

Carson dismounted, his jaw still set and grim. He motioned for her to get up into the saddle. Heart hammering, Nola mounted, snugging herself forward as close to the saddle horn as possible. She felt the saddle leather strain to the left as Carson put his weight into the stirrup and swung into the saddle behind her. Then he was behind her, close and warm and solid against her back. His right arm came around her, tight, and he held the reins firmly with his other hand.

"Ooh!" Nola clung to the horn as the mare stepped sideways in a wide circle and took a series of stiff-legged hops. A preliminary to bucking?

Carson cursed again and she felt him drive his heels into the mare's side, causing her to leap forward. Nola's head was flung against Carson's chest by the unexpected movement and for a few stomach-fluttering seconds she reveled in the sensation. The mare's leap forward, the man solid and strong behind her, holding her tightly, her head resting against his chest and her hair, loosened from her braid, flying in the wind. The mind-freeing sense that she was safe as a baby, totally under someone else's direction. If she'd dared, she would have looked up at him—she knew exactly where his hard, unshaven rigidly set jaw was, just by her right ear. If she'd dared . . .

Carson wheeled the mare and returned to the clearing to reach for the lead rope tied to Ted's bridle. He wrapped the rope twice around the saddle's horn and they set off. So far he hadn't said a word. She felt the mare quiver under the saddle and watched her flick her tawny ears forward and backward nervously.

"Easy, baby, slow down. You're going to be all right, sweetheart. Shhh . . . whoa, now."

Nola heard the words, deep and intimate in her ear, the rumble in his chest behind her as he spoke. Then she realized he was talking to the mare. For one or two crazy seconds . . .

After they'd been on the trail about ten minutes, she felt his arm tighten infinitesimally around her waist. "You okay?" he muttered gruffly in her ear.

What could she say—that all she could think about was how intimately connected they were in that saddle? How terrified she was that he would hear the pounding of her heart? Or feel the searing heat of her body as she flushed through and through with embarrassment, every nerve afire with consciousness of him, his body behind her, cradling her, his chest against her back, his thigh against her thigh? She'd had to tuck her toes behind his legs to keep her balance. Otherwise she'd have had to surrender herself wholly to the sway and rhythm of his arms as they moved together, as one, on the mare. To relax, secure and safe in his arms. And she wasn't quite ready to do that . . . couldn't. Her hands felt slick with nervousness as she clung to the horn.

"I— I'm fine,"she managed to whisper. Somehow they made it back to where he had left his packhorse. Nola practically fell into Carson's arms when he'd dismounted and reached up for her. And perhaps she'd imagined it, but she felt before he let her go—her legs stiff and weak at the same time—that he'd held her a few seconds longer than was necessary to steady her, that he'd bent his head to hers in an unexpected gesture of tenderness before he'd released her abruptly.

"Maybe you could start a fire," Carson said, tossing her a box of matches and nodding at a pile of dead wood she saw thrown down near a tree. Then he left to see to the horses. Nola saw him wipe both horses down before examining Ted's leg again carefully, then he hobbled the mare and turned her loose.

Within half an hour, she had a mug of instant chicken soup cradled in her hands, made from a packet she'd found among the supplies in the packsaddle. She sipped the hot liquid and watched Carson.

He hadn't said much since they'd arrived, but she'd watched with interest as he packed Ted's injured hoof with a concoction he'd made out of a plant he'd told her was yarrow, then proceeded to scrape, crush and boil the root of another plant he'd gathered, a plant he said the Blackfoot called *po-kint-somo*. He boiled and stirred the crushed root for a few minutes in a tin can over the fire before binding the mixture in a cloth and tying the poultice securely to Ted's bruised fetlock. Ted snorted and blew at his bound foot for a few moments, under Carson's watchful eye, then moved off to graze.

"Where did you learn Blackfoot medicine?" she finally ventured, looking up at him when he'd returned to the fire. The more she learned about this white man, the more she realized she knew nothing about him.

"Here and there," he said, hunkering down by the fire and reaching over to take her mug. She released it, curious, then watched as he refilled it from the pot of soup on the fire. "I learned a little about Indian food and Indian medicine from an old Flathead I knew in the Bitterroots a few years back. It's come in handy."

"The same Indian you got your jacket from?" she guessed.

He gave her a lightning glance. "The same." Then he raised the refilled mug in her direction, catching her eye across the fire. "Sorry. We'll have to share," he said with a smile. "I've only got one mug with me. I wasn't expecting company."

He took a sip of the hot soup, then another, then handed it back to her. She took it, stunned at the easy, friendly gesture of sharing the soup. Of course he wasn't expecting company, she'd messed up his plans as well as her own ... and Augustus's.

"I don't know what to do about Augustus," she said, chewing her bottom lip. "I know he's going to worry."

"He was expecting you back tonight?" Carson looked up. His face was hard again, the friendliness had disappeared.

"Yes," she replied softly. She made a weak gesture toward Ted in the distance, toward her saddle under the tree. "All this is completely my fault, he told me not to go chasing after you without knowing where you were camped or anything, but—" She remembered that they'd tried to reach Carson on the mobile phone. "Have you got your phone with you?"

Carson showed her the mobile phone and left her to contact Augustus. By the time she'd talked to her father and accepted his thorough scolding, relieved that at least now she knew he wouldn't worry—that "she was in good hands," as he'd said, although she wasn't so sure about that—Carson had erected an exceedingly small blue nylon tent that didn't look as if it would accommodate more than one medium-size person she realized with dismay, and he'd started supper. The tantalizing aroma of frying ham and potatoes, bubbling baked beans and campfire coffee made her realize just how hungry she was.

"Can I help?"

"Maybe you can round up some plates." She found only one plate in the packsaddle but she also found an enamel bowl that could do double duty.

A few minutes later they were eating their meal in silence, Carson sitting on the ground leaning against one tree and Nola leaning against another, a good five or six feet away. Nola didn't think she'd ever had a meal outdoors that tasted as good. Nothing improved the appetite more, she thought with an inward wince, than the prospect of missing a couple of meals.

"So, Nola..." Carson got to his feet and poured some coffee into their mutual cup, then came back and sank down onto the ground beside her, stretching out his long legs with a sigh. He crossed his feet lazily and looked at her, his green eyes glinting in the late evening sun. "I'm awful curious about something."

She felt her heart leap into her throat as she held his gaze.

"Just what could be important enough to bring you chasing all the way out here after me?"

Chapter Ten

"I don't flatter myself for a moment that it was my company you missed," he drawled. He took a sip of the steaming coffee, his eyes not leaving hers over the rim of the mug.

She'd ignore that. She put her bowl down. She hadn't finished her beans, but suddenly she was no longer hungry. She knew her cheeks were hot, but she couldn't avoid the issue any longer. She sent up a quick prayer to any Blackfoot spirits that might be lingering in this place for their help in convincing the white man of the rightness of her cause.

"I— I'm not sure whether Augustus has mentioned it or not," she began, "but maybe you've gathered that I haven't been too keen about you prospecting up here—"

"You could say I'd noticed," he said dryly.

She met his gaze quickly, then dropped hers to the ground in front of her. She picked at a stalk of grass, then another, and twisted the stems between her finger before going on. "Partly it's because I've been worried about my father—we talked about that—"

"I thought I'd put your mind at ease about Augustus."

"You did. At least as far as your dealings with my father go, although I'm not happy about that. I still don't think he needs any more disappointments at his stage in life and, as far as I'm concerned, some pie-in-the-sky prospecting scheme pretty much means exactly that." She held his gaze resolutely, her own chin squared in response to the flicker of amusement she saw in his eyes. But he said nothing. "I worry about Augustus," she went on, frowning and twisting at the grass again. "Maybe more than I should. You have no idea of the kind of crackpot schemes he's managed to get into over the years. Martha had her hands full keeping him out of trouble while she was alive—"

"And now you figure it's your job," he said bluntly.

Nola considered. She'd never thought of it that way, but she supposed that he was right. What she felt for Augustus went beyond what she imagined ordinary daughterly duty to be, whatever that was. She almost felt she was the parent and he was the child sometimes. She nodded. "I guess so... partly at least."

"You didn't ride out here hell-for-leather to tell me that."

"No." Nola paused, and took a deep breath. "Okay. I suppose you've heard of pictographs before? Indian rock paintings?"

He nodded slowly.

"I know there are quite a few sites in Montana," she went on, "and other places in the States. Well, there are some here, too, in southern Alberta, and one of the more important sites is apparently right up here on the Wild Plum Creek."

"It is?" He looked very serious, and Nola felt a flood of relief. His interest gave her the courage to rush on. At least he was listening to her; she'd been afraid he wouldn't even listen.

"The tribes that I'm working with this summer—the Blood, the Peigan and the Blackfoot—all have a lot of stories in their oral culture about this place, a place they call the Painted Rocks. The first written records came from anthropologists back at the turn of the century who'd collected the stories from old Indians. The Painted Rocks are supposed to be a collection of figures and abstract designs, circles and stuff and, according to legend—"

"Supposed to be?"

She shot him a glance and mentally crossed her fingers. This was the part that no one bought. "Apparently they're hard to see. In fact, according to Ben's grandmother, you can't see them unless you're an Indian and you know exactly what to look for."

He was staring at her. She wished he'd say something, ask her a question ... anything. The grass plait in her fingers broke in two.

"And, uh, well, I'm worried that if you go prospecting around here before the Painted Rocks are definitely located and mapped so that steps can be taken to preserve them, they might end up being destroyed."

"Destroyed ... how?" He was frowning.

"Well, you know what will happen if the mining community gets wind of some mineral deposit up here, which they will the minute you stake a claim." Once a claim was registered, its location was public knowledge. "Other prospectors will be up here like a bunch of army ants, staking claims all over the place. There'll be no stopping them."

"But they could be stopped."

"Well, yes," she admitted grudgingly. "Maybe...at a lot of expense and a legal battle that could go on for years. Nobody wants that to happen. Sure, mineral rights belong to the Crown—I know that. But there are other rights at stake here, First Nations' rights. I know Augustus would have a hard time stopping anybody who wanted to stake mineral claims on his land. That's why he's so damn happy about you—" Nola caught back her words. But it was too late.

"Happy about me? And why is that?"

"Because he thinks you're a totally trustworthy guy and a real gentleman just because you bothered to look him up and ask his permission to scout his land!" she said with heat. She threw down the two pieces of plaited grass.

"I take it you don't."

"Well, let's put it this way. *I* know you couldn't stake a legal claim as an American citizen. *I* know you needed Augustus's cooperation to get what you were after, more, in fact, than just his cooperation—"

"You mean you don't think I did it because I'm a trustworthy guy and a real gentleman?"

He was laughing at her... although when she looked at him she saw only the faintest glimmer of a smile. She scrambled to her feet, reaching for her bowl and fork. She tried to walk with dignity to the fire, to pick up the coffeepot, to walk back calmly and offer him some in a desperate effort to regain her poise and purpose. Damn the man, anyway! She was way off track....

"More coffee?" she offered sweetly. She hoped he didn't see the venom in her eyes.

"Thanks." He held up his cup, and she poured shakily.

When she'd returned the pot to the fire, he offered her the cup. "Your turn."

"No, thanks," she said, sitting back down. "I'd never be able to sleep if I drank all that coffee this late."

Nola glanced nervously at the small tent. Somehow she didn't think she was going to sleep, anyway, although after the day she'd been through, every muscle, every bone cried out for rest. She felt stiff and sore all over. It had been years since she'd ridden as hard as she had today. And then... She shuddered as she remembered the added nerve-snapping tension of riding double with Carson, every fiber of her body on fire. Even now, if she closed her eyes, she could feel his arms around her....

Now, this... this business of saving the Painted Rocks. She suddenly felt incredibly weary. Not for the first time she wondered why she struggled as hard as she did, fought tooth and nail for the things she believed in. She wasn't even getting paid to do this! Her job was researching legal challenges to the Crown in certain areas of specific histor-ical documents. The Painted Rocks was another crusade, one no one had asked her to take on. And yet, deep down, Nola felt it was as important—maybe even more impor-tant than the dry, dusty legal work she'd been hired to do. She was doing this to prove something to herself, and to save this precious place for future generations, for future Indian children to gaze at in wonder... perhaps even her own child one day.

She was getting nowhere fast. She had to get back to the point. She had to convince Carson Harlow. She watched as he threw back his head to drain the rest of the coffee from the mug and then, before she could speak, he turned to her, eyes serious.

"So I take it you want me to hold off on my prospect-ing?"

She felt her breath suddenly squeeze in her throat and she quickly crossed her fingers behind her back. "Yes," she whispered.

He shook his head and her heart sank. "Sorry. 'Fraid I can't do that." He got to his feet, stretched briefly, then held out his hand to her.

She ignored his offer of help and scrambled to her feet on her own. She uncrossed her fingers. Lot of good it had done. One chance in ten, that's all she'd told herself she had. Yet it was a bitter pill all the same. Reason had told her what to expect, but reason didn't make it any easier to swallow. She felt quick tears spring to her eyes and she turned away from him. She'd take the dishes down to the creek and wash them. By the time she returned, she'd have her emotions well under control again.

"Nola?" He put his hand on her shoulder as she swept by him. She turned, angrily pulling away from him.

"Hey, you didn't really think I'd agree to quit prospecting up here, did you? Not after all I've put into it already?" His eyes, dark in the last shafts of the evening sun, looked solemn...compassionate.

The last thing she wanted was his sympathy. "No," she managed, blinking, her voice as hard as she could make it. Hot tears welled up and it was only a desperate effort of will that kept them back. "No, I didn't really believe you would."

But it was a lie, a total lie, her heart told her as she stumbled blindly down the grassy path to the tiny creek at the bottom of the coulee. *She had believed he would—she had.* The tears finally spilled down her cheeks and she made no effort to hold them back.

It had been one hell of a day, and she deserved it.

But the day wasn't over yet.

When Nola carried back the clean dishes, it was nearly dark. She noticed that Carson had tidied up, all signs of debris from their meal had disappeared and a couple of blankets had been laid out under one of the trees near the fire. For her? The fire was blazing; she noticed he'd thrown on a few more dry branches. She put the dishes back into the packsaddle and then stood nervously watching him.

"Sit down." He indicated a space by the fire. "Or maybe you're tired...do you want to turn in?"

She edged toward the fire. Night had fallen suddenly, as it did in the summer. The firelight beckoned. Far off in the hills she could hear the yip, yip of a coyote, then another, closer, answering, then a third.

She shivered. Somehow with the dancing fire, the luminous eyes of the horses in the distance, the brilliant carpet of stars in the black sky above and the presence of this man standing tall and strong beside her, it was as though she'd been swept back to an earlier time, a time when people had lived on this land as nomads, hunters...warriors. It had been the way of life of the Plains people since time immemorial, since long before the white man arrived with his diseases and his one god and his insatiable greed for the land of her forefathers. Mother Earth, the land and all its bounty, which before had been shared by all, was surveyed and divided into something that belonged to a few. Wire fences had sprung up, crisscrossing the land where once the Blackfoot had roamed as free as the buffalo they hunted, and the people, her people, her mother's people, had been crowded onto reservations, caged like so many wild birds, to end their days—for too many of them—in despair.

The buffalo were gone; and the dreams of her people had been broken. It was up to the current generation, people such as her and Ben to help rekindle the spirit of the Indian people. One way was to demand justice, through legal challenges to ancient treaties; another way was to preserve such spiritual heritage sites as the Painted Rocks.

For Nola, it was almost too hard to bear that the future of this one site, the Painted Rocks, should be held so completely in the hands of this one man, this stranger, this foreigner...this white man. This man, in whose presence she felt so powerless. *This man,* whispered something deep and urgent in her soul, *who has marked you with his blood. Marked you forever.*

Suddenly she shivered violently.

"Cold?" Carson poked at the fire, sending up a shower of fiery sparks into the night air.

"No," she said, and wrapped her arms around herself. The heat from the fire warmed her skin, but nothing could warm her soul. It was not the chill of the night air that had made her shiver. It was the sudden blinding realization that this man, this white man, presented a far deeper, darker threat to her personal future than simply as the person who held the key—one of the keys—to saving the Painted Rocks. Even if the Painted Rocks were saved—or lost, she suddenly realized—the personal danger this man presented to her would still exist. Nothing between them would have changed. Would ever change.

What was between them, he'd once said back when they were haying. He hoped he wouldn't have to spell it out. She took another deep, shaky breath as the full import of his meaning struck her. Dear God! Nor would he have to spell it out.... She'd seen it for herself, felt it when he'd kissed her, when he'd held her in the saddle in front of him, when their fingers had touched that first day she'd met him, in Augustus's kitchen. She was deeply, fundamentally, irrevocably attracted to him...to a white man. And nothing—*nothing*—had ever frightened her more.

"...and you can take the tent," he was saying. She hadn't realized he'd been speaking.

"It's not that big but it should be fine for you." His gaze traveled lightly, swiftly, over her. "You're not that big."

He was telling her that she should take the tent. She had to force this craziness from her mind, these other foolish thoughts, she told herself, squaring her shoulders. Sure, she was attracted to him. What woman wouldn't be? But she wasn't a victim of her hormones, certainly not. She wouldn't allow herself to be a victim. She must get a grip on herself, pay attention to the here and now...never mind the erratic thumping of her heart.

She cleared her throat. "I'll take the blankets, Carson," she heard herself say. "I insist. I can't turn you out of your own bed. I've caused you enough trouble as it is. I'll be fine sleeping outside—really."

He tossed another stick on the fire. "No," he said flatly. He didn't look at her. "You'll sleep in the tent."

As though there would be no more discussion; as though it had been settled already—by him. As it had, she realized, pulling her knees up and wrapping her arms around them. She needed to choose her battles carefully with this man. There was no point—and nothing to be gained—by arguing with him now. It was such a small, foolish thing, really . . . where she slept.

Carson had leaned back against a tree trunk, just out of the firelight, so that she couldn't see his face clearly. She sighed and hugged her knees.

"What makes Nola Snow sigh?" he asked softly.

She smiled. "I was thinking of how bossy you are."

She heard his deep, quiet laugh. "*I* am?" was the lazy response from the darkness.

"Yes, you," she repeated. "And it annoys me that I keep giving in to you on these little things . . . like sleeping in the tent for instance."

"'Fraid you might end up giving in to me on the big things?"

She looked at him. *What big things?* She wished she could see his expression more clearly. Then again, maybe she was glad she couldn't. She felt less inhibited when she didn't have that sardonic glance to contend with, that smoky green gaze that went straight through to her soul. "Not really."

"Funny, you should say that," he said. "I've been figuring you're a pretty bossy lady yourself."

"Bossy?" She felt faintly offended. "I wouldn't say 'bossy,' really. I know what I want, if that's what you mean."

"And you generally know how to go about getting what you want," he said. "Any way you add it up, it comes up bossy."

"I can't agree," she said, holding her head a little higher. "I haven't managed to get anywhere with Augustus on this business of you prospecting up here and getting him to make any promises about the Painted Rocks. And I haven't gotten anywhere with you. I wish what you said was true, but it isn't."

There was silence for a moment or two, as though Carson was making up his mind whether or not he'd bother responding. The fire crackled noisily. A pocket of pitch burst somewhere in the hot center of the flames and sent a spray of sparks shooting sky high, giving enough light for a second or two for her to see his face clearly. And the expression on his face—thoughtful, inward-looking, pained—astonished her. Then it was dark again.

"That Painted Rocks business means a lot to you, doesn't it?" he said.

"Yes."

There was nothing more to say. It was a bitter disappointment but she hadn't given up yet. She didn't need to tell him that, not just yet.

"I suppose it's pretty important to the Indian people, of which," he drawled, "you consider yourself one."

"I *am* half Blackfoot—"

"But only half," came the swift interjection.

"My mother was a young Blackfoot girl who was taken advantage of by a white drifter. I never even knew his name, but my mother's people have always been good to me. They've treated me like one of their own, and I have to say, yes, I consider myself to be an Indian. And some-day—'' She stopped herself.

"Someday what?" He spoke softly in the darkness. "Someday you'll be a whole Indian? Someday your fa-ther's white blood will no longer run in your veins? Some-day you'll be someone you're not?"

"Of course not. Nobody can change who they are,'' she said. "But a person can make the right choices. And that's what I intend to do. I'm not going to make the kind of mistakes I've seen other people do—"

"Mistakes of the heart? Mistakes somebody like your mother made?"

"Leave my mother out of this! I don't know how or why she got involved with my father but I don't suppose too many of the advantages were on her side. They wouldn't have been, would they?"

Nola felt her heart pound as she thought about what she had decided she must tell him. Especially now. She'd thought about her plans for a long time and her mind was settled. He might as well know...it might make a differ-ence.

"Even if what you say was true, I know myself well enough to know I'd never make the same mistake.'' She wished he hadn't referred to it as a mistake of the heart. What had happened to her mother had not been, she was certain, a matter of choice. "I intend to look for an Indian husband someday, someone I respect and who has the qualities I admire in a man—"

He laughed, but it was a hard sound. "Sounds pretty cut and dried. What about love, Nola? I thought that's what women wanted?"

"Most women do. And so do most men, probably.'' She shrugged. "I don't believe in falling in love, or even if such a thing exists. Anything could happen that way. The kind of love I believe in is something that grows between two people. I believe I could grow to love a man I respected, a man of my own choosing—"

"Like Ben?" It was more a statement than a question, and his voice had an odd note in it, a note she didn't recognize.

She nodded. "Someone like Ben, yes. And my children will be brought up as Indians, they'll never know that . . . that—"

"That their mother was a half-breed." She heard the note of pure disgust in his voice. "That their grandfather wasn't worth knowing about, just one more lowlife white man. So much for all the high-held principles of the lady lawyer!"

"You make it sound a lot worse than it is," she said quietly. He said nothing, then she saw him rise to his feet in the darkness. His shadow loomed over her, black and tall and straight against the night sky.

"You'd better turn in," he said brusquely. "You've got a long ride back tomorrow."

Without another word, he moved off into the darkness and by the time Nola finally fell into a fitful sleep, lulled by the far-off yip of the coyotes, by the wind in the cottonwoods, he still had not returned.

Carson was up before she woke the next morning. She could smell coffee brewing and, by the time she'd wriggled into her jeans in the cramped space of the little blue tent, and re-rolled his bedroll and stowed it neatly, then wriggled out of the narrow tent door, her stomach was growling with hunger pangs.

"Good morning," she said shyly. She resisted the temptation to smooth her hair with her palms. She knew she must look a wreck, and Carson's quick impersonal survey from her mussed hair to her bare feet poking out under wrinkled jeans, did nothing to reassure her.

"Morning." He gestured toward the small campfire flickering palely in the morning light. She could see steam rising from several pans, and sniffed appreciatively.

"Looks like breakfast is ready," she said with a smile. "I'll have a wash in the creek and be right back."

He said nothing, but when she risked a glance over her shoulder when she was nearly at the bottom of the coulee, it was to see him standing there, staring grimly after her.

"What a grump!" she muttered to herself, then shrieked as she splashed icy water over her face and neck. Maybe he hadn't slept that well. Neither had she, at least at first. Then sometime after midnight she'd fallen into the deep, deep sleep she'd longed for, her mind full of images of warmth and security and comfort. This morning she felt great.

Nola didn't stop to brush and rebraid her hair. She was too hungry.

"Here." Carson handed her a plate. At her questioning look, a smile, as sweet and rare as a sunbeam, broke through his grim expression. "My turn for the bowl," he said. She laughed and took the plate.

There was fried ham—again—and pancakes from a mix, and coffee, of course, and maple syrup and butter from a tin and canned blueberries to go on top of the pancakes, and hot pickled peppers. Pickled peppers?

"What are these?" Nola said, holding one up on her fork.

"Jalapeños," he said, with a sheepish grin. "I don't leave home without them. You Canadians don't seem to have a true understanding of peppers, I'm afraid. Must be the climate."

She laughed out loud. The sun seemed brighter, the air cleaner and purer, and the antics of the horses as they play-kicked and nuzzled each other seemed funnier. Even the famous Alberta sky seemed bigger and bluer.

All because you've got a full belly, she told herself, with a mental pinch to remind herself of what she had ahead of her today. And tomorrow...and the next day. She'd try a new tack, consult the elders, see what insight Ben had to offer.

After the meal, Carson insisted she leave the dishes. He saddled Ted for her and checked his foot again. The gelding wasn't limping and the swelling on his fetlock had gone down.

"He should be okay if you take it easy going back," Carson said, patting the gelding's glossy brown neck. "Don't push him." He held out his hand to give her a leg up. With one swift movement she was up and in the saddle.

"Thanks, Carson," she said, pulling down her hat to shade her eyes from the morning sun. She touched his shoulder lightly. "You've come to my rescue again...I guess I still owe you."

She couldn't resist reminding him, especially when it got the glower from him that she knew it would.

"Don't be ridiculous. You'd have been fine on your own, even if I hadn't come by," he growled, looking up at her, his green gaze holding hers. "So don't bother thanking me."

"What does it take to get you to accept a person's thanks gracefully, Mr. Carson Harlow?" she asked, teasing him a little. "Cheerfully, even?"

"I don't know," he said, finally giving her a reluctant grin. "Maybe you oughta try me someday."

"Well...goodbye, then," Nola said, gathering up the reins. She felt oddly reluctant to say the word, oddly reluctant to leave him.

"Something else, Nola," he said, putting one hand on Ted's bridle, the other on her knee. "I've thought over what you said about the Painted Rocks. I've changed my mind." His voice sounded gruff. "I've decided that—"

"What?" Oh, thank heavens! He'd changed his mind. He was leaving the Wild Plum, the area where the Painted Rocks were thought to be! Was he leaving Alberta altogether? And why did that thought hurt so suddenly in her chest that she could barely breathe?

"Hold on—listen what I have to say. You might not be so pleased when you hear my conditions. One, I'm not going anywhere, I'm going to keep prospecting in the area—"

"Oh." Was that a bubble of joy that had risen suddenly in her midriff, letting her breathe again?

"I'm giving you—you and whoever else you can round up—two weeks to find this Painted Rocks place before I make up my mind on staking a claim. If you find it, you have to agree not to tell anyone else about it without my permission. If you don't...well, I guess I can go ahead and finish what I set out to do when I came across the line."

"Oh, Carson..."

"Do you agree?" He looked as grim as he had earlier.

"Yes, yes...*yes!*" She knew she'd find it, now that she had a reprieve. Two weeks was plenty of time. She'd get Augustus and Jimmy and Nelson and anybody else she could find— "Of course, I agree! Carson, thank you so much. You don't know what this means to me, to all the Peigans, to the Bloods, to—"

"Get!" Carson waved his hand at Ted and the gelding threw up his head and bolted, bridle jangling. Nola reined him in.

"I'm serious, Carson Harlow," she shouted, struggling to control the plunging gelding and to stop the crazy impulse she had to laugh and cry and jump off her horse and hug the man who'd been the cause of nothing but trouble for her ever since she'd laid eyes on him. "One of these days you're going to have to let me thank you—"

"*Ayieee-hah!*"

Carson slapped his hat across Ted's rump and the gelding jumped and broke into a dead run, Nola grabbing for her hat and her reins at the same time, and laughing like a girl, the hair she'd forgotten to braid flying out behind her like a magpie's wing in the morning sun.

The man at the head of the coulee stood, his hands jammed into his pockets, his shoulders hunched, watching horse and rider until long after they'd disappeared into the haze.

Chapter Eleven

Two weeks. Fourteen days.

Two weeks gave her time to reschedule the work she was doing with the band, delegate some extra research to Marie back at the Lethbridge office, and make a quick trip to the provincial capital, Edmonton, before launching the hunt for the Painted Rocks. Ben had said he'd go along with her, and offered to help round up a search party from the reserve while she was away.

In Edmonton, Nola spent a lively evening at a nightclub with her ex-roommate and a group of young lawyers who'd been in her graduating class, among them a few young men she'd dated off and on in the past couple of years. She'd been looking forward to a little shoptalk and reestablishing contact with some of her colleagues and classmates.

And she was curious: would she feel the same interest in these men she'd once felt? After all, they were accomplished, up-and-coming professional men. Two were of native ancestry, handsome, assured men, the sort of men who turned heads in any room. To her dismay, her main problem throughout the evening was masking her yawns as her colleagues wrangled old court cases among themselves. Had they always been this self-preoccupied? Or perhaps in those heady days a few years ago, she, too, had enjoyed nothing more than the thrust and parry of rehashing old court battles with her colleagues. Now she was merely bored. Now the thought of the genuine, vital importance of the Indian cause for justice, and of the Painted Rocks, and of her father's worrisome future...well, she felt as if she'd grown up all of a sudden.

And lingering, always, on the edge of her consciousness, no matter how she tried to squeeze her eyes tightly and ignore it, was the ghostly image of Carson Harlow in his beaded buckskin jacket. There, behind her at the bar, a glass of whiskey in his work-hardened hand, a cheroot in his straight, white teeth, eyes narrowed against the smoke in the noisy room and a faint smile of irony on his handsome face as he watched the antics of the group at her table. A man among boys.

Her stomach sank. She knew she'd never feel the same about her colleagues again...she'd left that part of her life behind her forever. Some part of her had grown up, and she'd never again be the lighthearted, laughing girl she'd been just those few short years ago. Nor would men like her colleagues ever hold her interest again. She was a woman now. And a woman wanted a man. The realization made her feel cold, cold all over. It made her stomach hurt.

Knowing the others wouldn't notice, wrapped up as they were in their boisterous debate, she shut her eyes tightly and clenched her fists on her lap until her knuckles ached. *No!* She wouldn't be swayed by any specter. She would force these—these crazy thoughts from her mind—she would! When she turned to face down Carson's ghost at the bar, to scorch it with her fury, she saw—as she'd known—that there was nothing there. Only a row of empty bar stools, a couple deep in conversation, and the questioning glance, the raised eyebrow of the man behind the bar. Did she want something?

She shook her head no, and turned back to her friends, shaken.

When she got back to Pincher Creek, she found that Ben had had some success in putting together a search party. Jimmy and Nelson had volunteered, and they'd strong-armed a friend of theirs, a neighboring rancher's son, into joining them. Nola wasn't sure about the wisdom of having three teenage boys along, especially the rancher's boy, Ross McFarlane, who had a reputation among the Pincher Creek youth as a party animal. Nola hoped the rumors were unfounded. Two distant cousins of Ben's also volunteered.

Augustus wouldn't join them.

"No way I'm gettin' involved in some hare-brained expedition looking for invisible rocks," he said. "Whether they're there or ain't there isn't going to make a bit of difference to the work I've got cut out for me around here. Besides, I'm too old for it."

Nola was disappointed but not surprised. Ever since Harlow had started prospecting, she'd felt that Augustus secretly wanted him to succeed. She felt hurt, in a way, that her own father seemed to have so much faith in this stranger, but at the same time she realized that Augustus wanted Carson's success because he—Augustus—wanted to be part of a venture that finally paid off. Once a prospector, always a prospector. Carson's claim was going to be the pay dirt Augustus had dreamed of all his life.

And Nola couldn't blame him. The ranch had never been very successful—too much land and not enough money or energy to put into it—and now that Martha May was gone, her father's life had to be a pretty lonely one up here. Not that she could imagine Augustus tucked away in some old folks home in Lethbridge or Pincher Creek. Still, her father was getting on. He'd be eighty in just over a year—his seventy-ninth birthday was coming up the end of this month. He was getting too old for the kind of life he led, and that was another worry.

"I'll trailer some of you up there, though," he conceded. Nola gave her father a hug. "Hey, now, never mind that...I'm offering as much to give the horses a break as to do a favor for you," he warned her gruffly. But she knew differently, and his offer to help warmed her heart.

As their plans came together, as she and Ben spent hours poring over aerial maps, Nola became more and more certain that it could be done—they'd find the Painted Rocks and...and then what? She'd promised Carson that she wouldn't take any action without consulting him. She had to keep that promise. If she didn't, he'd just go ahead and stake his claims and the Painted Rocks be damned. Even she wasn't foolish enough to think that the provincial government would protect the site if the historic designation got in the way of a potential mine development.

What was Carson looking for, anyway? Nola bit her lip as she checked though her pack for the last time. They were taking enough provisions for a week-long trip. Carson had always been so cagey about telling anyone what he was after. As far as she knew, he hadn't even told Augustus.

Gold, probably. She frowned as she heaved her bedroll up to secure behind Ted's saddle. Wasn't that what all prospectors were after? He'd admitted that himself, even though he'd said he wasn't looking for gold. 'Course, she thought, raising one brow cynically and tightening the buckles that secured her pack, it wasn't too likely he'd ignore gold if it turned up, was it? What gambler would? And that's what all prospectors were at heart . . . gamblers. Carson Harlow was no different.

For the first day or two after Carson knew Nola's search party was in the area, he tried to keep his mind on his work. He continued to scour each box canyon carefully and thoroughly, as he'd been doing all summer, noting outcrops, rock slides, places where boulders had been dislodged by the kind of flood that occurred once, maybe twice, in a century. He walked up each dry creek bed, searching for clues to the geology, to the bones of the earth buried deep within the shape of the land. By long habit, he took samples everywhere he went, examining some on the spot, stowing others in his pack for later examination. A few he'd keep; many he'd toss away.

At night, at the camp he'd established in one of the box canyons, he'd go over his samples, split some, make notes of others, make color streaks on a special white unglazed tile he carried that showed up colors characteristic of the mineral. Hematite, for instance, which had a lot of iron in it, left a red streak. It didn't matter what he was looking for, by long habit he noted the presence of everything he came across, minerals, even fossils. Every clue gave him a piece of the puzzle he needed. A strike was a wonderful thing, but it was the puzzle, the feeling of piecing together and unraveling one of Mother Nature's secrets, that drove him. It was what brought him back to prospecting again and again throughout his life when other ventures soured, when other pursuits paled, it had been that way ever since he was a boy and had picked up his first Shoshone arrowhead on the bank of the Salmon River.

Still, no matter how he pushed himself to focus on what had brought him across the line in the first place, he couldn't forget, not for an hour, that *she* was back in here somewhere, too. In some canyon, in some coulee. That she was looking for the Painted Rocks.

Not much chance of that, he thought with an inward smile, trying to bury the unease he felt. She and that motley bunch she'd gathered together would never find the Painted Rocks. He was pretty sure of that. Otherwise, would he have offered her the chance to find the site? Not likely. This way, she'd get it out of her system and maybe move on out of his life, feeling she'd done everything she possibly could.

Besides, he had to admit, in addition to the uncomfortable feeling of having the hottest case of sheer animal lust he'd ever felt for a woman—which was more than reason enough to keep clear of her—Nola Snow, and just what it was that drove her, was beginning to intrigue him. More than intrigue him. He didn't think he'd ever met a woman with more single-minded passion. He sighed and smiled wryly to himself. Too bad it wasn't for him. Too bad it was over dusty old Indian rights and wrongs, ancient treaties with a long-dead English queen, a future for her people that no one—including her—could see.

Still, he admired her. That's what it amounted to, he decided. As for what she did to his hormone levels, hell, he'd just been in the bush too long. Admiration, that was it. She had grit. Tremendous grit. And courage. And passion. He even admired the ornery way she refused to give up. That was the problem—she just plain wouldn't give up.

By the fourth day, Carson knew his particular problem wasn't going to go away on its own. That was the day he found himself tethering the mare to a deadfall deep in the canyon—he'd left the packhorse hobbled back at his camp—while he climbed up a precarious rockfall, binoculars on his belt. That was the day he found himself moving from one vantage point to the next, systematically scanning the area for her party.

He wanted to know where she was. He wanted to know what was going on. The fact that he couldn't spot any sign of them angered him. The fact that he was looking for her in the first place angered him. The fact that he'd more than once contemplated calling Augustus on the mobile to find out what he knew about their plans, angered him. He hadn't called. Nor would he.

Damn! he thought, scanning the horizon. Where were they? It was near evening and he thought they might have camped for the night. Surely he'd spot evidence of a campfire or something.

Nothing. He saw nothing. Then he noticed, way in the distance, the thin plume of a campfire, and felt the tension in his chest ease. More a bonfire, he thought with grim satisfaction. Must be, to see it from this distance, certainly not the sort of fire an experienced outdoorsman would build.

Then ...

He never knew what made him pause before he dropped the glasses, what made him swing slowly to the north, scanning automatically as he did so. There was another thin plume of smoke. The unease he'd felt deepened.

What had they done, split up? With a curse of exasperation and frustration, Carson slung his binoculars back on his belt and scrambled recklessly down the hillside. He knew where they'd camped yesterday, two nights ago. That southeast fire made sense. Maybe that fire to the north was somebody else altogether, a camper, a fisherman ... maybe even another prospector. News spread; in this business, it couldn't be helped.

He had another hour of daylight left, maybe two. As he untied the mare and swung up into the saddle he felt the solid, deep surge of strength inside himself, felt his own power, and realized that, contrary to all his better judgment, contrary to all his best intentions, contrary to everything that instinct told him, he'd come to a decision. He was going to find her. He was going to see with his own eyes that she was all right.

He couldn't spend another night not knowing. He couldn't spend another night just wondering.

He had to know.

Carson walked the last hundred yards toward the camp-fire he'd spotted. He tied his mare to a branch on the other side of the ridge, knowing she'd signal his arrival if she sensed the presence of other horses. He still wasn't sure he intended to show himself. Of course, if she had whinnied a welcome to the other horses, he'd have come forward. He had nothing to hide, and they knew he was in the region. On the other hand, he hadn't made up his mind whether to drop in on the search party or not; he wanted to leave that option open. He didn't want it jeopardized by the mare.

One thing he knew for damn sure: he wanted no compli-cations. The last thing he wanted was to be drawn into her search for the Painted Rocks. All he wanted was to satisfy himself—under any pretext, any pretext at all—that she was all right.

Why it mattered so much he didn't dare ask himself.

He could see the fire from his vantage point, and a woman's back as she bent over the fire. She had a frying pan over the fire and he could smell the good scent of fish frying. Then she turned and—

It wasn't Nola.

His heart in his throat, he watched as she straightened and waved. A man walked from the shelter of the trees. He was carrying a forked stick with four fish dangling from it. He had a fishing rod over his shoulder. He smiled and waved back at the woman and held up his catch. It wasn't Ben Walking-Bow. He'd never seen this man before, nor this woman.

"Hello," he called out, stepping forward. He held up his hand in a friendly gesture. The woman turned to him. She was a native woman, well into middle age, he'd guess, although it was hard to tell. She wore her hair in a long braid, and the man had his in two long, thin plaits.

"Hungry, mister?" said the man, laughing and holding up his fish. He stepped forward. "You're welcome to join us."

"Thanks, I've had my supper," Carson said. He looked at the man closely. "You with the party looking for the Painted Rocks?"

The man nodded, and the woman's face broke into a wreath of smiles. She giggled.

"Yeah," she said. "Me and my old man are looking for the Painted Rocks. But we're takin' the time to fish along the way. The fishin's good, if you don't mind grayling."

Carson smiled and nodded. Where were the rest? Where was Nola? "I'm Carson Harlow. I'm prospecting in the area—" The other man nodded again, as though he'd heard of him. "Your party split up?" He hated to ask questions. It went against every unspoken code of the wild to ask questions, to stick your nose in another man's business. But he had to, he had to find out what had happened.

"Yeah." The woman giggled again. "You could say that. Ben and Nola and the three boys headed off this morning. The boys got a little liquored up last night, and Nola told 'em they'd have to go back. She said she didn't intend to baby-sit no teenagers on this trip."

Carson's jaw tightened. Sounded like her, she was pretty easygoing, but he knew this quest of hers for the Painted Rocks meant everything, and she only had a week left to find it. He knew she'd feel responsible for the boys.

"Jimmy and Nelson?"

"You know them?" The man sounded surprised.

Carson smiled and nodded. "Yeah. I hayed with them two weeks ago at the Lazy J. They're pretty good boys—"

"Not when Ross McFarlane's with 'em." The woman laughed. "He's a wild one, that one is."

"So." Carson still felt uneasy. "You say they left this morning?"

"Yeah. Nola tried to get Augustus on the radio to get him to meet the boys and take back their horses, but I don't think she got hold of him."

Which meant they'd have to ride back. It would take the better part of the day over that rough country. Not much chance they'd return before tomorrow. She'd be fine; she was with Ben.

Carson's jaw tightened again. That's just it—it was none of his business, none at all, but he didn't want to know that she was somewhere out there, maybe camped for the night with Ben Walking-Bow. Still, that was the reaction of a crazy man. What had got into him? He took a deep breath.

Okay. So now that he knew she was all right, he should be able to go back to his camp and get a good night's sleep. Right? Now that he knew she'd lost a day, maybe two, thanks to a couple of rowdy teenage boys who were more interested in partying than looking for Indian rock paintings, he should be pleased. Right? It was just that much less likely that she'd stumble across the Painted Rocks before her two weeks was up.

And, as for Ben, he hadn't forgotten what she'd told him ten days ago. Ben Walking-Bow was exactly the kind of man she wanted in her life. He should be happy for Nola Snow, if he cared about the well-being of his partner's daughter at all. Which he didn't. Which he did, damn it. Of course, he did....

So why did he suddenly feel like smashing something? Why did he suddenly feel like getting on the buckskin and riding like hell, not stopping until he'd crossed back into

Montana? Why did he realize suddenly that nothing he might do—neither busting something up nor running away—was going to make a damn bit of difference?

When he found her, finally, it was already dark.

At first he hadn't cared how much noise he made approaching. What he was going to say—bursting in on her and Ben—he didn't know, didn't care. He'd think of something.

Then he changed his mind. Maybe he'd try to catch a glimpse of her from a distance. He'd know if she was all right just if he saw her. And, he reminded himself, that's all he wanted to know. After all, he'd feel pretty foolish if he burst in on them when she was...if they were... He felt his blood pound again. Nola. Nola and Ben Walking-Bow. He thrust the image from his mind.

He tethered the buckskin with shaking hands and crept silently toward the campsite, thankful, not for the first time, for his Flathead moccasins. Hell, he was probably overreacting. He wasn't even positive this other fire was from her camp. *Their* camp, he reminded himself. Maybe they'd stayed at the Lazy J. Probably had, when a man took the time to think about it, when a man used a little sense, when a man got past this crazy fury that had fueled his breakneck ride through the bush.

He reached up to rub his face where a branch had slapped him smartly in the dark. Lucky he hadn't lost an eye, or that the mare hadn't broken a leg, riding hell-for-leather through the near dark as he had. It shook him that he'd been so irresponsible...it wasn't like him. He *always* looked after his animals first, he *never* took such crazy chances. And over what? A woman.

And maybe he'd been dead wrong. He suddenly wanted to laugh. Maybe this was just some innocent fisherman about to get the scare of his life when he charged out of the darkness. He smiled to himself, but it was a grim smile, mainly nerves. He'd never felt so damn mixed up in his entire life.

Then, suddenly, there she was. He froze, stopped breathing.

She was sitting beside the campfire, a stick in her hand, with which she drew idly in the ashes at the edge of the fire. From time to time she raised her head and glanced nervously toward the darkness, pushing her hair back with her hand with a quick movement that he'd seen before. A movement that did something strange to his heart.

There was no sign of anyone else. No sign of Ben. The weakness, the flood of utter relief that swept through him when he realized Ben wasn't there turned immediately to fury. What kind of man who called himself a man would leave a woman alone like this in the bush?

Dumb, Harlow, he told himself, real dumb, feeling his knees sag as the realization swept through him that she was all right. Nola Rosa was all right. She was fine, she was alone, but she was in no danger. And now that he was here, he'd make sure of that.

Real dumb. She wouldn't appreciate his concern. She'd think he was hopelessly old-fashioned and out of date, thinking for a moment that a woman wasn't just as capable as a man at taking care of herself alone in the bush. But he couldn't help the way he felt, could he? All he wanted to do was step forward, wrap his arms around her, kiss her soft mouth and promise her anything. Promise her that he'd take care of her. Promise her that he'd never leave her, that he'd make all her dreams come true. But he couldn't do that. No one could do that for another person. We made our own dreams come true, each of us. Wanting it to be otherwise didn't make it so.

The surge of tenderness he felt toward this woman in the firelight made him take a deep, shaky breath. What the hell was going on?

But he knew. He knew. Deep in his heart he'd known since the day he'd seen her reaching up for those dishes of her mother's in Augustus's kitchen, the day he'd offered to get them for her. She'd let him help her then. Would she let him help her now? Probably not. And that hurt.

And then he realized that he knew something else, something that plain scared the hell out of him.

This woman was in his blood... just like the bulls had been, like the search for silver and gold, like his hunt for sweet green peace somewhere in the hills. All those things were part of who he was... and now this woman was, too.

He must have made a noise, for he saw her glance fearfully in his direction. And then he heard the soft nicker of welcome from her horse in the darkness. It wasn't fair to frighten her this way.

He stepped forward into the circle of firelight. He saw the fear on her face turn to delight, to gladness in an instant. He felt his heart squeeze with happiness. It was a few short seconds he knew he'd treasure all his life.

"Carson!" She was on her feet, her hands outstretched, her face wondering. "What are you doing here?"

It would have been so easy to step toward her, to take her in his arms as he longed to do. But he didn't move.

"Hello, Nola," he said, as though they'd seen each other only that morning on the streets of Pincher Creek, or over breakfast at her father's ranch, as though there was nothing more between them than passing friendship.

And that was exactly the way he intended to keep it.

Chapter Twelve

She couldn't believe this man!

That he could step out of the darkness and just stand there in his beaded jacket, staring at her across the fire, his face a mask, his eyes hidden. The way he'd spoken...as casually as though they'd met over their respective shopping carts that morning in the Pincher Creek supermarket!

Her heart was pounding through her ribs. Her mouth was dry. Her palms were damp with sweat. She'd been utterly terrified when she'd heard the snap of a twig, the footsteps in the darkness. A grizzly? A cougar? Or—she had to admit, her twentieth century woman's heart no more proof against the terrible fear all women had known since the dawn of time—an unknown man. A man. The creature who could step from the darkness to the fireside and use his superior strength to protect her and her children, or the creature who could tear them limb to limb, who could destroy them all. The not knowing had always struck terror in a woman's heart...which would it be? Protection or destruction? To touch a man in his deepest core and show him, as women had always done, the infinite possibilities that existed between a man and a woman, through love. To banish the fear, to reveal the healing, positive power of love: it was a woman's way. It had always been her greatest challenge and it would always be her greatest triumph.

"Carson!" she said again, feeling her mouth tremble as she tried to smile, her voice not much more than a croak. "For heaven's sake. You frightened me half to death." She felt weak with the vast relief of seeing him there, after the nightmare she'd been through in the past couple of days. And then, especially now, tonight, the regret she'd felt that she'd insisted on continuing the search by herself, letting Ben escort the boys back to the Lazy J. All of it...

It was only the grim expression on Carson's face that stopped her from throwing herself into his arms. Still, she told herself, she would have felt that way about anyone who showed up about now to keep her company...Ben, Augustus, even Grizzly Sawchuck.

"I apologize if I frightened you," he replied, squatting down by the fire and pushing one of the sticks of wood farther into the center. "I didn't mean to." A shower of sparks flew up, lighting his features. Nola felt her heart give a sudden lurch. *Oh, thank goodness, he'd come....*

"Did...did you walk here?"

He glanced up. "No. I left Shasta on the other side of the coulee," he said, and then stood suddenly. "I'd better bring her in." With that, he plunged back into the darkness.

Oh, still my trembling heart, dear Lord. She stirred the fire with her stick. She'd make a pot of tea, that's what she'd do...had he had supper? There was stew left over from the tin she'd warmed up for her meal. And she had buns that were still relatively fresh. Was he heading somewhere tonight? Would he stay the night with her?

Nola glanced at her tent. Hers, unlike his, was large enough for two, in a pinch. Should she offer? She swallowed and stood as she heard Ted whinny and Shasta answer. She wiped her hands along the sides of her jeans.

"Would you like some tea?"

Carson glanced up from unfastening the cinch on the saddle. He smiled, and she thought her heart would thump right out of her chest again. "Sure." He lifted off the saddle and began to wipe down the mare with a clump of long grass he'd twisted into a knot. "Tea sounds fine."

"How about some stew? I had some for supper and there's some left over. It's not that great, really, but I could warm it up in a minute." Nola suddenly felt shy, realized that she was babbling. Came from spending too many hours alone, she decided. Besides, anyone would sound like a babbler around a man such as Carson, she thought. He was definitely one of the West's strong, silent types. She watched as he stowed his saddle and bridle under a tree, not hurrying in the slightest, then fastened the hobbles before he slapped the mare's rump fondly as she moved off to join Ted grazing a few yards away.

He turned to her finally. "A plate of stew'd be great, Nola." He stood tall and straight, not more than ten feet away from her. Then he smiled. He looked like another man... handsome, relaxed, happy.

"Oh, Carson!" Nola took a flying leap and threw her arms around his neck. She buried her face in his shirt. He staggered back a step, but his arms held her, tight and warm and secure.

"Hey, hey... what's all this about?"

She looked up, smiling and wiping tears against his shirtfront at the same time. "I— I just am so happy to see you," she managed, sniffing to hold back a sudden out-and-out desire to break into tears. "To see s-somebody. I— I—"

She couldn't finish, and buried her face against his chest again, and sobbed. She felt his arms tighten like bands of steel around her. She heard the low rumble of his laughter.

"Okay, okay," he murmured, and she felt his hands, warm on her back, as he slid them up to her shoulders. He patted her left shoulder awkwardly. "You're all right now, girl." She'd heard him soothe his mare using just that tone.

He cleared his throat. "Hey," he said softly, and his voice was gruff. "Better not let that stew burn." He held her slightly away from him, his hands firm on her shoulders, his eyes hooded, and Nola immediately stepped back. What had she been thinking of, throwing herself at him that way?

But the awful tension of his arrival had been broken, and the overwhelming tide of conflicting emotions that had washed through her had begun to turn. Nola busied herself around the campfire, pouring the tea, one mug for him and another for herself, and ladling the stew onto a plate. Warmth and simple happiness swelled inside her.

"Here," she said, handing the plate to him. She smiled, not caring in the least if he smiled back. He regarded her through narrowed eyes and she smiled again. Brilliantly. Suddenly she couldn't believe how glad she was to be alive!

"Thanks." Carson sat down a few feet from the fire and gave his attention to his meal. Nola carried over their mugs of tea and sat near him, on a stump she'd dragged up to the fire earlier.

"How'd you find me?" She poked at the fire with the stick.

"I spotted your campfire a while ago. Tracking you down was fairly straightforward."

"In the dark?" She looked at him, one eyebrow lifted.

He cleared his throat, and studied the forkful of stew he'd lifted. He smiled a little. "Actually, I got a little side-tracked. I tracked down another fire first. A couple. They said they were with your party."

"That'd be Wilfred and Lucy. Ben's cousins." Nola sighed. She kicked absently at one of the rocks that rimmed the fire. "Carson, I can't begin to tell you how much trouble I've had in the last couple of days. I suppose they told you about Nelson and Jimmy and that little rat Ross McFarlane from Pincher Creek?"

Carson nodded, and took another mouthful of stew.

"Ross brought a couple of bottles of applejack with him in his saddlebags. I didn't know or I'd have made him take them out. Then he and the other two got stinking drunk last night. And sick?" She turned to him, and he met her gaze, then looked back at his plate. "They were sicker than dogs. Well, no wonder, considering how much they drank. They could barely ride this morning. Can you believe it? A couple of underage boys and *I'm* the one responsible for them—"

"What about Ben?"

"Well, Ben and I are both responsible, I guess," she admitted. "But I feel this was all my idea. What are we going to tell their parents? I wish I'd never brought them along, but I had the idea they were really interested in finding the Painted Rocks. Not Ross—" she gave him a dark look "—but the other two. I thought it mattered to them, that it meant something to help rediscover some of their own heritage." She was silent for a moment, drawing a stick figure in the ashes. "I guess I'm just fooling myself that finding the Painted Rocks is as important to them as it is to me."

Carson looked at her. "What about the other two?"

"Oh, they're more interested in catching trout than they are in looking for the Painted Rocks," Nola said, throwing down her stick in disgust. "That's not fair... they're interested, I guess. But they're not in any hurry. I can't seem to make them understand that we haven't got much time." She glanced sideways at Carson. After all, *he* was the one who'd set a deadline for finding the site. Maybe he'd...

"What about Ben?"

He'd hesitated as he said Ben's name. Nola frowned. "Ben's been terrific, he really has," she said softly. "I don't know what I'd have done without Ben on this trip." Had it been her imagination, or had Carson's jaw tightened in the firelight? "But there's only so much the two of us can do. And now he's taken the boys back."

"Back to the Lazy J?" Carson frowned. He set his plate on the ground and stretched out his legs, finally looking up at her, a long, steady gaze that she felt somewhere deep, deep inside.

"Yes," she said. "That's where they left Jimmy's dad's horse trailer. He probably won't make it back up here until tomorrow."

"You're meeting him?"

"No." She looked uneasily at him, then back at the fire. This was the hard part, this was the part she wished now she'd let Ben talk her out of. "He's going to meet up with Wilfred and Lucy and I'm going to keep looking on my own."

Carson turned to face her. He didn't say anything. Finally, his silence got to her.

"I can, you know."

"I didn't say you couldn't."

"I used to fish up here all the time with Augustus."

"That was a long time ago, Nola. When you were a kid."

"I know. But I can do it all the same. It makes sense," she said, repeating what she'd told Ben. "We haven't got much time and this way we'll cover more ground." She raised her chin, and hoped her voice didn't betray her. She wasn't nearly as confident anymore as she'd been that morning when she'd argued with Ben, who hadn't wanted to leave her on her own. "I'll manage. I'll be okay."

She picked up Carson's plate and rinsed it off. Then she dried it carefully and put it back in her pack. He stayed by the fire, leaning back on his elbows on the grass, long legs stretched out. She could feel his eyes on her, following her, watching everything she did.

"Where are you camped?" she asked lightly. It was time to change the subject.

"Couple of miles from here."

"Are you planning to spend the night here with me? Or go back?" she added hastily as she realized how her invitation sounded, feeling her cheeks flood with heat. Thank goodness he couldn't see her in the darkness. Still, he couldn't go back to his campsite now, it was too late. And he'd already unsaddled the buckskin.

"I could stay here," he drawled, then added, "with you. Or I could go back. You want me to stay?"

"You might as well stay," Nola said, hoping her offer didn't sound too churlish. The fact was, she desperately wanted him to stay. If she spent the night alone here she knew she wouldn't get a wink of sleep. But he didn't need to know that. She made herself add, hospitably, "I've got extra blankets. And the tent's plenty big enough for two."

Carson didn't answer for a moment, then when he did, her cheeks burned. "That's a mighty attractive offer, Nola Rosa, and I can't say I'm not tempted. But I believe I'll sleep under the stars, just the same. Alone." There was a pause. "Thanks."

The air between them hummed with tension. Suddenly he wasn't just an itinerant prospector, a stranger passing through, a friend of her father's, a man she was beginning to know and, she had to admit, like a little. Suddenly he was what she'd always known him to be, deep in her woman's soul: he was the man ghost at the bar, he was the gambler in the bunkhouse, he was the rugged, virile, confident man who wanted her, she knew, the way she wanted him. She closed her eyes tightly, wishing it were otherwise, but she couldn't deny it: some part of her wanted this man more than she'd ever wanted any man before. Appalled at her thoughts, completely flustered, Nola hurried to get out an extra blanket, then watched as he spread it and his Navaho saddle blanket under a nearby tree.

"I, uh, I guess I'll turn in now," she said, hoping her voice sounded normal, not knowing what else there was to say, yet reluctant to leave. "Well . . . good night, Carson."

"Come here," he said. His voice was deep and dark.

She walked toward him.

"Look." He put one hand on her shoulder and tipped up her chin with the other, so that she had to look up at him. His features were sharp and shadowed in the light from the fire and the light from the stars above. "I'm glad I found you, Nola. I was worried about you. I haven't been able to keep my mind on my work the past couple of days knowing you were out here, not knowing what kind of trouble you might have got yourself into—"

"I'm not in any—"

"Shh." He placed his thumb, rough and hard and gentle at the same time, on her lips for a few seconds. She swallowed, her heart pounding in her ears. "Listen. You're determined to find the Painted Rocks, aren't you? Come hell or high water."

"Come—" She licked her dry lips and nodded slightly. Her voice was shaky. "Come hell or high water."

"I'll take you there. Tomorrow."

I'll take you there? Had he known all along? "You'll take me there?" she whispered. "You know where they are?"

"Yeah. I do."

He studied her in the moonlight, never taking his eyes from hers, and she felt hers fill with tears. She blinked hard, trying to stop them from spilling over. She should not feel gratitude that finally, after all this time, she would see the fabled Indian rock paintings she'd seen only in her dreams, she should be blinking back tears of anger. Anger that he'd kept it from her. How long? Maybe since she'd met him . . . ?

"You want me to take you there?" he repeated.

"Yes," she managed, feeling her anger rise finally and spill over. "Of course I want you to take me there. *Damn you, Carson Harlow!* How long have you known about the Painted Rocks?"

"Since a couple of weeks after I crossed the border this spring." His hand slid to the back of her neck, his long fingers pushing under her tangled braid. His hand was warm, so warm, and his thumb stroked the skin at the side of her neck lightly, so lightly. She tried desperately to ignore the sensations that shot through her body. His eyes were still on her face, on her eyes . . . then they slid to her mouth.

She was furious. "But . . . but that was ages ago! Why didn't you tell me this before? Why have you been playing me for a . . . for a *fool* all this time?" She felt his fingers tighten slightly on her nape as she spoke. Her heart was pounding. She tried to step back, but he held her firmly. "Do you realize what you've done? These past couple of weeks have been hell for me, Carson Harlow, *absolute hell—*"

"That makes two of us," he said softly. He bent and placed his mouth warmly, lightly, on hers for the briefest of moments, stilling her angry words. Nola felt her knees weaken, and for a few crazy, sweet seconds she was lost. "They've been hell for me, too. *Sheer, bloody, living hell!*" he whispered again hoarsely, his breath hot against her mouth. "And you're looking at another fool," he added savagely. "The biggest kind of fool. The kind I never thought I'd be.'' His lips met hers again in a brief, hard kiss, then he let her go so abruptly that she staggered back. She felt as though she'd been pushed, although she knew she hadn't. It was only that her legs would barely support her.

His final words floated out of the darkness to her as she fled, stumbling a little, toward her tent. ''Good night, Nola. I'll see you in my dreams.''

He was trying to get her lost.

There was no doubt about it; they'd been around this hill before. She was positive she'd noticed that particular clump of black poplars before, the one with the lightning-blasted stump in the middle. But perhaps this stump wasn't as large as the last one had been....

She didn't know anymore. She wished she didn't care. She was tired and hot and hungry, and saddle-sore. And cross. Carson had been pushing on like a mad man ever since they'd broken both camps this morning. And she could have sworn that Carson had known that that last canyon, the one they'd followed up and had had to turn around and follow out again, had been a box canyon, a dead end. If he'd known, why had he made her follow him up it? What was he trying to do, drive her crazy?

She leaned forward and patted the darkly sweating neck of her gelding. ''Good old Ted,'' she muttered. At least the horse hadn't lost his spirits. He must be getting tired, too, yet each time they turned to skirt a copse of trees, or climbed a ridge to get over the next hill, he pricked up his ears with interest, curious to see what lay ahead. But then, she thought with a frown, Ted had always been a pretty easy horse to please.

If Carson was trying to get her lost, he could quit trying—she was already lost. Sure, she'd been up in this country many times before, on fishing trips with Augustus, as a girl. But Carson had been right: that was a long time ago. She'd forgotten the landmarks, the creeks, the coulees, if, in fact, she'd ever paid attention to them. No doubt she'd relied on Augustus to get her safely home again back then and hadn't even bothered to notice where they were going. Funny, how patchy a person's memory could be. You remembered what you wanted to remember. Had Carson known that? Is that why he'd finally decided to take her to the Painted Rocks—he didn't trust her knocking around out here on her own?

But why would he care? Probably didn't want her stumbling around and maybe finding out what he was up to out here. Prospectors were notoriously suspicious men. He probably had her pegged for a spy, she grumbled blackly to herself, knowing the idea to be complete and total nonsense yet enjoying feeling misunderstood and put upon at the same time.

"Ready for a bite to eat?" Carson had pulled up the mare, Buddy contentedly bobbing his head behind her, and waited until Nola caught up to him. "There's a creek just up here. It might be a good place to stop for a while."

"A while?" Nola wailed. "I thought we were nearly there." On the one hand, she wanted to stop and rest; on the other hand, she wanted to get to the Painted Rocks as soon as possible. "I thought you said it was only a couple of miles."

"It is." Carson grinned. "As the crow flies." If she could have reached him, she would have smacked him. "I thought you might like to see a little bit of the country while we were here anyway," he drawled, still grinning.

She made a rude sound, and he threw back his head and laughed. Seeing him laugh that way made her want to laugh, too, but she restrained herself, with difficulty.

"All right," she said grudgingly. "We might as well stop for supper." She patted Ted's neck again. "But I'm not sure you're going to get me back up in this saddle again," she warned Carson. "I'm not used to riding all day like this anymore."

"Not much farther," he said, pushing his hat back. "We'll eat, and then we'll get up there and set up camp. You'll be able to see the Painted Rocks by sunset. That's a promise."

The buckskin tossed her head impatiently, bridle and bit jangling, as though she sensed they were near their journey's end. "You'll be safe and sound back at the Lazy J tomorrow." He touched his heels lightly to the mare and she sprang forward, Buddy lumbering behind.

Yes, but is that where she wanted to be, back at the Lazy J? Nola thought with dismay. Tired and hungry and sore as she was, she had to admit this was a bit of an adventure. And she liked any kind of adventure. Grousing about it was part of the fun. Still, he was right. Once she'd seen the Painted Rocks, she had no more reason to be out here.

And maybe that's really why he'd offered to bring her: the sooner she satisfied herself about the location of the rock paintings, the sooner she'd go home and leave him alone. That thought depressed her vaguely, particularly since the more she thought about it, the more she realized she was probably right.

I'll see you in my dreams, he'd said. *His* dreams! That was another thing, she hadn't slept all that well last night. She'd had a hard time getting to sleep, imagining him stretched out under the stars only a few yards away. Was he sleeping? What was he thinking about, looking up into that big, black, starry sky?

Then, when she did finally fall asleep, she'd tossed and turned, cursing the thin foam pad between her and the hard ground, cursing the full moon for shining through the thin nylon of her tent and keeping her awake. As for her dreams . . . she blushed to remember them.

They stopped by a fast-flowing stream that she didn't remember seeing on the map. Most of the meltwater from the mountains had already come down and it was unusual for such a small stream to be so full of water at this time of year, unless it had its source in a spring somewhere up-country. The water was clear and cold, and Nola waded in in her bare feet. She had the beginnings of a blister on one heel and the icy water felt good.

Within minutes, it seemed, Carson had a fire going and a pot of coffee bubbling. He pulled out a frying pan from one of Buddy's packs and they had reconstituted, freeze-dried pork chops, which she had to admit tasted pretty good, with bean salad, hardtack and canned cherries for dessert. Thank goodness Carson appreciated a somewhat varied diet on the trail. She remembered many a fishing trip with Augustus where all they ate was fish, if they caught any, otherwise it was raisin bread and tinned corned beef. Augustus had always told her you couldn't get better fare than that: you had your protein, your carbohydrates and your fruit. That, and a mug of heavily sugared tea, and a man couldn't ask for more. Vegetables, he'd told her with a conspiratorial wink, were highly overrated.

Nola volunteered to wash the dishes in the stream, since she hadn't contributed anything toward their meal, and Carson stowed the supplies back in the packsaddle with the same speed and economy of movement that he'd un-packed. Just think, Nola told herself, he's done this thousands of times. This was his life. He'd told her that he moved his main camp every three or four days, using Buddy to carry his tent and supplies. Between moves, he'd hobble the horses and sometimes go out on foot with just his tools and a pack on his back, and sometimes take the mare if he was working at a distance from his camp. He could have worked with an all-terrain vehicle—many prospectors did, he'd told her, but he liked horses. Home was where he laid his head. Home, at least home as she knew it—the Lazy J and her passion to secure the ancestral land claims of her people—meant nothing to him. He was a rambler; he followed his heart wherever it led him.

Nola shivered as she pulled herself into the saddle once more. She wasn't cold, but it was as though a shadow had fallen over her. Had it been her thoughts? She looked up. There were clouds gathering to the northwest, she'd noticed them earlier. Perhaps they were in for a summer storm. If not tonight, perhaps tomorrow. She hoped the rain would hold off or blow over, at least until she got back to the ranch.

Just when she was about to despair of Carson ever stopping for the night, he pulled up.

"We'll pitch our tents here," he said. "There's a good spot here and shelter for the horses." He looked up at the sky.

"Is...is this where the Painted Rocks are?" Nola looked around her in amazement. They were at the head of one of those box canyons again, and she couldn't see anything anywhere that looked like the rock face where the paintings were supposed to be—according to Ben's grandmother.

"No," Carson said, and dismounted. He tossed down the reins and walked over to her. He held up his hand. "Here."

She took his hand, and then, when she'd raised her weary right leg and swung it over Ted's rump, she practically fell into his arms. Her legs were weak, her knees were sore, her ankles were sore.

"Hey," he said softly, holding her upright for a moment. She wished she didn't long to stay exactly where she was, in the safe circle of his arms, to lay her head against his chest, to hear his heart beat, deep and strong, to feel the rumble of his laughter...but she did.

Drawing on every ounce of energy she had left, she pulled away. "Thanks," she said, mustering a light smile and stamping her feet to get her blood moving. Neither she nor he had referred to the night before. Neither she nor, in all probability, he would ever mention it. It was best that way, she'd decided the moment she'd awoken from her restless sleep. Ignore it, pretend he hadn't kissed her, it hadn't happened, that was the surest way to make sure a fellow didn't get the wrong idea. *A fellow? And just what idea would that be?* asked a tiny voice inside her heart. She ignored that, too.

It was eight o'clock. Nola gnawed her bottom lip. At this rate... But within half an hour they had pitched their tents, Carson had chopped a stack of firewood under a tree where it wouldn't get wet even if it rained and he'd hobbled the horses and turned them loose.

"Ready?" Carson looked down. "Got anything you can wear besides riding boots?"

"Why?"

"We've got a little climbing ahead of us and I don't think those boots would be the best choice for hiking." She noticed that he'd taken off his riding boots and put on moccasins, the moccasins she'd seen him wear before.

"Carson Harlow," she said, her hands on her hips. "Just what do you mean by 'a little climbing'? I've got some sneakers. Would they be better?"

Carson nodded. "Better than those boots. It's not far, Nola. Just up this hill. I promised you I'd get you there by sunset and I will, even if I have to carry you to the top."

"You won't have to do that," she grumbled, and went to her tent to dig through her pack. She found her sneakers and took off her boots, leaving them just inside the door.

"Okay," she said. She met his smile with one of her own. She had to admit, she was enjoying the challenge of keeping up to him. And the mystery of where it was he was leading her. And she'd keep up to him, too, or she'd die trying. "I'm ready. Lead on."

She followed him up a heavily treed hillside, around a ravine, over a low ridge and then across a rockfall. At the edge of the slide she twisted her ankle, barely stifling a howl of pain. Carson was a good ten yards ahead of her and she was sure he hadn't heard her. Her ankle hurt like crazy, but she gritted her teeth and pushed on. This was turning into a comedy of errors, she thought, her eyes watering with the pain of putting down her foot. She looked up. Carson had stopped at the top of the hill and was looking toward the northwest. The evening breeze blew his hair around his face. He'd taken off his hat. The setting sun shone on his face in profile to her and she bit her lip. Nearly there! Her heart fluttered in her chest, and it wasn't only that she was out of breath from the climb.

She was here...she was finally here. The Painted Rocks. She'd only dreamed of seeing them one day. Her heart swelled with pleasure and anticipation. Thank goodness Carson had brought her here. She never would have found this place, not in a million years.

Nola tried to mask her limp the last few yards, hoping he wouldn't notice that she was favoring her right foot. She didn't want anything to spoil this moment.

He turned, his face shining, his eyes alight. He held out his hand, to help her over the rocky lip of the plateau he was standing on. She grasped it, and he hauled her up the remaining few feet.

Then she was standing beside him.

"Look, Nola," he said, throwing his arm out in a wide gesture. "The Painted Rocks."

Chapter Thirteen

They stood on a narrow plateau, perhaps twenty yards across, covered with short, brown, windswept grass and studded with rocky outcrops, some big boulders, some piles of rock cracked and crumbled by the forces of weather over the centuries. The plateau overlooked a sizable canyon, with sheer rock faces and wind- and rain-sculpted rock, smaller versions of the fantastic forms she'd seen in the dinosaur hills near Drumheller, or the Hoodoos of neighboring southeastern British Columbia. They could see for miles in any direction from where they stood. To the west and south and north were the snowcapped peaks of the Rockies, the Livingstone Range, to the south-southeast she saw the long lumbering form of the Porcupine Hills, and, even more distant, Chief Mountain on the Canada-U.S. border. She hadn't realized how high they were.

"Come on," Carson said. He grinned at her, his face alive with interest and enthusiasm. Nola had never seen him like this before. "Let's go over to the other side and find a place to sit down out of the wind. You can see them better from over there."

So far, Nola wasn't quite sure what he was talking about. The sun was lower now, but still well above the horizon. All she could see were rocks, rocks, and more rocks. She began to follow Carson, then yelped with pain. She'd forgotten, in the excitement of the moment, about her ankle.

"Hey, what's wrong with your foot?" Carson came back to where she stood favoring her right foot. He was frowning as he bent to examine it. He looked up. "What happened?"

"My ankle, I think. I twisted it a little." She bit her bottom lip. "Back on that rock slide we climbed over. I don't think it's sprained. It'll be fine if I just rest it a bit."

Carson stood, and before she realized what he intended, he'd swept her up into his arms. "Hang on."

"Oh!" She grabbed his neck. He grinned, his teeth white, his eyes shining, his face close, too close, to hers. "Didn't I tell you I'd get you here even if I had to carry you?"

He strode over to the western side of the plateau, and, after turning this way and that, stopped at a place near a big, sun-warmed boulder with a clear view to the north. "This looks like as good a place as any."

But he didn't put her down... not yet. He looked at her and for a moment she tried to ignore him, knowing how very close his face was to hers. She looked down at her knees, then at his shoulder, encased in creased blue chambray, then... unable to stop herself, at his face.

She took a quick, deep breath. He was smiling and he looked so handsome and so strong and so... so utterly perfect, the clear green of his eyes so intense, the red bandanna that he'd worn as a sweatband restraining his sun-bleached hair, shaggy and tossed by the evening breeze. The deep blue of the evening sky was behind him, framing his face perfectly. She'd never seen any image so magnificent, so male and so utterly perfect in this one particular setting. This is where he belonged. Carson Harlow was made for wild places, for mountaintops and for lonely hills.

"Well? Are you going to put me down?" she finally managed to say, hoping he hadn't seen the hunger in her eyes that she knew was there although she'd tried to mask it, a spiritual hunger that was as biting and strong and demanding as the need for food.

"In a minute." He shifted and held her tighter. Her eyes widened. "I've been here quite a few times since I came across this place. It's one of my favorite places in the whole world, I've decided. Until I find a better one. But I'd never dreamed I'd ever be here with a beautiful woman in my arms." His eyes darkened, and she looked down. "I think I like the feeling. Hey," he said softly, "you're blushing."

He teased her by holding her a minute longer. Then he took a step forward, bent down and deposited her by the boulder. He hunkered down beside her, all business now, and gently, carefully, removed her sneaker. Then he peeled down her sock and lightly touched the side of her foot. Her ankle was only slightly swollen, but she had a scrape on the side where she'd slipped.

"That's going to hurt for a while," he said, frowning slightly and replacing her sock. "You've got the start of a nasty bruise there."

"I'll be okay," she said, and replaced her shoe gingerly. She didn't bother with her laces. Never mind her foot, where were these famous Painted Rocks he was going to show her?

"So where are the rock paintings?" she said lightly. She had a queasy feeling in her stomach, a feeling of mounting unease. And she didn't think it had anything to do with the clouds that were gathering in the northwest or the pain in her ankle.

He'd sat down beside her while she was putting her shoe back on and now he turned to her in surprise. He waved, an expansive gesture toward the rock face on the other side of the canyon. "Over there."

She shaded her eyes from the sun and peered in the direction he was pointing. "Look, Nola, over there, by that column of reddish rock to the left, just there—" He leaned toward her and put his left arm around her, steadying her and putting his face next to hers to show her exactly the direction he meant. "Do you see those circles? About twenty, maybe twenty-five feet off the ground. Let's see, there's one, two...looks like five of them from here. Drawn in thick red lines, what the Indians used to call 'spirit paint'."

Nola squinted. She shaded her eyes with both hands. She looked to the left of where he was pointing—she'd seen the column of red-brown rock—she looked to the right. "No," she said finally in a small voice. "I can't see any circles."

Nola remembered how Ben's grandmother had told her the story of the Painted Rocks in her own tongue, the Blackfoot language. She'd told Nola that the paintings changed, according to ancient legend. She'd told her how in the spring there might be pictures of tepees and of people wearing war bonnets, hunting buffalo. Then, perhaps in the summer, all the pictures would change and perhaps a house with a bell on top would be drawn, a white man's house, perhaps a church, a full moon, would be clearly visible. Then, sometimes, later, there would be figures of men on horseback shooting all the mountain animals: goats, sheep, bears and jumping deer. Sometimes circles that indicated the moons would be drawn, she'd told Nola, and seven moons with seven marks on the rock might mean good luck in seven months' time. There was an element of prophecy involved, and vision-seekers might go to the

Painted Rocks to seek special dreams, visions that they'd then keep secret.

All of that—the secrecy, the magical nature of the paintings, the fact that they were drawn in special red paint, that they changed all the time, that they appeared higher on the mountain than any man could reach—had made the Painted Rocks the special, magical, powerful place that it had come to be in legend. No one Nola knew had ever seen it.

In fact, Ben's grandmother had told her sadly, people—Nola believed she meant white people of a generation or two before—had seen these places and made fun of them. That is why, she'd said, very few people today can see such a thing, and the paintings have moved higher and higher on the mountain. According to her, though, the rock paintings had been known among her people for many generations.

Nola felt the first fingers of fear clutch at her midriff. Why could Carson see these things? Why could he see images that she couldn't see?

"Who told you about spirit paint?" she asked, wanting to maintain some semblance of normal conversation with Carson, wanting to ignore the feeling of panic she felt rising in her middle. Perhaps she'd see the images if she kept her gaze trained on the rock. Perhaps it was a question of changing light, perhaps she'd see something as the sun sank toward the horizon.

Carson took a deep breath, held it for a few seconds, then began to speak. She had the clear impression that he didn't want to talk about it with her. "Old Jim told me about it," he said finally. "He told me about the rock paintings, too. He was a Flathead Indian, from the Bitter-roots, but his first wife was a Blackfoot from Browning, and she'd told him about it. Her grandfather's cousin had seen the rock paintings. Old Jim had always wanted to travel up here to Alberta to look for them, but he never did.'' Carson paused, and she sneaked a sidelong glance at him. His jaw looked tense.

"After Old Jim died, I decided to come up here and see for myself," he finished.

"Sort of a pilgrimage," she ventured softly.

He turned, his eyes searching hers. Then he nodded. "Yes. As a sort of a pilgrimage."

"Does—" An idea had suddenly struck her. Augustus had talked about some secret map or something that Carson had, something that had convinced her father that his new partner had an edge in finding whatever it was he was looking for up here. Maybe that old Indian he'd known had told him something. "Does this have anything to do with your plans for staking a claim up here?"

He gave her a quick, hard look. His jaw was tight again. "Maybe. Maybe not."

"You're still not telling," she said flatly. His refusal to tell her what he was really doing in the area had begun to anger her. She didn't for a minute buy the idea that the Painted Rocks were all that had brought him here.

"That's right," he said flatly. "I'm still not telling." He stared toward the face of the canyon. The breeze lifted a lock of his hair and let it go again. She had a sudden physical longing to reach up and touch him, to bury her fingers in his hair.

He turned to her suddenly. "Do you accept that?" His voice was hard.

She forced herself to laugh, wishing the ache in her belly would go away. "I guess I have to, don't I?"

"Yeah," he finished softly, "you do."

They were silent for a few long moments. Nola watched the sun sink lower in the sky and crossed her fingers and prayed fervently that as the sun went down she'd see the rock paintings. She'd heard—who had told her?—that the paintings could be seen best just at sunset. Carson had leaned back against the boulder she rested against, and his shoulder touched hers. She was very aware of the warmth of his shoulder, of his whole body next to hers. She sat, legs drawn up, ankles crossed, and waited. *Creator Sun, Mother Earth, listen to your daughter whose mother was one of your people. Please reveal the secrets of the Painted Rocks to one who will treasure the knowledge....*

"Old Jim told me once that one of his father's cousins had died because he'd told the secrets of the vision he'd had at another one of these sacred spots," Carson said softly. "Somewhere in Montana. That's what a lot of the Indians believed would happen." He wasn't looking at her. He was gazing toward the rock face where he said he'd seen the paintings, and he was smiling slightly to himself.

Suddenly he tensed. "Look there, Nola. There!" He grabbed her by the shoulders and turned her slightly so that she could see where he was pointing. "Horsemen, three of them. You can see the feathered bonnet that one of them is wearing. It must be because the light has shifted a little now, the sun is lower. He's carrying what looks like a rifle, definitely not a bow and arrow—*Hey, what the hell's the matter—?*"

Nola had twisted from his hold and leapt to her feet, ignoring the pain in her ankle. Then she'd thrown back her head and screamed, a high-pitched unearthly sound that ended in a wail. For a split second, it shocked her, too, as though what she'd heard had come from the mouth and heart and soul of someone else. Carson leapt to his feet and she felt him seize her by the shoulders. "Let me go!" She clenched her fists and struck out at him, her heart bursting with pain and rage, but he held her too tightly and she could only struggle to free herself.

"Don't tell me what you see. Don't you *dare* tell me what you see! You're lying...there's nothing there. You're lying to me!'' She sobbed, violent, dry, hacking sobs, and tried to hit him again and again. His arms tightened around her, trapping her against his chest, and she shook her head wildly, her hair flying free. Somewhere, somehow, the end that secured her braid had come undone.

''Stop it!'' His voice was hard and merciless. ''Stop it right now.'' He shook her.

''No! Let me go, leave me alone—'' She was crying now, great horrible gulping sounds. Her rage had given her the strength of a madwoman and she twisted wildly to free herself, but still he held her. ''You can't see those things you say you can...*you can't. You're* not an Indian and *I am! I'm* the one who's supposed to see the Painted Rocks, not you—'' Her voice broke and she collapsed against him, tears streaming down her face. ''I— I can't bear it, I can't! It's so unfair....''

She felt his arms loosen around her, but he didn't let her go. When she tried to push away from him, she found she couldn't. She bent her head against his chest and sobbed, and now her arms were still, her fists unclenched, her palms flat against his chest. She felt the tears run across the back of her hand, and she didn't care. She had nothing left. She wanted to die. She wanted never to return to the Lazy J, to the reservation. She wanted never to face Ben again, or the elders.

Her life was a sham. A charade. She was no more an Indian than Carson Harlow was. She was an outsider, neither Indian nor white. Sure, her mother's people had been good to her, but it wasn't the same... it wasn't the same as knowing you belonged. She'd built her life on a lie, a lie to others who depended on her, who counted on her, and worse, she'd built her life on a lie to herself.

Her mother hadn't been an innocent girl from the reservation who'd been ravished and abandoned by an evil white man. Her mother had left the reservation behind her by her own choice to make another life for herself, she'd wanted to escape, as Nola had escaped with her fine college education. But her mother had had the bad luck to end up pregnant by a man who'd run at the first sign of trouble, a drifter who couldn't handle the consequences. The responsibility. He hadn't cared enough. Or... or maybe he'd never known he'd fathered a child.

No, Nola, she told herself bitterly, let it go... stop pretending, stop hoping. She clung to Carson's shirtfront as though to life itself. Her face was wet, his shirt was damp from her tears. She felt his arms around her, sheltering and strong, and she no longer felt trapped by them, only warmed and comforted. She felt the low rumble of his voice through his chest, murmuring words, she knew, of reassurance and comfort.

She trusted him... God help her, but she trusted this man. Her sobs quieted, and she felt herself simply weep now, endlessly, until she trembled with exhaustion. And it was cold, too. She shivered. With an enormous effort, she raised her head from Carson's chest and looked up. His eyes were dark and serious and the concern she read there made her cry again. Then she saw that it had started to rain a little, soft, cold drops from the dark clouds that had gathered above.

"W-we'd better go back," she whispered. Her words were hoarse; she barely recognized her own voice.

"Yes," he said. But he didn't move, except to raise his right hand and push back her tear-dampened hair from her face. He traced the tears on her face. She knew her eyes must be red and swollen and she must look an absolute mess, but she read none of that in his expression, which was half wondering as his eyes followed the path his own thumb made on her skin.

Then he buried his hand in her hair and held her face steady as he looked at her, looked at her in a way she'd never been looked at before—strong, steady, intense, with an openness that made her heart ache. He looked briefly at her lips, before lowering his head and covering her mouth with his. He folded her gently into his arms again, so strongly, so surely, so warmly that she felt she'd melded with him right there under the lowering sky. She felt the chill of raindrops striking her face, and the warmth of his breath on her skin and the heat of his mouth on hers.

He kissed her warmly, deeply, thoroughly, and then, slowly, ever so slowly, he raised his head.

"Nola Rosa," he said, his voice tight with emotion. "Your hurt rips me up inside. It makes me want to leap over rivers and vault mountains and rage and storm and tear apart whatever it is that has made you so unhappy. And I would, if I could. If your hurt was the kind of thing a man could shatter, I'd shatter it."

She was drowning in the deep fire of his eyes. She could not have looked away from him if the earth had opened up and swallowed them both right then.

"Your tears make me want to weep with you and I haven't cried since I was a teenager. Your dreams are my dreams." He bent his head again and kissed her gently, reverently. Her heart squeezed unbearably inside her breast and she felt the tears flow afresh. Then he said, "I'd do anything I could to make you happy. Just tell me what you need."

"I— I don't know what I need," she whispered, her voice breaking. It was the God's truth . . . she didn't know.

He kissed her again and when he raised his head this time, he was smiling. "One thing I know we both need," he said, "is the sense to get out of the rain."

He didn't know how he'd made it down the hill, slipping on the rain-slicked earth in his moccasins, stumbling over rock slides with her on his back. She had taken a few faltering steps with his assistance at the top of the hill, but he'd soon realized they weren't going to get anywhere with her walking.

Then the skies had burst. Rain pelted down. A flash of lightning and a crack of thunder nearby helped him make up his mind, fast. The high, exposed plateau was the last place to be in a summer rainstorm. He'd carried her in his arms to the edge of the plateau, then shouted at her, over the wind, to climb onto his back and hold on tight.

She'd looked frightened, her hair wild and clinging to her face and his as the rain lashed at them both. Her fear, after the tears she'd already shed, ripped at his heart. He'd never forget that wail of anguish, that scream of a mortally wounded animal for as long as he lived. He wanted to protect this woman, to help her, to make sure nothing ever would—ever could—harm her again. The deep well of feeling that had overcome him as he'd held her in his arms, he didn't stop to consider. He only knew it was right. He only knew that what he'd said to her, the pledge he'd made to her, had been the truth. And, to Carson Harlow, that was a commitment. He'd given her his solemn word. He knew he'd walk through the fires of hell for her.

Now, if only they could get safely back to their camp....

He tensed as he steadied himself and leapt to a safe foothold. He grunted under the strain of balancing with her on his back, her arms so tightly around his neck that she nearly choked him. He tried to hold her legs steady, to secure them where she'd wound them around his waist, but he needed his arms free to maintain his balance. The rain blinded him, as did her hair, which swung free, and more than once he'd had to reach up to pull the clinging black veil from his eyes.

"Hang on!" he shouted back to her as they entered the trees and he increased his pace to a sort of staggering trot. He could feel the shudder of her body against his as she sobbed softly, could hear the fear in her voice as he leapt down a small decline, grabbing at small bushes to steady himself.

He knew he'd get her back safely; he had to. He suddenly realized that he felt strong, that her weight was nothing on his back. He was a giant. He felt stronger than ten men, and he wanted to throw back his head and roar his defiance at the rain and the wind and the lightning. He'd matched them, he'd snatched this woman from the mountaintop, he'd taken her for himself, he'd laughed in the face of all that nature could throw at him, with her thunder and her lightning bolts.

It was sheer craziness; he knew that. And he savored every moment of it. He felt full of the strangeness of the situation he found himself in, of the fierce, primitive urges that had been unleashed in him with the coming of the storm and with the awareness of what he felt for this woman.

And he'd won.

He burst into the clearing, panting heavily. There were the tents, fly sheets rattling in the wind. There were the three horses, huddled under the trees, their backs turned to the lashing rain.

"Nola," he said softly, reaching back to touch her face. "We're here. We're home."

Home. Soundlessly, she slipped from his back and he turned to catch her in his arms. She was shivering violently. Chill, from the rain, and shock, from what had happened to her on the hill. He had to get her under cover, get her warm and dry, tend to her ankle.

"Here..." He picked her up without the slightest protest from her and strode over to the door of her tent. He fell heavily to his knees, balancing her weight awkwardly with one arm, and fumbled with the zipper.

"I— I'll be okay," she said, her teeth chattering so hard he could barely make out her words.

"Get in." He held the door open for her, then followed her in.

It was nearly dark in the tent, his eyes used to the dusk outside.

"Here." He quickly unbuttoned his shirt and tossed it at her. Most of his shirt was still dry, where her body had shielded it from the rain. "Take off your shirt and dry yourself with this. I'll be right back—"

"Where are you going?" The fear in her voice was unmistakable.

"Just to my tent. I've got a first-aid kit there with a bandage in it that we could use for your ankle. And I want to make sure the horses are all right." He paused. He only saw her outline against the lighter nylon of the tent behind her. He could see that she was struggling to get out of her wet T-shirt. "Don't worry," he added softly. "I'm not leaving you."

Then he pitched back into the dark and wind and slash of the rain. He was instantly wet, the water running in rivulets from his bare chest. He checked the horses. They seemed fine, and had some shelter under the trees. He checked their hobbles. They were secure. Then he scooped up her saddle and his where they'd left them under the trees and carried them over to his tent. He opened the door and shoved them both in, crawling in after them.

"Where the hell's that kit," he muttered to himself, feeling in his pack for the first-aid kit and the flashlight he knew was there. "Damn!"

He picked up the entire pack, and, after a few seconds' reflection, grabbed his sleeping bag, still rolled in its waterproof nylon sack. Then he backed out of the tent and fastened the door securely. He wasn't coming back here tonight. Then, taking a deep breath, he sped across the few yards of sodden ground that separated her tent from his.

Her ankle had swollen slightly and was bruised. He cleaned the scrape as well as he could with some antiseptic he had in his kit and carefully bandaged it. Then he found the tension bandage he'd been looking for, and gently wound it around her ankle, trying not to look beyond the pool of light from the flashlight that she held steady for him. She'd put on one of his dry shirts he'd tossed her as he'd rummaged through the pack, and he didn't think it was possible for a woman to look more desirable or more lovely, clad as she was in nothing but his much-washed red flannel shirt, her hair still hanging in damp strands, her eyes red and swollen with the tears she'd finally managed to stem.

Lord, he thought, *I must have it bad.*

"Okay," he said, leaning back on his heels. "I think that's going to be all right like that. I'll check it in an hour or two to make sure the elastic bandage isn't too tight." He paused, aware suddenly that he was damp, his jeans were soaked, and he was still bare-chested. He reached for his pack.

"Stay with me."

He hesitated, then continued to dig for a dry pair of sweatpants he could put on. He didn't look at her; he didn't dare. "I'll stay with you, Nola. I said I wouldn't leave you and I won't."

He heard her sigh of relief, although he could also tell she'd tried to hide it from him.

"Turn off the light for a minute, will you?" He didn't know why he should feel shy in front of her. Still, wriggling out of soaking wet blue jeans could not be done with any sort of dignity. She shut off the light. Quickly he peeled off his jeans and pulled on the sweatpants. They felt warm and dry, and suddenly he realized how tired he was. It had been a long day, and the emotional upheaval of the past hour, plus the physical exertion of getting down from the mountain had taken its toll. He didn't know what time it was, but he wanted nothing more than to sleep.

If sleep was possible, that is, lying all night stretched out in the same tent as Nola Snow.

"I'm freezing," she whispered as he began to lay out his sleeping bag. He reached out to touch her arm. She had goose bumps, and her teeth were still chattering slightly. Shock. She needed to get warm, fast. He wished he'd brought his tiny Sterno stove with him from his tent; he could have heated her up a cup of tea or some instant soup.

He unzipped his sleeping bag, then unzipped hers. He was fumbling to match the zippers in the darkness when she spoke. "What are you doing?"

"I'll zip these bags together. That way I'll be able to make sure you're warm enough." Thank God, it was dark! He actually felt himself flush. Thank God, he wasn't a woman and had to deal with lines like that....

"D-don't you think you should ask a lady's permission b-before you get into bed with h-her?"

He grinned in the darkness. Her sense of humor was coming back...that was an excellent sign. "Ah..." The zippers finally mated and caught. He zipped them up.

"I usually do." He lifted her feet, rubbed them both lightly between his palms—they were icy cold—and tucked them under the top sleeping bag. He could just make out the outline of her face, pale and round beside him. He'd thought the mountain had been a challenge; it was nothing to what the challenge this night was going to be. To lie here beside her, with the most honorable of motives, and simply warm her by lying next to her, as he'd said he'd do. So that she wouldn't go deeper into shock, of course. No other motive whatsoever.

Sure, Harlow, you're all gentleman.

"May I come into your bed, law lady?" He swung his feet around so that he could ease them in beside hers. He felt her hand touch his bare chest, and he stiffened. Lord! He didn't know if he'd be able to take this. It was going to be a long, long night.

"You may," she answered softly, with a tiny giggle. He inched down until he lay fully beside her. He could sense her body, every inch, lying there beside him. Then, taking a deep shaky breath, he turned toward her and gathered her into his arms. She came readily and snuggled her head under his chin. He was glad he'd put the sweatpants on; he wished now he'd put a shirt on, too.

He could feel her breathing soft and warm against his skin. He could breathe in the sweet scent of her hair, all sunshine and spring water.

"Carson?" she murmured, nestling closer.

"Mmm?"

"Make love to me."

Chapter Fourteen

The rain pelted down so hard on the fly sheet above them that at first Carson didn't think he'd heard her right. He couldn't have . . .

Maybe if he ignored her. Maybe if he let on he hadn't heard her. But he couldn't ignore the intense male reaction of his own body to the whispered invitation. What redblooded man could? All he could do was hope she hadn't noticed. He cursed the twisted series of events that had landed him in her bed in the first place.

"Mmm?" Her voice was soft and sleepy.

Maybe she was just kidding. "Go to sleep, Nola." His voice sounded rougher than he'd intended.

"I will. But first I want you to make love to me."

There was absolutely no mistaking her meaning, none at all. "Look, Nola. I—I don't think that would be the best idea. Under the circumstances."

"What circumstances?"

"Well, you're exhausted. We both are, physically and . . . and emotionally. You're upset. You've had—"

"Don't you want to make love to me?" The thread of sadness in her voice nearly broke his heart.

"Don't want to make love to you?" he growled. "Damn it, Nola. I've dreamed of making love to you a thousand times, at least a dozen times a day since that first day I met you. There's something between us, God knows why, that's damn near unstoppable. You know that. I feel you inside me. You're in my blood, my bones, like no other woman has ever been before, and I can tell you that if everything was equal and considered, the last damn thing I ever thought I'd be doing if I ever found myself in your bed was just lying here like a gentleman holding you like this, just to keep you warm—"

"You told me once you were no gentleman." He heard her soft, sleepy giggle, which made him feel a whole lot better. Not physically, the ache in his groin wasn't going to be easy to forget about. . . . But at least she sounded as though she accepted his explanation. His excuse. God knows, he'd never thought he'd need one.

There was a long silence, a silence during which he thought—hoped—she'd finally fallen asleep. But when she spoke, he realized, like him, she'd been thinking.

"What am I going to do, Carson?" Her voice was very small. "When I get back? What am I going to tell the others?"

"Why don't you worry about that tomorrow, after you've had some rest? Cross that bridge when you have to." He shifted, drawing her even closer into the circle of his arms. He wanted to comfort her, make all her demons go away. The feel of her breath, the sound of her words muffled against his chest—he'd never realized that just holding a woman could be so damn sexy.

"What will I tell Ben?"

Ben! It was the dash of cold water he needed.

"Why do you have to tell Ben anything?" Surely she meant what would she tell him about the Painted Rocks. Surely she didn't mean what should she tell him about spending the night in his, Carson's, arms. But...maybe she did. It'd be a whole lot better, all the way around, if that's what she did mean.

"I feel I owe him some kind of explanation. He's wanted to find the Painted Rocks as much as I have. How can I tell them that I couldn't see any rock paintings, I couldn't see *anything—*"

So that *isn't* what she meant. Carson's relief was completely mixed up with his concern for her state of mind, his concern for the fresh flow of hot tears he felt trickle down the side of his chest. "Shh, Nola," he said gruffly, tightening his arms around her. "Just go to sleep."

And eventually she did. But not before telling him how so many of the dreams she'd held all her life had died that night, the instant she realized that her Indian blood meant nothing. The legendary figures of the Painted Rocks obviously were not revealed to just anyone with Blackfoot blood. They were magic, just as Ben's grandmother had said. And yet he—Carson—had seen them. How could that be?

She'd wanted to become a real Indian all her life, in every way, and now she realized that she'd built her life on a lie. She was only half Indian; the other half of her was white. She could no longer deny it. Now she wondered how many other lies she was living, how many half-truths, how many more dreams would slip away from her.

He listened, and then, when she'd finally fallen asleep, he thought about what she'd told him for a long, long time before he was able to sleep, too. Nola Rose Snow. It was a cold name for a woman with fire in her soul. He'd never known anyone with so much passion, so much single-minded intensity, so much courage. Even if she'd been dead wrong about every crusade she'd taken on, he'd have loved her for the passion in her that burned so bright and so true. And those who felt the most, as Nola did, were the ones who hurt the most, too, when things went wrong.

He knew what she said was true: some of her deepest, dearest, most precious dreams had been shattered that day. But he also knew that he could have warned her it might happen. Not that she'd have paid attention, of course. Nor would he have, if he'd been in her place. In fact, he *had* tried to warn her, the night he'd brought her to his camp after Ted had picked up a stone in his hoof. When she'd told him how she intended her children to be brought up as Indians—all that pride in her voice—how they'd never know their real grandfather had been a white man, a drifter who'd had no name. It had made him angry. Although he understood the hurt she was trying to put behind her, he deeply resented what he saw as a far too simple view of the reality they both lived in. And he was a white man, too. She'd condemned him, too, for the color of his skin. So he'd scorned her for her denial of who she really was.

Still, broken dreams hurt. He'd had his share. All the Harlows had. He knew that nothing—ever—hurt a man more. And he also knew that sometimes it was out of the deepest, worst kind of hurt that true healing began. He'd spent a lot of his life, most of his youth, looking for that kind of healing, and now, after years in the mountains, he'd begun to find it. After all these years... Carson sighed. Maybe it was time to come down from the hills. Maybe the hills and the people of the hills he'd loved and trusted, people such as Old Jim, had taught him all he could learn. Maybe it was time to start a new chapter in his life....

No sense thinking about that now. There was plenty of time to think on that another time, maybe after he got back to Montana this fall. He yawned hugely, and tightened his grip on the sleeping woman in his arms, thinking that the Lord—and the hill spirits—could not have blessed him more.

A clap of thunder woke him. He had no idea how long he'd slept, but when he awoke the rain was still spattering against the fly sheet and distant lightning lit up the night sky, what he could see of it through the thin nylon of the tent. It seemed lighter in the tent, perhaps the stars were out now that the main part of the storm seemed to have moved on.

He turned. Nola had shifted away from him sometime in the night, she'd probably been too hot, and had pushed aside the sleeping bag. The shirt she wore, his, was tangled around her waist and several buttons had come undone at the neck, showing him the faint soft swell of her bosom glowing palely in the dim, filtered light of the stars.

He looked down at her for a long, long moment and then bent to touch his lips softly to the skin of her breast. She stirred slightly and he caught his breath. Damn! he cursed himself. *What the hell are you doing, Harlow?*

I'm making love to the woman I love, something deep inside him answered faintly, something he didn't really want to hear. He bent his head and kissed her softly again, leaning over her, not touching the rest of her. He felt the surge of sheer, primitive, white-hot desire rush through him as he breathed in the sweet sleeping scent of her skin. He remembered how it had felt to have her pressed against him in the saddle that day he'd found her in the coulee, how it had nearly driven him out of his mind feeling her cradled tight against him that way, her soft breasts pressed against his arm, the scent of her hair filling his brain. He'd tried to keep his mind on controlling the mare, and somehow he'd managed. Not that it had made much difference in the end.

Nola stirred again, and half turned toward him. He heard the sound of his name escape her lips on a sigh. It did powerful things to his libido.

"Yes, sweetheart?" he said, kissing her softly again. To hell with it! His lips moved up, inch by tantalizing inch, until he'd reached the juncture of her throat and shoulder. Impatiently he swept aside the tangled veil of her hair with his chin. He felt the drag of his unshaven jaw against the velvet of her skin and heard her sharply indrawn breath in response. He kissed her throat again, and again, the crook of her shoulder, he was hungry for her taste, for her scent, for everything that was her....

"Carson?"

"Mmm?" He'd turned to her fully now, and no living, breathing, red-blooded woman could be unaware of his intentions.

"You're going to make love to me?" It was a rhetorical question, he knew.

He raised his head and looked down at her. Her eyes glowed. She was smiling and her face looked soft and open and vulnerable...and so incredibly desirable that he wanted to pull his shirt off her and make love to her right then, that very instant, plunge inside her body in a hot, fierce coupling—a mating—that would blot out his world—and hers—for a time. A mating that was long, long overdue.

It was a time out of time that he needed. A healing time, a spiritual time. It had nothing to do with the real world. And he knew she needed that time, too. She needed him.

"You said I was no gentleman," he growled softly, and boldly pushed his hand up under the shirt until he felt the soft side of her naked breast against his thumb. He stopped.

"No. Definitely not a gentleman," she whispered, and raised her hands to frame his face as he looked down at her. "Thank heavens for that." Her hands trembled. He felt the trembling start in his own frame, as the thought of what she wanted—of what they both wanted—overwhelmed him.

"You're sure?" His voice was ragged. *Lord*...

She pulled him down until his mouth nearly touched hers. "I'm sure," she whispered against his mouth, then her lips touched his. With a groan, he pulled her into his arms, tight, tighter, until she gasped. He kissed her again and again, fiercely, deeply, feeling that rush of heat he'd felt when he'd kissed her before, back down by the creek, back at the Lazy J... all the times he'd kissed her in his dreams.

She took what he offered, her need matching his. She fed his hunger for her, each tiny moan, each muffled whisper telling him that he was the one she wanted, only him. Nothing—*nothing*—mattered more. This flesh-and-blood woman in his arms was more responsive, more eager, more utterly and completely desirable than the woman ghost who lived in his dreams had ever been.

Which was right; which was exactly as it should be.

Just as he felt he was nearly lost, that he wouldn't be able to impose his will on himself any longer, he somehow found the strength to raise himself, to rear back and fumble for a few seconds in his pack for the store-bought protection he usually carried. A man never knew...

Could he have dreamed that his practicality, his foresight, would ever have been so important? Considering her background, and the future she wanted for herself, there was no way he could take the chance of one glorious night of lovemaking resulting in a child. A child would change everything... especially for her. No matter how much he knew he'd welcome that child and the responsibility that was part of becoming a father... no matter how much he realized that he'd never known a man could ache to make a child as much as he did right now. And that this woman, this woman watching him from their tumbled bed on the hard, cold ground, was the woman with whom he wanted to make that child. It was truth to him, truth not to be questioned, as hard and real as the mountains behind them, as clear and bright as the stars above.

She was naked; he was naked. The smooth, warm length of her body against his was more wonderful than anything he'd imagined. He kissed her again, deeply, holding her head still as she writhed and twisted under him.

"Oh, Carson...*yes*," she gasped, and yet as he rose to position himself, as he focused his entire being on joining her, becoming wholly, utterly joined to her, as a man wanted to merge himself, his body, his spirit, with the woman he loves...he felt her freeze. And her gasp, as he thrust forward with one smooth powerful motion, was more than a woman's gasp of pleasure as she welcomes the man she knows she wants and has the courage to invite to be her lover. He heard fear.

Two equals together; this is what he expected. This, he realized instantly, is not what he had got.

He trembled violently, forcing his mind to overtake, to control his body, his body that wanted only to seize the satisfaction too long overdue. He forced his body to remain still, when all he wanted was to plunge wildly inside her, to receive all her softness, her warmth, and to give her pleasure, to satisfy her beyond her dreams, to offer her all of himself.

But her rising whimpers of pleasure as she writhed under him, her hands frantic on his rigid back, on his loins, urging him against her, closer, closer, was almost more than he could bear. Then, as a shard of lightning split the sky, her final cry came, wild and high and all alone, and he could bear it no longer. He moved within her. Once, twice—it was only a matter of seconds—and his groan, deep and raw and ancient, came on the last crack and roll of the thunder that followed.

Streaming with sweat, shuddering in the afterthroes of his own pleasure and the knowledge, sweeter than anything else a man knows, of his woman's pleasure, Carson collapsed. He shifted sideways, gathering her into his arms, careful not to burden her with his weight, yet still unable, unwilling, to be separated from her. He felt the small shudders of her shoulders as she wept, and gathered her in even closer, protecting her, sheltering her, cherishing her. He knew why she wept; he knew her tears had nothing to do with being sad.

He stroked her damp, tangled hair, smoothed it from her face, ran his hand down her back in long, light strokes, ending by just holding her motionless in his arms and waiting for her tears to pass. He felt his own heart thundering in his brain. He'd never felt such calm, such joy, such utter completeness and peace as he did at this moment. What he felt was beyond—far beyond—physical release. His hunger for her—no, that hadn't passed, and never would, he knew—came from someplace deeper, some lonely place in his soul. That was the particular shape of his own sadness, he knew, that was the reality he would have to face. Tomorrow.

As for now...the night was his...and hers.

Nola's shoulders had been still for some time before she finally raised her tear-stained face. She kissed him lightly on the side of the neck, and he bent his head and kissed her more thoroughly. She reached up one hand to trace his jaw.

"That...that was wonderful," she whispered, her voice soft as the last drops of rain falling outside.

"Mmm..." He kissed her again, and felt the stirrings of desire reawaken. The night belonged to them. He had so much to share with this woman, so little time. But first...

"Nola?" He cleared his throat.

"Yes?" He could see one delicate eyebrow arch as she looked at him, her eyes pools of darkness searching his.

There was no way to mince words. "Why didn't you tell me I was the first man you'd ever made love with?"

She said nothing for a few seconds, but he felt her stiffen slightly, felt the quickened breath of embarrassment, saw the quickly averted eyes. "How did you know?" she asked softly.

He laughed, just as softly. "A man has a way of knowing these things, Nola Rosa. It's not as though it's a big deal, just..." Well, hell. It *was* a big deal. "Still, a man likes to know. It might..."

Now her continued silence and the way she was determinedly tracing and retracing some invisible design on his forearm, was beginning to embarrass him. "It might make a difference in the way he...well, in the way he makes love to her."

"Did it make any difference to you?" Her voice was so soft he barely heard it.

He thought about that for a moment. Then he turned to face her fully, held her face steady in one hand. "I couldn't have done anything much different if I'd wanted to. Sure it made a difference...it's special, it's important, it's—hell, I can't tell you how much it mattered to me. I was...well, honored seems like a pretty stupid word for what I felt, but it was that, and amazed and delighted—idiotic as I know that is...and...and—" He stopped and kissed her soundly. "Hell, I was bowled over, that's what."

She giggled, then began to trace a pattern on his chest that made his blood throb heavily. "It seems kind of crazy to be a virgin in this day and age, I know that," she said softly, thoughtfully. She silenced him by putting a finger to his lips when he would have said there was nothing crazy about it at all. "I wasn't, well, *saving* it for anything— I just had never met anyone I wanted to...well..." Her voice trailed off, then strengthened. "I wanted you to be the first, Carson. I don't know why."

Her calm, clear eyes sought his and he thought he'd drown in them. "I knew not long after I met you that you were the man that I wanted to...to be first. That's all." She lowered her lids again and studied her own hand on his chest.

His arm tightened around her. "Well, I'm honored. I am." And he was, nothing had ever touched him as deeply as that simple statement that she'd wanted him to be the first. And—the knowledge suddenly hit him like a ton of bricks—he realized he wanted to be more than her first lover, he wanted to be the last lover she'd ever have, too.

But that was too ridiculous to waste time thinking about. "Look, I want you to know there's a lot more to making love than what happened just now," he said, shifting against her so that she couldn't help but feel the evidence of his interest. Had she actually blushed again? Delightful woman! He leaned over and kissed her hard on the lips. "Interested in finding out?"

"Why do you think I picked you?" she said slyly.

He grinned. Lord, she was good for his ego! "Well, first of all, I can tell you it doesn't get any better than that, what happened just now between us. In a certain way, special way, it doesn't get any more wonderful. But I got you figured for kind of a skeptic, law lady. You strike me as a woman who doesn't believe everything she hears, am I right?"

He grinned down at her in the semi-darkness and saw her smile back. "You need proof, right? The facts. Hard evidence."

She nodded.

"I figured that. So, I've got an idea that I think might just interest you."

"What's that?"

"Why don't we do some investigating of our own and find out if I'm right. Or wrong."

She laughed again, a delightful sound that made his chest swell until it felt as if it would burst. She wriggled deliciously against him. "You're on, mister. I invite you to prove your case."

That is exactly what he had intended to do. And that is exactly what he did.

Chapter Fifteen

When Nola awoke, dawn had broken. She could hear birds chattering in the trees outside and sensed a kind of expectant hush, as though the world was waiting for her to emerge and join the morning. There was a new day out there, a new dawn. It was a feeling that made her glad to be alive.

If, she thought, looking at Carson's sleeping form, if it was possible to feel more glad to be alive. She studied him, his hair mussed and shaggy on the pillow, his face softened with sleep, lashes longer than she would have thought, one tanned and muscular arm outflung to where she'd lain. It pleased her that she'd awoken first; she wanted this time to look at him without him observing her, to study each tiny feature in a way she'd never before been able to do, she wanted this time to hold the revelations of the night close to her heart and treasure them privately. Last night had changed everything. Besides, he needed his sleep.

Nola felt herself blush, even alone as she was and unobserved. She quietly began searching for something to put on. She was naked, as was he, and her skin tingled in the chill of dawn. Every nerve ending in her body sang, in a way she'd never felt before, and her skin felt almost too sensitive, as though the cotton of the T-shirt that she pulled on would feel coarse and scratchy, as though her jeans and panties were too rough and awkward to put on.

She wriggled into her jeans nevertheless, as quietly as possible, wincing as Carson stirred slightly once and frowned. Then his expression cleared and he slept on and she let out her breath slowly. She reached for her packsack and fumbled in one of the side pockets for a pad of paper and pen she knew she'd put there.

She was going back up the hill. Sometime last evening she'd lost the hammered silver clip that had held her braid, perhaps by the boulder where... where they'd sat. Nola frowned as she remembered what had happened there only last evening. What had happened between her and Carson up on the hill seemed so very long ago, and yet the memory of her bitter disappointment hurt as much now as it did then.

But she had to find that clip, it was one of the very few things she had that had belonged to her mother. She didn't even have a photograph of her. She wrote the note quickly and left it folded on her pillow, a few inches from Carson's outstretched hand. She had the sudden impulse to bend and press a kiss into his palm, but she managed to restrain herself. The night was over. And it wasn't something, she knew deep in her heart, that would ever be repeated.

Outside the tent the air was fresh-scrubbed and still, cleansed of every possible impurity by the fierce summer storm the night before. Nola drew deep breaths, relishing the clean, cool mountain scents and the joy there was in raising her arms luxuriously over her head, every fiber of her body supple and strong and aching to stretch. Even the weariness she knew she should feel from a night spent with so little sleep, and the definite feelings of tenderness in various parts of her body, only served to remind her of what had happened between them, and to deepen her blush. Carson had been the lover she'd only dreamed of, and she had to believe him that, yes, it didn't—couldn't possibly—get any better than that.

Gingerly, she stepped forward and put all her weight on her sore ankle. It was much better than it had been the night before. She'd noticed that the slight swelling had gone down, and all she had to show for her carelessness scrambling over the rock slide last night was a bruise and a nasty scrape. She'd live.

Resolutely, Nola set off on the same path she'd traveled the evening before, once on her own two feet, once rather ignominiously on Carson's back. She felt again, in her belly, the movement of his strong back under her as she clung to him. She felt again the depth of the trust she'd instinctively offered him when he'd told her to climb onto his back and hang on, that somehow, come hell or high water, he'd bring her safely down the mountain. Now, she thought, that even then they'd merged somehow, melded, that it hadn't taken a night of glorious lovemaking—sex, she reminded herself firmly—to achieve that sense of oneness. She'd already given herself to him when she'd trusted him to carry her off the mountain.

Was it always this way between a man and a woman? Her limited experience had not prepared her for her new knowledge about the needs and aches of her own body, nor the perfect fulfillment she'd discovered it was possible to find in a man's arms. She was not naive enough not to know that most women her age had already had several lovers.

Perhaps it *was* this way between the sexes, physical love. She bit her lip. If so, most women were made of stronger stuff than she. How could they stop themselves from falling in love, if every lover made them feel the way she'd felt last night in Carson's arms? Not, of course, that the falling in love part applied in this case. There was no question of that. It was simply that the whole idea interested her. It was just that, in her usual way, she had to study what had happened, analyze it, and parcel it up to try to fit it into her own experience.

The parched ground had absorbed the night's rain and the going was relatively solid underfoot. It wasn't as far to the top of the plateau as she'd remembered, nor was the climb as difficult. Perhaps it had been only in her eagerness last night to finally see the Painted Rocks that she'd cursed every rock slide that slowed her progress, every gully that had had to be detoured.

When she reached the top, panting slightly, the morning sun had gilded the plateau, its rays spilling over into the canyon where Carson had said the Painted Rocks were. Below, all was in dark and shadow. Above, the side of the canyon blazed with light and with the colors of the rocks: gray and tan and rust-red, sandstone and the hard glow of granite. Nola approached the boulder slowly, her heart thumping in her breast.

Perhaps the much repeated legend had been wrong. Perhaps the time to see the rock paintings was not sunset, perhaps it was sunrise.... Nola came to a halt and slowly, ever so slowly, studied the rock face across from her. She examined every square foot of rock surface. She squinted her eyes and looked this way and that, thinking that perhaps it would help her to see ... to see what it was that others had seen before her. To see what it was Carson had seen.

Then the pain of disappointment stabbed at her once again. It was no use. She saw nothing, nothing that could even vaguely be taken to be rock paintings. She couldn't even lie to herself, tell herself that some rock formation, just there, perhaps there, looked a lot like— No, there was nothing to see. Nothing.

Nola bit back the pain. She had to accept it now. The vision of the Painted Rocks was not hers. The spirits, the keepers of this sacred place, in their wisdom, kept it from her. She was not strong enough, or wise enough, or whatever it was that enabled the seeker to find the vision....

Nola felt suddenly very old, very much older than her twenty-five years. She bent to examine the grass where they'd sat. The entire area had been flattened by the rainstorm and Nola finally had to get down on her hands and knees and pat the grass, hoping to feel the hard edge of her hair clip. Not there, not there, either ... perhaps closer to the boulder.

Finally she felt it, a hard lump under the grass. But there were two lumps.... Nola dug under the grass with her fingers and felt her heart lighten. There was the silver clip that her mother had once owned, bits of grass stuck to its hammered silver surface, a little debris caught in the mechanism that snapped it tight.

Pleased, Nola pulled a wide-tooth comb out of her back pocket and made herself comfortable in the sunshine, crosslegged, warmed by the rising sun, and began to comb out the tangles in her hair. It was a slow job, one requiring patience. Many times in the past it had been a task that had made her impatient and she'd yank at the tangles, causing tears to spring to her eyes, and she'd curse her hair and swear she'd get it cut next trip to Lethbridge. But she never did. And today she took her time, combing her hair out dreamily, ending by braiding it neatly into a full, single, shining braid, and fastening it with the silver clip. She double-checked to make sure it was secure, then sat for a few moments longer, absorbing the sunshine and thinking about making the trip back down the hill to the campsite.

Carson would probably have awoken by now. She wanted to see him; at the same time she did not want to see him. She did not want to have to explore any further the feelings that had risen between them last night. She wanted that particular episode of her life to be over, to be behind her, to be neatly tucked into the past. It *was* the past; the future was what she needed to think about.

She put out her hand to help herself rise and again felt the hard lump under the grass she'd felt when she found the clip. Curious, Nola parted the grass and dug underneath with her fingers. Whatever it was was half buried, half covered by the flinty soil. She scraped at it with her fingernail and finally it came free.

What in the world was it? She lifted the small stonelike object in her hand and examined it closely. It seemed to be some sort of a rock, but a rock unlike any other. It had the weight of a small stone, yet looked on the surface like a shell, with striations and glints of something that looked almost like mother-of-pearl. Idly, Nola brushed the debris from the object, and as its shape became clearer, her heart suddenly stopped beating.

The spirits had not forgotten her.

It was an *i-nis'-kim*. She felt her blood run cold. Yes. There, clearly, was the shape of the buffalo. There was the lowered head. There, the humped shoulders and the short back.... Nola's fingers closed convulsively over the precious amulet and she closed her eyes. Tears of joy leaked out from under her eyelids; she turned her face to the rising sun.

"Thank you, thank you, Creator Sun. Thank you Mother Earth for giving me this *i-nis'-kim*, symbol of plenty, of food for the children and the old people, this promise that the buffalo will never forsake the one who finds the *i-nis'-kim....*"

Nola's tears broke out afresh. This was dearer, this was more precious than the rock paintings could ever be to her. This was the tiny object that had started her on her search for her identity, for her Indian roots, all those many years ago when a visitor to the ranch had shown her an *i-nis'-kim*. That one had been larger and darker in color but, like hers, it held the spirit of the buffalo...the buffalo without which her people would have died out thousands of years ago. The buffalo, which the Blackfoot called "real food."

Of course, the buffalo were gone now. Exterminated. And the Indian people had not been able to depend on the buffalo for more than a hundred years. So, too, was their way of life gone. But still, the spirits had given her the *i-nis'-kim* for a reason. She must know, she must find out what that reason was....

Nola suddenly paled. No...it couldn't be. *No!* She opened her hand and stared in horror at the tiny stone buffalo. It was telling her what she didn't want to hear. It was telling her she had to destroy every last remaining dream she had. She couldn't—*she wouldn't*—listen to the song of the *i-nis'-kim*.

She was a modern woman, after all. She was educated, she was a grown-up, she didn't believe in all this hocus-pocus. She didn't believe in magic. She wasn't superstitious, not in the slightest. Her interest in the Painted Rocks had been to preserve them for future generations, as Head-Smashed-In Buffalo Jump, near Fort Macleod, had been classed a world heritage site not that many years before. Places such as this were part of the true history of her people, after all, not to be destroyed by willy-nilly development or mining interests. As for the *i-nis'-kim*, it was no more than a piece of fossilized ammonite, preserved from the millions of years before when this entire area had been covered by vast inland waters. How it had ended up here on a foothills plateau so close to the Rockies, she had no idea. Perhaps some Indian had lost it here many generations ago. Perhaps he'd come to this hill seeking a vision and had left his medicine bag here and had never been able to find it again.

That's all. That's all it was.

But as she stood to begin making her way down the hill, she realized her knees were shaky and her hands still trembled. Could it be? Could it be that the spirits were telling her that she belonged to Carson Harlow? That now he no longer had only brought her to the place where she had lost her dreams of seeing the Painted Rocks, but he had her heart, as well?

If she hadn't lost her mother's clip, if she hadn't *worn* it yesterday. If Carson hadn't brought her to sit by just that particular boulder... Still, she felt the eyes of the ancestors on her back as she made her way down the hill. She shivered in the brightness.

Love this man...this white man? It was impossible! But in her heart she knew different. It was true. She loved him. She loved Carson Harlow with all her strength and soul. She'd known from the moment she'd met him that he was different somehow, that something bound them as tightly and closely as it was possible for man and woman to be bound. Last night had proved it to her. As thunder and lightning, they could never be separated.

No...no! Nola forced the very thought of what the *i-nis'-kim* might mean from her mind as she picked her way carefully down the hill. No accidents, no stumbling that would mean *he'd* have to come after her and rescue her again. She gritted her teeth. She'd make it on her own. Just as she'd done all her life. She knew what she wanted and she knew how to fight for it. She was a rational woman, and a rational woman did not give up all her carefully laid plans because she found an old stone under a clump of grass. And what made her say it looked like a buffalo, anyway? It was like looking for the pictures in clouds, anyone could see anything.

She'd never see the Painted Rocks, she could accept that now. She had to believe the evidence of her own eyes. But she wasn't giving up everything else—her dreams of marrying an Indian man someday and securing for her children the birthright she'd never had.

No man—not even a man like Carson Harlow—could make her give up that dream.

Carson cursed as a piece of rusted barbed wire snapped and bit into the flesh at the base of his thumb, even through the thick hide of his rawhide gloves. He didn't think it had pierced his glove, but still, it hurt like hell. He tossed the broken wire down in disgust. He couldn't blame Augustus: the man was getting too old to keep up with this kind of work. And some of these fences were an awful mess....

Most ranchers hated mending fence; most ranchers hated anything that couldn't be done from the back of a horse. But it still had to be done. There were miles and miles of fencing to keep up on an ordinary spread. And with so much deeded high range land backing right up to the Rockies, the Lazy J crew had a big job cut out for them.

Carson straightened and wiped his brow with his sleeve. He settled his hat again and shrugged irritably. He'd got a haircut in Calgary last week and was reminded of it every time he took off his hat and felt the wind on the back of his neck. He set his jaw grimly... would it make any difference if she knew he could look half civilized if he put his mind to it? Not likely, not when he couldn't do anything about the color of his skin.

"Goin' to Augustus's birthday party, Carson?" Mort Slade was helping him on this section of fence and he had a couple of other hands, Tom Spanner, the dour, tobacco-chewing Pincher Creek man, and another hand he'd hired out of the hotel bar last week, working another section, just ahead. He'd told Augustus he'd give him any help he could in the week or ten days left before he headed back to Montana.

"Maybe," he replied tersely, scowling to himself as he hammered in a couple of fence staples. "Maybe not. Haven't made up my mind yet."

He aimed to leave Alberta the week after Labor Day. Head back across the line. He'd already made arrangements to leave his horses behind. He hated to leave the line-back buckskin, felt as if he'd just begun to make some real progress with her and he still had a long way to go. He'd always liked horses, and helping the wrangler had been his favorite kind of ranch work back on the Double H where he'd grown up. Leaving the mare half trained and just getting used to him was an abuse of trust, he felt, just like leaving the old man in the lurch the way he was planning to do.

That's why he'd volunteered to do what he could to get his fences in shape before winter. Sure, Augustus had a hired crew to do it, but Carson wanted to make sure it was done right.

He stood for a minute and looked around, at the heat shimmering off the parched grassland, at the brilliance of the snowcapped Rockies that reared up behind the ranch. It was pretty country, no doubt about it. He wished he could say he was glad to be leaving it behind. But he'd known Nola Snow was trouble the first time he'd seen her and the only thing left to him now was what he should have had the sense to do in the first place: run. His continued presence was just an embarrassment to them both.

He sighed and picked up his hammer again. Hell, no man

could have made a worse mess of things. He drove in a couple of staples savagely.

"Okay, let's move on down," he said to Mort. The other man tossed his hammer into the toolbox.

"Gonna be fun. I hear Nola's got a coupla fiddles organized and a squeeze box. And there'll be women there."

"You going?" Carson asked suspiciously. He frowned. He'd never gotten over his feeling about Mort Slade, who was basically a likable fellow and a hard worker. Carson respected that. But something about the man had always rubbed him wrong.

"Wouldn't miss it for anything. You betcha. Even Grizzly's gonna be there. Me 'n Tom got a small wager going on whether or not he changes his shirt for the occasion." Mort grinned. "Besides, I figure it's one way to get me a dance with Nola. How could she refuse?" He winked at Carson.

She damn well could refuse! He just remembered what it was about Mort Slade that rubbed him the wrong way. After checking the sudden urge to hit him—no man had ever unknowingly come as close to getting hit as often as Mort Slade had, he was beginning to think—Carson made up his mind. Maybe he would show up. It'd be the last chance he had to see Nola before he left. Why not show himself, say goodbye like a man, wish her happiness?

Some men sure are suckers for punishment, he thought, grimacing as he slammed the pickup door shut behind him. And he was one of the prime ones. He watched in the rearview mirror as Mort climbed onto the bed of the truck box and yelled as a signal for him to let out the clutch.

He'd seen Nola a couple of times—well, three times to be exact—since the night they'd made love, and each time it had ripped him up so bad inside that he swore he'd make sure he never saw her again. He'd been cool and careful, and so had she. And then, each time he had the chance to see her again, he took it.

Why couldn't he just damn well let her go? Forget her, as he'd already forgotten a lot of women in his life? But it didn't seem to work that way; he couldn't forget what had happened between them. He'd thought it had meant something. He'd thought this time was different. What a fool he'd been. When he'd awoken that morning to find her gone, before he'd seen her note, he'd felt as though he'd taken a kick in the stomach from a runaway rodeo bronc.

Then, when he'd seen her emerge from the trees finally, her hair all neat and tidy, her modest jeans and T-shirt hiding all evidence of the eager young woman he'd held in his arms all night long, the woman he'd kissed, caressed, made love to, held close . . . he'd smiled. Pride, pleasure . . . He didn't think he'd ever felt so happy before; never would again.

Then he'd seen her face clearly and he knew that it wasn't going to be the way he'd begun to hope it might be, the way he'd begun to hope it could be. . . . He'd never forget that moment, either, not for as long as he lived.

Her face was pinched and pale, and she held something clutched in one hand that she wouldn't let him see. "I want to go home, Carson," was all she'd said. Then she'd begun to pack up her gear without another word.

Home? Where was home? The Lazy J? The band site? He'd turned back to the fire where he'd started breakfast and poked at the ashes. So that's the way it was. All she'd wanted from him is what she'd got—a man she'd decided she wanted to be the first. Probably part of the complicated plan she'd laid out for her life. He felt the way he figured a lot of women must feel sometimes . . . used.

But knowing that made no difference. He was crazy about her . . . he couldn't stop thinking about her. And he couldn't stop hoping that he'd been wrong.

Is this what had happened to his brother Boone back when he'd first met Lucie? Had Boone lost **all his** good sense the same way, just like that, over a woman? Everybody in the Sawtooth Valley had known how bedrock sensible his brother was. Maybe some men had sawdust for brains when it came to women. Maybe the Harlows were among them. Maybe it had just taken this long for him to find out.

A week or ten days. It wasn't that long now. He'd been up to Calgary, talked to the district geologist there and had made up his mind. He couldn't say Nola hadn't had anything to do with his decision—she had. But there was no need for her to know why he'd done what he'd done.

Carson sighed again and pulled his hat lower against the red of the setting sun. They had another half mile of fence to check before heading back to the ranch. How the hell had his life gotten so damn complicated all of a sudden?

And Augustus. Damn, he felt bad about the old man. Augustus had counted on partnering a winning proposition. And the cards were there, too, if he—Carson—would pick them up and play them right. But he couldn't do it, not now, no matter how much Augustus tried to convince him to stay.

The fact was, he hated himself for what he'd had to do to the old man. His guilt had brought him back to the Lazy J to offer some help mending fences, making sure the Lazy J was set up for winter. He'd let his brother down all those years ago, he couldn't let the old man down, too. Augustus had counted on him, too, just as Boone had.

Tomorrow Augustus was turning seventy-nine. It would mean a lot to the old rancher to have his friends there to celebrate, even though Carson didn't know if Augustus knew about this party Nola was planning.

Carson hit the brakes and got out of the pickup. The sun had nearly set. He and Mort were nearly finished the job they'd set out to do.

Would he be there tomorrow, at the party? Yeah, he'd be there. Wild horses couldn't keep him away.

Nola glanced over her shoulder at the open door of the bunkhouse. It wasn't the first time she'd looked that way that evening and she was pretty sure it wouldn't be the last. Was Carson going to show up? She'd heard from Mort Slade that he intended to come, but thinking about maybe coming to her father's birthday party and actually showing up was a different matter.

Augustus, at least, was in seventh heaven. She glanced over to the corner of the bunkhouse, which had been cleared out to make room for a table of party food, a hastily rigged bandstand and a space for dancing, where her father was holding court with Grizzly Sawchuck—resplendent in a brand new bandanna although it didn't look as if he'd changed his shirt for a month—and a couple of the widow ladies from the neighborhood. Augustus's white hair was flying, his leathery cheeks tinged pink with pleasure. And heat.

Hot! Nola blew at a strand of hair that had stuck to her cheek. She'd worn it loose tonight, with one wing at the side pulled high and back and fastened with her mother's silver clip. For whose eyes? she asked herself, knowing full well the feminine pleasure she'd allowed herself at the thought of dressing for a certain pair of green eyes. The silver clip that had brought her to the *i-nis'-kim* ...

She'd never told anyone about what she'd found on the mountain. She'd never told anyone about the Painted Rocks, although Carson had made it clear to her on the way back to the ranch that day that he was leaving it entirely up to her whether or not she told anyone. Why had she kept the information to herself?

"Hot?"

Ben's voice, coming next to her ear, caused her to start. "Mmm. I think I'll sit out the next one."

She'd almost forgotten that she was dancing with Ben, which was a pretty poor state of affairs considering she'd once thought of him as the epitome of the man she'd one day marry. The way she felt now, she could have been dancing with a brother she'd never had. The fact was, only one man had ever tripped her heart into double time. Only one.

Who could blame him if he didn't show up? She'd treated him badly. But she'd been so frightened when she'd first found the *i-nis'-kim* that she hadn't known what else to do. The very thought that even the last of her dreams was about to splinter, coming on top of the bitter disappointment of her failure to see the rock paintings, had been too much to bear. Now... Could she say things were really any different now?

She knew only one thing: her heart ached and she'd shed many, many tears. And still she did not know what path to take. Except that she needed to see him, to talk to him again...to say goodbye. She'd figured from Augustus's gloom and occasional remarks regarding the American, that he was ready to head south. She'd noticed his horses in Augustus's back pasture, and had the sneaking suspicion maybe Carson was leaving them behind.

Automatically, she touched the leather thong she wore around her neck. Unseen, under the silk of her blouse, the *i-nis'-kim* rested between her breasts in its own soft leather bag. Her medicine bag. Since she'd found the *i-nis'-kim*, she had never been separated from it. Superstition? Perhaps. But it also symbolized the special time in a woman's life when she finally meets a certain man, fully, equally, intimately. A coming of age. It isn't often the man she marries; but it's a man she never forgets.

Suddenly she froze.

There he was . . . he'd come. He was standing in the doorway, hatless. . . . Why, he'd had a haircut. He looked different, but the same somehow. A civilized man in civilized clothes. He was wearing khaki-colored pants and a white shirt, and slung over his shoulder was his buckskin jacket. No, he wasn't Carson Harlow without that jacket. He hadn't seen her yet.

"Something wrong?" Ben murmured.

"Carson's here, Ben," she said, hoping the breathlessness she felt wasn't evident in her voice. "He must have decided to come, after all." But her nervousness must have shown, judging by Ben's understanding smile and the raised eyebrow—which irritated her. It was one thing for her to feel the way she did, it was another for everyone else to be aware of it.

"Looks like Marie could use some rescuing, anyway," he said with a smile and a nod across the room toward where the researcher from Lethbridge danced with Mort Slade.

Nola winced. Perhaps "dancing" was stretching the meaning of the word as it applied to Mort's technique. Ben had shown up at the party with Marie Crowfoot, much to Nola's delight. Somehow knowing that Ben was involved with someone else helped relieve the guilty feelings she had about him, not that she'd ever let him know what she'd once been planning for him. Yes, that was about it, Nola, she realized grimly, you'd once been planning Ben's life for him, just the way you thought you could plan Augustus's and your own. Life, she'd discovered—certainly matters of the heart—just didn't fall in nicely with anyone's plans.

Just as Ben grinned down at her and let her go, Nola happened to glance over at the doorway. For a split second Carson's image hung before her—his stiffness, the shade of indifference that had come down over his features as he'd spotted her with Ben—and then he was gone.

He couldn't leave . . . he just couldn't! Nola pushed her way frantically through the couples on the dance floor—half of Pincher Creek had turned up to her father's party, it seemed—but when she reached the doorway, she couldn't see him anymore.

He'd disappeared.

Chapter Sixteen

"Carson!"

She burst out the door, not caring that her behavior was less than dignified, neither as hostess for her father's birthday party nor as a respected member of the legal profession. She was a woman, too. Carson was nowhere in sight, but his dusty red pickup was still parked in the yard, pulled up behind a dozen or so other pickups. He was still here... somewhere.

Her heart pounded, terror mixing with relief. The relief that washed over her brought it home to her yet again that she could no longer ignore what she felt. Perhaps he was on his way back to Montana, out of her life—she deserved no less, and, of course, those had always been his plans—but she couldn't deny what these past few weeks had meant to her, no matter where her future lie. What he'd meant to her. He was the first man who'd made love to her and the first man she'd loved, the way a woman loves a man. Life went on. Of course, it did. Yet, no woman could ever forget that kind of man. Nor would she.

She didn't find him by the corral where she'd found him once before. He wasn't in the barn—she even peeked in the darkened blacksmith shop, not really expecting that he'd be there, but a memory of how she'd once happened on him shoeing the mare there, brow clear, half-naked body utterly magnificent, purpose dead-calm and absolutely certain, twisted her heart.

"Carson!"

He never answered, yet something drew her to the hay shed that bounded the ranch yard to the north. There she found him, leaning against the big timbered gate that closed the shed, gazing to the west and north, to the Rockies, to the canyon of the Painted Rocks, to the last golden rays of the sun as it slipped down behind the mountains.

"Are... are you coming to the party?" she finally ventured, feeling her heart pound in her breast and feeling anger at herself for coming out with such a remark. She hadn't followed him here to invite him back to the party.

He turned. "Sure," he said easily. "Couldn't miss the chance to wish your father a happy birthday, could I?"

His casual reply, no more than anyone would have given, gave her confidence. She took a deep breath and stepped up beside him to lean back against the gate, too, one sandaled foot going up behind her to hook onto one of the crosspieces. She'd noted Carson's quick appraising look at how she was dressed. He'd never seen her in anything but jeans. She was wearing a skirt today, for the party, and still felt terribly self-conscious in it. She didn't think she'd worn a skirt more than a dozen times in all the years she'd grown up on the Lazy J.

"I—I'm glad you came...." Her words faded. She *was* glad he'd come, of course, but that wasn't—

"I had to come," he said, and his voice was rough. He turned to face her fully, leaning with one shoulder against the gate. "I don't know if Augustus said anything or not," he went on, "but I'll be leaving in a week or ten days, as soon as I finish the fence mending I promised him."

"I kind of knew you were," she answered, her voice very small. She couldn't bear to meet his gaze. She plucked at the material of her skirt with one hand and twisted it. *So it was true then, he was leaving!* Yet she'd known, hadn't she? This came as no surprise.

He cleared his throat. "So I came to say, so long, Nola Rosa, and tell you that...well, that this summer has meant a lot to me." He smiled, and she felt the tears rise in her throat. "I'll miss you."

"I want to tell you how sorry I am for what I said when we were up on the mountain," she whispered, her voice trembling. "What happened between us meant—it meant a lot to me, and I treated you badly and I'm so sorry and...I'll miss you, too." Her voice wasn't much more than a croak.

Nola Rosa... He'd always called her that. It used to make her mad; now she didn't think she'd ever heard a name that sounded sweeter to her ears, more intimate.... She turned away, not wanting him to see her tears. She blinked fiercely, desperately trying to regain control. It didn't help. Something was shattering inside her. Something clear and hard, like glass. She felt it crack and break apart slowly, inexorably, inside her very soul, and she suddenly realized that whatever it was should have broken and been swept from her life a long, long time ago.

"Carson," she said, and her voice broke on his name. "Carson, this is awful...just hold me. Please."

He cursed savagely, caught her in his arms and hauled her tight against his chest. "Damn it, Nola." His voice was strained. "Don't do this to me. Don't cry like this. I can't stand it. I can't stand to see you hurting like this—"

"I'm not crying," she lied, somehow managing to hold back the sobs. It felt so good, so incredibly good to be this close to him again, to be held by him, to feel his strong arms around her, to hear him muttering familiar cowboy curses into her hair. He smelled like laundry soap and horses and leather and all the wide open spaces that had spawned his wild wanderer's soul.

She'd known him and she'd loved him, and she had to let him go. It wasn't... it wasn't fair.

"Look, Nola," she heard him mutter. "I told you once that I'd do anything I could to make you happy. That your dreams were my dreams. And I meant what I said, damn it. You said you didn't know what you wanted then, what you needed—"

"I don't. I mean, I do..." she whispered, shocked that she even dared to think the thought. "Kiss me, Carson...just kiss me one more time."

With a growl of impatience and frustration, Carson held her head steady with one hand and covered her mouth with his. His mouth felt hard, it felt demanding, it felt so warm, so familiar...it brought everything back to her, the night they'd spent together, the soft words of passion he'd whispered over and over to her in the dark of the night while the storm raged around them. The memories, so bright and vivid, unleashed feelings in her that she'd thought had been frozen and stopped up forever. *Yes, yes! This is what she wanted.*

Their tongues touched and twined and Nola felt the flame of desire, rich and ready, rise within her the way it did whenever she dared to touch this man, whenever he kissed her this way. She kissed him back, strongly, fiercely, hungry for his taste, hungry to imprint everything about him in her memory, so that she'd have him always....

"Lord, Nola..." he growled, lifting his mouth finally from hers. He'd pulled the clip from her hair and it had fallen wild and free around her face. He brushed back a strand with his thumb and kissed her again. Then he held her face firmly and said, "This isn't smart, Nola."

"No," she managed.

"This isn't wise." His voice was unsteady.

"I know," she whispered, and reached up to link her arms around his neck and pull him closer. Again and again their mouths met, hungry, each kiss promising more...and more. Finally he pulled back, and held her clamped tightly against his chest so that she couldn't reach up and kiss him any longer. She closed her eyes and heard the thunder of his heart, blended with the thunder of her own heart, crashing inside her head.

"Nola," he said. He paused, then went on. "I didn't come here to do this, even though this is what I've wanted to do every time I saw you these past couple of weeks. That's why I haven't come down to the ranch more than I had to, lately. I wanted to see you and yet seeing you, knowing I had to leave...well, it was just too hard on me. I couldn't stand seeing you and not having you."

What was he talking about? Nola raised her head. His eyes were clear and green and full of the deep hunger she'd seen in them the night they'd made love up on the mountain. A hunger she knew he needed her to satisfy just as he filled the ache and emptiness that had always existed inside her. Who could say why these things were the way they were?

"I made up my mind that I'd come to your father's party tonight. But I wasn't coming here just to see him. I wanted to be able to say goodbye to you properly, after what we'd—what we'd gone through. What I like to think we shared. I didn't want it to seem like I'd just run out on you. I wanted you to know my reasons."

"Carson . . ." she whispered, a dawning sort of wonder in her voice. *Could it be . . . could it possibly be?* She reached up one hand to touch his jaw as he spoke. He turned, pressed a kiss into her palm, then went on.

"I know how bad it was for you when you couldn't see the rock paintings. I know it was something you'd worked for all your life. If I could have made you see them somehow, I would have. You know that, don't you?"

He smiled slightly and she nodded. She realized suddenly that tears were trickling down her face, but she made no move to wipe them away. The tears were carrying all that broken glass out of her soul, they were washing away something that had hurt her all her life, although she hadn't quite known it until now.

"But there is something I can do for you, Nola." He gave her a very serious look. "There is a dream you still have, I know you have because you've told me." He took a deep breath. "I know how much it means to you to find yourself an Indian husband someday and have children that you can raise in the tradition of your mother's people. That dream is still there. It's yours. You can make it come true.

"God strike me for a liar if I say I wish you success in finding that man someday, because I don't. I wish to God that I was that man. But I know I'm not."

Nola's tears began afresh. Carson wiped the path of her tears with his thumb, and his faint, crooked, self-mocking smile as he looked down at her nearly broke her heart. "The way I figure it is, you're one determined lady. I know you'll find that man one day, and settle down and be happy, knowing that at least one of your dreams came true. It might make it a little easier to accept what happened up at the canyon."

She shook her head unsteadily. "I— I can't—"

"Yes, you can." He smoothed her hair back from her face. "You're beautiful." She shook her head, but he smiled and went on. "You're young, you're the smartest woman I ever met, with the most grit and the most hellfire and passion for what she believes is right. I know you'll get what you want. That's just the kind of woman you are. That's why I—" He stopped abruptly, as though catching back something he hadn't planned to say.

She shook her head again, unable to speak.

He shook her gently. "You damn well better, Nola," he growled, "because I sure as hell wouldn't be giving up my stake in this business between you and me if I thought you were going to end up with somebody else someday. Maybe somebody just like me.

"If I thought that was the case, I'd be offering you second best right now. A man who isn't an Indian but who loves you as much as I figure it's possible for a man to love a woman." His voice was gruff. His eyes met hers, she saw the light in them shining strong and true. "I love you, Nola. I love you for the woman you are right now, right here in my arms, not for where you came from, or who you think you'd like to be someday. I wish to God I was the man who could make you happy, the man who'd make your dream come true."

"Are...are you—?" She couldn't say anything more, she felt utterly stunned. And happy, deliriously happy. This man loved her...*her, Nola Rose Snow.* Could it be possible? Her natural caution told her she had to make sure. "What are you saying?"

"I'm tossing my cards on the table, Nola. I'm saying, you can take me or leave me. If you want me, I'll promise to love you and cherish you forever, for as long as I've got blood and breath."

He paused, then went on, his voice a little rougher. "If you want to follow your dream, I'll understand. And I'll just head off south like I planned, give myself a little time and, hell, try to remember to keep my head up and my eyes open for whatever else life decides to throw at me." He shrugged slightly. But he hadn't slackened his hold on her, not the slightest bit. And she could see the shadow of pain, deep pain, in the back of his eyes.

"Oh, Carson," she breathed. "I never thought you felt that way about me. I never thought you could love a woman like me. I thought you...I just thought you lived a life that was too wild and free to ever want to be tied down—"

"I always have," he said. "That doesn't mean a man can't change. Especially when he meets the woman he figures it wouldn't be too terrible bad to be tied down with—"

"Where...where would we live?" Ever practical, Nola had to find out everything she could before she could really believe that what she was hearing was true. *That he loved her—*

"I've had a few strikes over the years. I've got some money put aside. I'd look around for a place near here, if you want to stay here," Carson said. "I have to admit I liked working at the hay with your father this summer, and mending fence isn't near as bad as I remember it. I guess ranching's in my blood as much as prospecting's ever been. I've been thinking for quite some time that maybe it was time for me to think about settling down, find me a place I could call home."

He paused and looked deep into her eyes, and Nola thought she'd die of happiness. "Never dreamed I'd be lucky enough to find a woman I'd want to share that life with. You interested?"

"Oh, yes, yes, yes," she said, suddenly feeling all her energy come rushing back into her body. "Oh, Carson...this is why I've been so desperately unhappy. I didn't want to love you, I didn't want to let myself love you. But

I just couldn't help loving you. I don't want to fight it anymore. Yes, I love you—''

"You do?" He sounded as stunned as she felt.

She laughed. "Surely you must know that—"

"I don't. I mean, I didn't." He tightened his grip around her until she nearly winced. She could feel his heart thumping nearly as wildly as hers. "Lord, does this mean...?"

"Yes, I love you, Carson. Yes, I want to marry you, if that's what you're asking me. And if we have children someday I want them to know about the part of me that is Indian. But I'll worry about that when the time comes. When they start asking questions. Besides, it seems to me that you know a whole lot more about the Indian way of life than I do, anyway—"

"Oh, Nola Rosa," he murmured, interrupting, and bent to kiss her again. This time she clung to him unreservedly, and when the fire rose again in them both, vital and strong and unquenchable, she had no objection when he led her into the shelter of the hay shed and in the privacy of the darkened shed, on the sweet-smelling hay, they reaffirmed their need for each other and pledged their love in body and in spirit.

Afterward, Nola lay beside Carson, her head on his shoulder, her hand on his bare chest. "Hey," she said slyly, "I thought you told me it didn't get any better."

He laughed. She saw the stars twinkle through a few damaged shingles in the shed roof and felt the hay prickle almost painfully against her back as he kissed her, and didn't care. "I didn't think it did," he growled, planting kisses on her bare throat and shoulders. "Which just goes to show a man can be dead wrong sometimes."

"Even you?"

"Even me." He lifted the leather thong she wore around her neck with one finger. "What's this?"

She told him about finding the *i-nis'-kim* the morning after they'd made love. She said she had realized then that she loved him but had been horrified at the implications of what it might mean to the plans she'd laid out for herself.

"But I was wrong, Carson," she said softly, tracing her finger along his jaw, then along his nose and eyes. How she loved this man! "Love is more important. Thank goodness I had the chance to discover just how wrong I was. Plans are just plans. Plans can be changed."

"Old Jim used to tell me that sometimes one dream has to die so that another one can get started," Carson said quietly. "He was a man with a lot of wisdom in his soul."

"You sound like you still miss him," she said.

"I do. He was the father I never had. I owe him a lot. My own father spent all his time up in the Sawtooths, sketching and painting pictures. My brother, Boone, and my grandmother raised us. I was hell as a kid, always raising one kind of trouble or another—" He gave her a sideways look. "You don't want to know about that. I've always been afraid I'd turn out too much like my dad, only with a pick and shovel instead of a paintbrush. Old Jim turned me around. Showed me some of the Indian ways, showed me what counted. Told me that what you didn't see sometimes counted for more than what you did see. Which, I guess, is what my father had been looking for, too, in his way. Except a kid doesn't understand that kind of thing the way a man does." He sat up and rummaged through a pocket in his buckskin jacket, which he'd spread on the hay.

"Here." He handed her a small, perfectly round, smooth object that felt like a stone, but she could see the iridescence, the lively sparkle of its surface in the faint starlight. "Put this in your medicine bag. It belongs with your *i-nis'-kim.*"

"What is it?" she asked as he took it from her and gently inserted it into the leather pouch around her neck.

"It's ammonite, too. A polished form of it. A lot of it is mined up here on the St. Mary's River. You probably know that."

She nodded. Ammonite had been mined for years on the Blood reservation near Lethbridge. Local companies made jewelry out of it and sold it worldwide.

"Old Jim gave this piece to me years ago, told me where I'd find the source up here in Alberta near the Painted Rocks. It's what I've been looking for this summer."

Nola felt the two objects in her pouch through the soft leather. Two forms of the same ancient fossil, buried under the vast inland sea seventy-five million years ago, in the age of the dinosaurs.

"Did you find it?"

"Hey, now, that'd be telling, wouldn't it?" She felt him smile at her in the darkness, and felt the joy of claiming this man and his love for her own. Not that it made a bit of difference . . . he still wasn't telling her any of his prospecting secrets.

He leaned over and kissed her briefly, warmly, loudly, on the lips. "Think we'll ever get to make love in a real bed, darlin'? I feel like a damn teenager fooling around in this hay shed," he said, then kissed her again, more thoroughly. "Much as I'd like to stay here and fool around some more, I think we ought to get dressed and get back to the party before Augustus sends out a search party," he finally said with a reluctance that she felt, too.

Nola quickly found her clothes and put them on, laughing as Carson picked the hay out of her hair. She walked back through the softness of the August darkness hand in hand with him, noting the big orange moon rising to the east. Harvest moon. We reap what we sow, she thought. And she found herself thanking the spirit of a dead Indian, his ghost departed to join the ancestors in the Sand

Hills many years ago, for sending a white man in a beaded buckskin jacket her way.

The party was still in full swing. Augustus led a loud cheer as they stepped through the doorway of the bunkhouse, blinking and grinning somewhat foolishly, Nola realized, in the bright light. It was hard to wipe the smile off her face, though. Nor did Carson stop smiling. She hoped no one guessed at what had transpired in the hay shed, and prayed he'd found and removed every bit of hay in her hair.

"Happy birthday, Augustus," she heard Carson say, and then clutched his hand a little tighter as she heard his next words. "Since I didn't bring you a birthday present, I thought I'd do you a favor and take your daughter off your hands." He grinned down at her and winked. "She's agreed to marry me."

Another huge cheer went up from the crowd. Nola looked at Carson with dismay. That isn't exactly what she'd had in mind in the way of a wedding announcement. He grinned a little sheepishly and shrugged his shoulders.

Augustus was ecstatic. He sent Mort Slade out to the barn for "a couple of bottles of Old Stump Blower," his best moonshine he'd been saving just for times such as this, he said, and he couldn't stop shaking Carson's hand or slapping his daughter on the back.

"I'm getting too old for this ranching, anyway. 'Bout time I took on a partner myself, eh?" He looked at Carson. "What about it, young fella?"

Carson looked at Nola. "Might be worth considering, Augustus, if you could stand having us around." He raised one eyebrow at her and she squeezed his hand. Having Carson stay right here on the Lazy J was more than worth considering, it was absolutely perfect! Even for her—she could live here with Carson and her father, and still keep on

with her work with the tribes of the Blackfoot Confederacy.

"No money in it, ya know that?" Augustus cautioned.
He looked dead serious all of a sudden, as though he
thought Carson might change his mind.

"You don't need to remind me of that, Augustus. Don't
forget I was raised poor in the Sawtooth Valley. Hell, we
were so hard up I was ten before I knew some people had
money that was made out of paper—"

"Aw, *hell,* Carson," Augustus roared. "Don't give me
none of your crazy American cowboy tall tales."

Carson grinned and winked at Nola. She was amazed
and delighted to see this side of the man she loved. She'd
never imagined him joking around with her father, with
Grizzly.

"Well, well," Augustus said, beaming and rubbing his
hands together. "Best damn news I heard since Old Man
Waldron told me looked like he might have a gusher on that
wildcat drilling prospect east of Twin Butte he talked me
into going in on. Turned out he didn't, but I remember the
feeling of thinking that he did, and it felt damn near as
good as hearing you two was fixing to get hitched.

"Remember that, Grizzly?" He turned to his old friend.
Grizzly nodded. "Say, how about you and me get our-
selves an outfit together and get out there and find what
what it was brought Carson up here in the first place. He
never did tell me what he was after, ya know."

"Didn't he, now?" Grizzly pulled at his beard and shot
a calculating look at Carson, then at Augustus. "Might be
something in that idea, Gus."

"Dance, Nola?"

"Thought you'd never ask." She felt her cheeks warm as
she met Carson's dancing eyes. She knew he was thinking
of the past half hour in the hay shed. He pulled her into his
arms and the band struck up a rather wheezy version of

"The Wedding Waltz," to the delight of the crowd. She saw Ben give her the high sign from where he stood in the corner with Marie, and she smiled, pleased to have her colleague's approval.

"I figured we could pretty well leave those two to fight it out over what they might or might not find up the Wild Plum Creek, hmm?"

"Mmm." She nestled close against him, feeling her body fit perfectly against his as they danced. "I didn't know you were such a good dancer," she murmured. "Got anything else you're hiding from me?"

"Fact is, Miss Law Lady," he said, pulling her into an intricate turn and grinning as she blushed at the whistles and cheers that went up from the crowd as her skirt flared out, "there's quite a bit you don't know about me."

Then he whispered into her ear.

"*Kit.* I'm going to be Mrs. *Kit* Carson Harlow." And his brother was *Boone?* "Just like the famous Wild West mountain man?" The man she loved was a mountain man, too.

"Yep. If you'll still have me."

"Just try and get away," she giggled.

He bent and kissed her thoroughly, not missing a beat of the music, to the accompaniment of another burst of catcalls and hoots. She saw several bottles of Augustus's moonshine being passed around. She realized, to her delight, that the man she loved was having a hell of a good time, this man she'd always thought of as a backwoods, high hills loner.

There was a sudden howl of outrage from somewhere in the room. "Hey, does this mean I *still* ain't gonna get to dance with her?"

It was Mort Slade. Carson gave him a triumphant grin and a nod over Nola's head. The crowd roared.

And the band played on.

* * *

They were married two weeks later. Three months after that, Ben drove up to the Lazy J to bring them some news.

After discussing the situation of the Painted Rocks with Carson and Ben, Nola had decided to tell the Peigan elders about the location of the sacred site and assure them that as long as she and Carson owned the ranch, the rock paintings would be safe. They agreed to leave it up to the elders to make a decision on whether to seek official historical site status for the Painted Rocks and perhaps open the way to commercialism and tourism, or whether to just leave the site as it was, hidden, secret and safe from all who might harm it.

When Nola saw Ben drive up, she and Carson were just sitting down to lunch and she went out to invite Ben to join them, sure that he was going to tell them what the elders had finally decided.

But that wasn't the news he'd brought at all.

"Nola," he began, and she could see the sparkle in his dark eyes. "You know how you always wanted to be part of the tribe . . . *really* part of it?"

She nodded, mystified, and glanced at Carson. He was looking at Ben, and she saw a tiny trace of the sadness that she knew he always felt because her love for him had denied her that particular dream.

"Well, I don't know what I'm going to call you from now on . . . Nola, *Mrs.* Harlow—" this with a grin at Carson "—or Nola Rose Tells-a-Tale, honorary member of the Peigan tribe."

"Me?" Nola felt her heart nearly jump out of her chest. An honorary member of the tribe? *That meant she was no longer the outsider, neither white nor Indian . . . she belonged.*

"Oh, Ben . . ." Tears sprang to her eyes.

"And this guy," Ben said, turning to Carson with a grin. "The elders asked me to welcome you to the Peigan tribe, Carson Walks Alone." He shook Carson's hand. "Welcome, brother."

Nola had never seen her husband look totally amazed. She did now. She knew, from what he'd told her of his relationship with Old Jim, just how much this would mean to him.

Later, after Ben left, she put her arms around him.

"I must be the luckiest woman in the world," she said softly, gazing into her husband's eyes. "I've chosen to marry the man I love with all my heart, a white man. And now the people I love with all my soul, my mother's people, have chosen me. And my children—our children."

She shook her head in wonder, her hand covering his as he held it over her still flat midriff. His child slept there. Not one hundred percent planned, but then a lot of the best things in life weren't. "Who in the world could be luckier?"

"Me," he said simply, and kissed her.

* * * * *

Take 4 bestselling love stories FREE

Plus get a FREE surprise gift!

Special Limited-time Offer

Mail to Silhouette Reader Service™

> 3010 Walden Avenue
> P.O. Box 1867
> Buffalo, N.Y. 14269-1867

YES! Please send me 4 free Silhouette Special Edition® novels and my free surprise gift. Then send me 6 brand-new novels every month, which I will receive months before they appear in bookstores. Bill me at the low price of $2.71 each plus 25¢ delivery and applicable sales tax, if any.* That's the complete price and—compared to the cover prices of $3.50 each—quite a bargain! I understand that accepting the books and gift places me under no obligation ever to buy any books. I can always return a shipment and cancel at any time. Even if I never buy another book from Silhouette, the 4 free books and the surprise gift are mine to keep forever.

235 BPA AJH7

Name	(PLEASE PRINT)
Address	Apt. No.
City	State	Zip

This offer is limited to one order per household and not valid to present Silhouette Special Edition® subscribers. *Terms and prices are subject to change without notice. Sales tax applicable in N.Y.

USPED-93R   ©1990 Harlequin Enterprises Limited

by
Laurie Paige

Come meet the wild McPherson men and see how these three sexy bachelors are tamed!

In HOME FOR A WILD HEART (SE #828) you got to know Kerrigan McPherson.

In A PLACE FOR EAGLES (SE #839) Keegan McPherson got the surprise of his life.

And in THE WAY OF A MAN (SE #849, November 1993) Paul McPherson finally meets his match.

Don't miss any of these exciting titles, only for our readers—and only from Silhouette Special Edition!

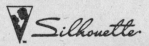

If you've been looking for something a little bit different and a little bit spooky, let Silhouette Books take you on a journey to the dark side of love with

SILHOUETTE® Shadows™

Every month, Silhouette brings you two romantic, spine-tingling Shadows novels, written by some of your favorite authors, such as Heather Graham Pozzessere, Anne Stuart, Helen R. Myers and Rachel Lee—to name just a few.

In October, look for:

THE HAUNTING OF BRIER ROSE
by Patricia Simpson
TWILIGHT PHANTASIES
by Maggie Shayne

In November, look for:

TREACHEROUS BEAUTIES
by Cheryl Emerson
DREAM A DEADLY DREAM
by Allie Harrison

In December, look for:

BRIDGE ACROSS FOREVER
by Regan Forest
THE SECRETS OF SEBASTIAN BEAUMONT
by Carrie Peterson

Come into the world of Shadows and prepare to tremble with fear—and passion....

SILHOUETTE.... Where Passion Lives

Don't miss these Silhouette favorites by some of our most popular authors!
And now, you can receive a discount by ordering two or more titles!

Silhouette Desire®

#05751	THE MAN WITH THE MIDNIGHT EYES BJ James	$2.89 ☐
#05763	THE COWBOY Cait London	$2.89 ☐
#05774	TENNESSEE WALTZ Jackie Merritt	$2.89 ☐
#05779	THE RANCHER AND THE RUNAWAY BRIDE Joan Johnston	$2.89 ☐

Silhouette Intimate Moments®

#07417	WOLF AND THE ANGEL Kathleen Creighton	$3.29 ☐
#07480	DIAMOND WILLOW Kathleen Eagle	$3.39 ☐
#07486	MEMORIES OF LAURA Marilyn Pappano	$3.39 ☐
#07493	QUINN EISLEY'S WAR Patricia Gardner Evans	$3.39 ☐

Silhouette Shadows®

#27003	STRANGER IN THE MIST Lee Karr	$3.50 ☐
#27007	FLASHBACK Terri Herrington	$3.50 ☐
#27009	BREAK THE NIGHT Anne Stuart	$3.50 ☐
#27012	DARK ENCHANTMENT Jane Toombs	$3.50 ☐

Silhouette Special Edition®

#09754	THERE AND NOW Linda Lael Miller	$3.39 ☐
#09770	FATHER: UNKNOWN Andrea Edwards	$3.39 ☐
#09791	THE CAT THAT LIVED ON PARK AVENUE Tracy Sinclair	$3.39 ☐
#09811	HE'S THE RICH BOY Lisa Jackson	$3.39 ☐

Silhouette Romance®

#08893	LETTERS FROM HOME Toni Collins	$2.69 ☐
#08915	NEW YEAR'S BABY Stella Bagwell	$2.69 ☐
#08927	THE PURSUIT OF HAPPINESS Anne Peters	$2.69 ☐
#08952	INSTANT FATHER Lucy Gordon	$2.75 ☐

	AMOUNT	$ _____
DEDUCT:	**10% DISCOUNT FOR 2+ BOOKS**	$ _____
	POSTAGE & HANDLING	$ _____
	($1.00 for one book, 50¢ for each additional)	
	APPLICABLE TAXES*	$ _____
	TOTAL PAYABLE	$ _____
	(check or money order—please do not send cash)	

To order, complete this form and send it, along with a check or money order for the total above, payable to Silhouette Books, to: *In the U.S.*: 3010 Walden Avenue, P.O. Box 9077, Buffalo, NY 14269-9077; *In Canada*: P.O. Box 636, Fort Erie, Ontario, L2A 5X3.

Name: _____

Address: _____ City: _____

State/Prov.: _____ Zip/Postal Code: _____

*New York residents remit applicable sales taxes.
Canadian residents remit applicable GST and provincial taxes.

SBACK-OD

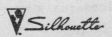